RACHEL —

So NICE TO GE ITM...

TO KNOW YOU A BIT.

YOU ENJOY THIS LITTLE ATT...

TO THINK ABOUT THE SOURCE ...

J3

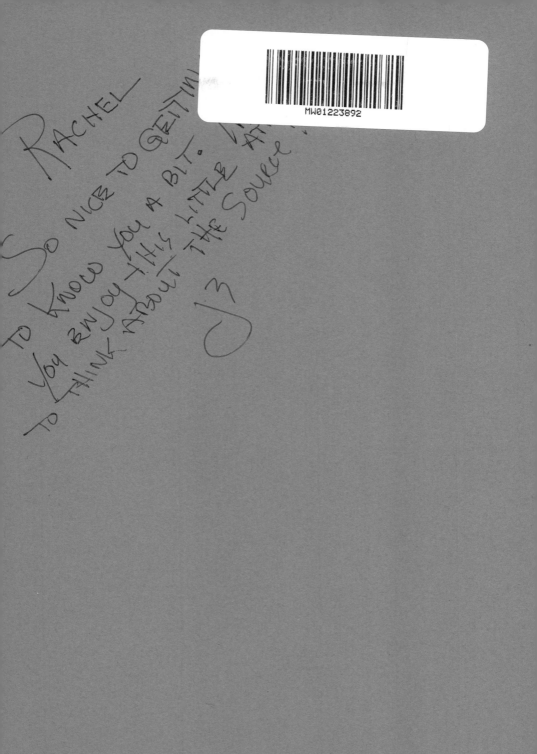

PRAISE FOR
ALL THE COWBOYS AIN'T GONE

"Epic adventure meets western cool. *All the Cowboys Ain't Gone* swaggers its way from page to page with thrilling action, likable characters, and a galloped pacing. Jacobson has a master's sense of storytelling, and he writes like he's having a hell of a lot of fun doing it."
—**James Wade**, author of *All Things Left Wild*

"How to read *All the Cowboys Ain't Gone*: get comfortable, take a deep breath, open to page one, and let 'er rip. You're off at a gallop on a grand adventure with the resourceful Lincoln Smith, who could give Allan Quatermain and Indiana Jones a run for their money. Smashing!"
—**James R. Benn**, author of *The Red Horse* and other Billy Boyle mysteries

"[A] rollicking debut...Lincoln is an old-fashioned hero worth rooting for. Jacobson ingeniously colors in Lincoln's adventures with elements of Dumas, Jules Verne, and P. C. Wren's *Beau Geste* mixed with much Indiana Jones–style derring-do. This is a ride worth taking."
—***Publishers Weekly***

"The kind of story we used to watch at the Saturday Morning Movies, one we hate to see end, and one we'd like to have return again and again in a series of sequels just as funny, exciting, and satisfying."
—***New York Journal of Books***

"Original, unique, adroitly crafted, and an inherently fascinating read featuring truly memorable characters, *All the Cowboys Ain't Gone* deftly showcases the impressive literary storytelling talents of author John J. Jacobson."
—***Midwest Book Review***

PRAISE FOR
CALIFORNIA FEVER

"Channeling the idiosyncratically whimsical voice of
Tom Robbins and marrying it with the SoCal surf scene,
John J. Jacobson's *California Fever* is a perfectly formed
overhead Rincon barrel groomed by an offshore zephyr."
—**Rex Pickett**, author of *Sideways* and *The Archivist*

"A humorous, light mashup of surfer culture,
mystery, and quirky characters."
—**Rick Bleiweiss**, author of *Pignon Scorbion*
& the Barbershop Detectives

"Having lived in the place and through the era, Jacobson
captures them both vividly and humorously. It was a time when
surfers really did rule; a time when surfers would avoid almost
anything (like a steady job) rather than risk missing a
day of good waves in the sun."
—**Rowland Hanson**, former Microsoft vice president
of marketing, and still a "surfdog"

"[A] laid-back, well-paced caper novel…This skillful farce is a perfect
beach read for Surf Dawgs and fans of P. G. Wodehouse alike."
—*Publishers Weekly*

Cupid on the Loose

BOOKS BY JOHN J. JACOBSON

NOVELS

Cupid on the Loose

California Fever

All the Cowboys Ain't Gone

JOHN J. JACOBSON

BLACK STONE PUBLISHING

Copyright © 2025 by John J. Jacobson
Published in 2025 by Blackstone Publishing
Cover and book design by Candice Edwards

"Wooly Bully" lyrics © Sony/atv Tree Publishing,
    Three Wise Boys Music LLC, Beckie Publishing Co., Inc.
"Hotel California" lyrics © Red Cloud Music, Fingers Music
"All I Have to Do Is Dream" lyrics © House of Bryant Publications

All rights reserved. This book or any portion
thereof may not be reproduced or used in any manner
whatsoever without the express written permission
of the publisher except for the use of brief quotations
in a book review.

The characters and events in this book are fictitious.
Any similarity to real persons, living or dead, is coincidental
and not intended by the author.

Printed in the United States of America

First edition: 2025
ISBN 979-8-200-96055-2
Fiction / Romance / General

Version 1

Blackstone Publishing
31 Mistletoe Rd.
Ashland, OR 97520

www.BlackstonePublishing.com

To AML

Lovers and madmen have such seething brains,
Such shaping fantasies, that apprehend
More than cool reason ever comprehends.
The lunatic, the lover, and the poet
Are of imagination all compact.

William Shakespeare,
A Midsummer Night's Dream

PART ONE

Love . . . Too swift arrives as tardy as too slow.
William Shakespeare, *Romeo and Juliet*

ONE

"What are we going to do with that grandson of yours?" Gwen Spiers asked Arthur Spiers, her husband of fifty-one years.

They were sitting on the eastern balcony of their old, stately home high atop the Palos Verdes Peninsula in Southern California. Often, in warmer weather, they would take their coffee there to catch the sun's early traverse across the morning sky.

"My dear, may I remind you that Billy is your grandson too?" replied Arthur. "What in particular are you concerned about today? His business seems to be doing fine. And from what he says, he's getting some interest in his writing."

"Yes, yes, but I dreamed about him again last night, and I fear he's on the verge of breaking up with, with . . . what was her name?"

"Her name is Jennifer. You speak of her as if she is already gone," said Arthur. "Do you really think it is up to you to do something?"

"It was in my dream, and my dreams are sometimes quite telling."

Two hummingbirds flew up to the feeder hanging from the eaves of the roof just above where they were sitting and hovered and darted in to take quick nips of nectar.

"I don't remember my own dreams, much less yours."

"Often I don't either, but I remember this one—it might be a sign. He was acting very strangely."

"So?" Arthur did care as much for their grandson as his wife did but wasn't so anxious about his love life.

"I think he has lost interest in her."

"What makes you think that?"

"I can tell."

"How?"

"Because at first he was crazy about her, then she was a definite 'maybe,' then she was just 'okay,' now he's 'just not sure.'"

"You don't like the pattern?"

"I don't know if it is right to call it a pattern, but I can tell he thinks there's something missing."

"Has he told you he thinks there's something missing?"

"No. He hasn't said so much as that. But I think he knows, even though he doesn't know he knows."

"I think I understand you, even though I doubt if he, or anyone else, would."

"Of course you would, my love." She reached out and warmly took her husband's hand. "It's not so much a pattern as the inconsistency. When love's arrow truly strikes, the wound never heals."

"Darling, if you recall, our relationship also had its ups and downs."

"Yes, I do recall," she said. Her smile grew into a chuckle as she remembered their early romance. "We did have something of a rocky start."

"Yes," Arthur said, "but it seems to have worked out all right."

"But he's already twenty-nine, and the years are catching up with him."

"He has plenty of time."

"And I want a grandchild while I'm still able to enjoy one."

"You already have a grandchild: Billy is our grandchild."

"Don't be difficult. You know what I mean."

"Of course I do. But I don't think it's wise to force things. It's a mystery how the type of love we want for him happens."

"Remember how it happened for us?"

"I remember it happened, even if I'm not sure *how* it happened." He paused and, feigning a look of pain, said, "And I'm still having a most difficult time getting over it."

She dropped his hand and pushed it away. "But there was something about that place."

"It was wonderful," he said, his grimace gone.

"It was magical. It was in my dream last night too. And also that man."

"Yes, he was an interesting fellow. He'd have to be quite old by now," said Arthur.

"I just remember the moment I saw you. It was all over for me."

"Well, you could have fooled me. You didn't show it."

"I was bursting inside. And when I saw the way you were flirting with that blonde, I nearly died. I came very close to attacking her."

"You're exaggerating. I don't think you noticed me at all."

"I more than noticed you; it just took a bit for me to notice how much I noticed you. I was numb at first. I was slain."

"It must have been painful," Arthur said.

"Stop it. It was wonderful," Gwen said.

"That blonde—it was only a slight infatuation. I hadn't seen *you* yet. But when I did, and I got to know you a little, it was all over for me too. I fear I made a fool of myself."

"*My* kind of fool. We were wonderfully silly. I wish I had written down all you said."

Arthur nestled closer and took her hand. "I'm glad you didn't. The wound you gave me still hasn't healed either." He backed off and dropped her hand. "Though sometimes . . ."

Ignoring his jest, she took a sip of coffee. "If there were only some way to get him up there."

"I doubt if it is even still there. Why don't we try something more subtle? Our favorite Shakespeare play is being performed this weekend at a little playhouse down in Culver City. I'll get him and Jennifer tickets. Maybe it will reignite things with them."

"That might work." She liked the play so much that she almost suggested they double-date with them, but then thought better of it. "I guess we can hope," she said.

»———➤

Two days later, Billy called his grandfather, thanking him for the tickets, but offered to return them. He had broken up with Jennifer and now didn't have a date. He suggested that he and Nana, as he called his grandmother, go instead.

Arthur declined. He said they were busy.

TWO

Despite his grandmother's concerns, Billy Spiers very much wanted to find a soulmate. But unfortunately—or fortunately, depending on the way one looked at it—he was also very much a romantic. He desired to see mundane things as new and exciting and life as an adventure, though it could sometimes be challenging or even perilous. He also had a somewhat idealized concept of, as the Italians call it, *amore.*

Growing up, he loved fairy tales, legends, and ancient myths. And also early on, the stories of knights whose quests were often motivated by amorous love for, or defense of, some wondrous maiden. The medieval and Renaissance literature he had studied in college abounded with these themes. In short—though he didn't necessarily realize it, or even try to be—regarding romantic love, he was an optimist, and he was vulnerable to "crushes."

He had at first been considerably attracted to Jennifer. But it became apparent that they didn't connect on what he thought were the most important levels. Their imaginations and what they wanted out of life were so different. He did try to gently break up with her, but as the old song says, "breaking up is hard to do." It didn't go well.

The breakup made the severe case of writer's block Billy was suffering worse. He had recently received some positive feedback on the manuscript he had submitted, but his agent told him it wasn't dark enough. Though his literary inclinations were more toward romantic adventure stories, the agent told him that if he wanted to get published, he needed something more modern. He was now painfully stuck on trying to make his story darker. He needed something.

It would take a lot of imagination for *A Midsummer Night's Dream* to be considered dark. But Shakespeare was a genius, and maybe the old romantic comedy featuring the king and queen of the faeries and Puck, Peaseblossom, Cobweb, Moth, and Mustardseed would jolt his creative juices. He decided to go to the play by himself.

The old, creaky makeshift theater was in an industrial part of Culver City, about twelve miles from his apartment. It was nothing like you'd expect of a playhouse so close to Hollywood. The walls and roof of the small building that used to store aircraft parts were made of corrugated galvanized steel. The ripples in the metal made for tremulous acoustics sometimes, and other times, at the right pitch, echoes that seemed enchanting. That night, there were gusts of wind that added to the effects.

The theater group renting out the place had put in a slightly elevated stage and, around it, five rows of tiered wooden benches. As he walked up to his seat, thinking about the story he was working on, a young woman with golden-brown hair stole his attention. They exchanged glances as he was sitting down. Fortunately, the bench seats didn't have armrests, or he might have sat on one.

A few moments later, Billy looked back at her. She was wearing white denim jeans and a navy blouse, the top two buttons unbuttoned, revealing a simple gold chain that hung down to the top of her well-formed collarbone. She seemed to be there alone, like he was. She caught him looking and smiled back.

He turned back to face the stage. If he had been wearing a heart monitor, it would have signaled danger. She was more than pretty. But there were lots of pretty girls. One of his favorite writers liked to distinguish between a woman being "beautiful" and being "attractive." There were many women who might be considered the former whom he was not attracted to at all. But it wasn't the case this time.

The production began, and though it was passable for a local playhouse, Billy was distracted through much of it. He couldn't get his mind off the girl behind him a few seats away. It was almost like he felt a current of electricity or some kind of energy coming from her.

Then came act 5 of the play. The actor playing the duke recited:

> More strange than true. I never may believe
> These antique fables, nor these fairy toys.
> Lovers and madmen have such seething brains,
> Such shaping fantasies, that apprehend
> More than cool reason ever comprehends.
> The lunatic, the lover, and the poet
> Are of imagination all compact . . .

The actor had only gotten that far in the speech before the lines sent Billy's imagination off. Maybe it was the wind outside, but the walls and roof and lights seemed to flutter with the words the actor spoke. The imagery of a "seething brain" particularly struck him, as it was what was going on in his. It wasn't just the brilliance of the words, their rhythm and imagery. He had heard these lines before. But, this time, what they did for him—or *to* him—was different. They seemed to crack open a door and let a foreign feeling in—like an ache, yet enormously satisfying. No, not quite totally satisfying because it tantalized, teasing of something beyond it, something greater, something slightly out of reach. It had very much to do with the girl he had just exchanged glances with.

The reverie didn't last long. By the end of the speech, trying to analyze what he was feeling had caused the vividness to fade. But there was enough of it left behind to remind him that he had had a trace of something like the feeling before, when he had thought he was in love, only to have the initial exhilaration fade.

His thoughts flew back to the girl whose smile had just pierced his heart.

>>——◆

When the play ended and the lights were turned up, a few people from the audience stayed for a discussion with the director and players. Billy waited a few moments before looking back, hoping the young woman behind him was staying and hoping she really was by herself. She was still there, and she was alone.

The discussion had just turned to whether it was right to take liberties with the Bard's texts, when a gust of wind shook the walls. The lights fluttered and went out.

When they came back on a few moments later, Billy and the woman were staring at each other. They both quickly looked away. He could feel his heart beating through his shirt.

"That was unusual," the person leading the discussion said. "The lights do flicker on occasion, but that's the first time they've ever gone out. Anyway, what about modernizing his language?"

A guy in the audience offered, "Ideas cannot be disassociated from the words that express them."

This was probably true but, at that moment, to Billy's frame of mind, way too bland. He wanted—needed—to say something witty that might impress the girl behind him. Without giving it a lot of thought, he came up with, "Anybody messing with Shakespeare's language will be haunted by Hamlet's ghost for all eternity."

To certain types of creative (in the sense of combinational) imaginations, this could possibly make sense. It did cause a bit of a stir in the audience—and a laugh, once the strained association was recognized.

Then a voice sounding like music came from behind him. "I totally agree. Changing Shakespeare's words should be a crime—and get thee, such criminals, to a nunnery." This caused a big laugh.

Billy turned, and their eyes met again. Her eyes sparkled with different hues of blue.

Another thought seemed to come to him from nowhere, and he spoke out: "It would be like the actors holding thunder in their mouths and braying like donkeys."

"Exactly," she agreed. "Like in act three, where Bottom gets turned into a donkey and brays like an ass." She said this so quickly after Billy that it seemed like their words were one thought. Her statement got not only another good laugh but some approving murmurs as well. She had a surprised look on her face, as if she didn't know where the idea had come from. Billy thought it not only brilliant but also merciful, as he hadn't noticed the connection between what he had said and act 3 until she brought it up.

After the buzz died down, Billy added, "And all those *doth*s and *thou*s and *est*s and *eth*s at the ends of words might be difficult but are important for the rhythm of the language." It wasn't easy for him to get the *est*s and *eth*s clearly pronounced without a lisp. "They're also good for articulation. I guess the trouble with my *eth*s makes my point." This also got a laugh.

He looked at her again. She was putting her hand to her chin with her index finger on her lips as if to hold back from giggling.

The discussion lasted another few minutes, with the purists winning the field. After it ended, Billy got up and took a few steps toward her as she was rising from her seat.

She noticed him approaching and smiled, the right corner of her mouth hitched a little higher than the left. It made her smile even more perfect. Her golden-brown hair was parted in the middle and fell a little past her shoulders. Under full eyebrows that were darker than her hair, her light-blue eyes shone with merry intelligence. She had become the most attractive woman he had ever seen. The ache he had experienced earlier returned.

He stopped about a yard from her. The height difference between rows was about eight inches, and Billy was six one. She must have been about five five as they were now eye to eye. Their eyes met again, and hers danced with a kind of joy. There was a moment of silence. Then both of them laughed.

"Cool tooth," she said, lightening the moment even more. She was referring to his gold-capped right cuspid. "Ken Kesey used to have one of those too."

Billy was quite proud of his gold tooth. "I played rugby in college," he said, finally able to say something. "You might be the only other person in the world who knows Ken Kesey had a gold tooth."

"Oh, there might be one or two others." She chuckled.

"Maybe one or two." Billy smiled back.

"Those *thy*s and *thou*s and *eth*s can be difficult." She also stumbled over pronouncing *eth*s, causing them both to laugh.

"Especially when you're under pressure," Billy said.

"Yes, when you're under pressure." She smiled shyly. "I'm Kari, by the way."

"I'm Billy," he said. "Making the connection of a braying ass with changing an author's words was amazing."

"I really don't know where that came from," she said. "It just popped into my head."

"I don't know where bringing up Hamlet's ghost came from either. It was just there all of a sudden."

"If you know Ken Kesey," she said, "you're either a teacher or a writer."

"Not a teacher. I've got a few things in the works. I got a pretty positive response from an agent the other day, but he says I need to get it more gritty." He didn't mention his major case of writer's block. "What about you? I can tell you love language."

"I'm working on a few things too," she said. "A children's book, and some other things a little more mature, some fun detective things. But I still have my day job."

"Yeah, I'm not quite ready to leave mine either."

"So, what do you do for your day job?" Kari asked.

"I have a little yacht-maintenance business that I run." A couple of years after he had gotten back from college, through his grandfather's connections at the King Harbor Yacht Club, Billy had started servicing yachts. This work mostly entailed cleaning the barnacles off the submerged hulls of expensive sailboats. As he was an experienced scuba diver, it was a good fit for him. After a year or so, he was able to hire a couple of divers he knew, who now did most of the work. The business wasn't exactly thriving, but it was consistent and paid well enough to support him while he pursued his passion to be a writer.

"What about you? What do you do for a day job?" Billy asked.

"I'm a flight attendant." Kari didn't seem all that excited about her job. "I typically work three days on and four days off because I don't have that much seniority. Most of my flights are short hops up and down the coast and the Northwest. But once in a while, I'll get a long one. At least on those, I get to read a lot."

"I love to travel. Do you get free flights to exotic places?"

"Sometimes. I like to travel too, when it's not on company time." Kari looped her purse over her shoulder. "Are you parked out in the lot? I don't feel that comfortable walking out there alone. Kinda a scary part of town."

"I'm down the street from it, so I'm going that way."

"I'd appreciate it."

As they walked, their conversation turned to books. A modern popular author they agreed was surprisingly good was Lee Child. Kari said, "His hero, Jack Reacher, is pretty cool—kind of a mix of Sherlock Holmes, an old-fashioned hobo, and the Terminator."

Hearing she was fond of another male, even a fictional one, stung Billy for a moment. But it passed.

When they reached her car, they both lingered, not ready to end their conversation. They would laugh at one thing and, the next moment, would touch on something they cared and felt strongly about. They couldn't stand modern superhero movies and liked most of whatever Kenneth Branagh was involved with. They didn't care for early Tarantino but thought some of his later stuff was good, and *Once Upon a Time in Hollywood* brilliant.

They connected on music too. Both weren't into modern pop and gravitated more toward Americana—John Prine and Alison Krauss, especially her song "Heartstrings," and sixties and seventies hippie music, like the Eagles, that their parents used to play. They agreed that the best were songs that told stories—some of Bernie Taupin's lyrics in Elton John songs were true poetry.

"Don't laugh," he said, "but 'Roy Rogers Is Riding Tonight' is one of my all-time favorite songs. Do you know it?"

"Are you kidding? I love that song; he totally captures the reality of old industrial life in New England: resigned but finding solace in old cowboy movies. I grew up close to one of those towns. But it's weird 'cause it isn't really that sad. I guess *sad* isn't the right word."

"Maybe the song is the only way to describe it."

"Yes, that's it," she said. "And when he says, 'Let's go shoot a hole in the moon,' it just strikes the perfect note. It makes me want to blast off and shake off the mundane." This last phrase came out with an exuberance that made Billy smile, not only on the outside. And not only smile—he had that feeling he got when he had heard those lines in the play that had set him off. He ached for this girl.

"You might not believe it," he said, their eyes meeting again, "but 'shoot the moon' is my email address."

"No!" she said. Her face lit up. Her heart warmed like it had never done before, and at the same time, she was having a hard time swallowing.

There were a few moments of racing thoughts in silence. He could hardly believe how perfect she was. She was not only incredibly attractive but smart and literary, and they cared about so many of the same things. They had chemistry—the kind that produces high-voltage electricity, at least for him.

"I'm really glad we met," Billy said.

"I enjoyed our talk very much," she said, able to talk again. "It was nice meeting you too."

"I'd love to see you again. Do you think I could give you a call?"

She sat down in the driver's seat without shutting the car door and pulled the theater program and a pen out of her purse. She wrote her number on the program and handed it to him.

"Please do give me a call, Billy." Her smile almost knocked the wind out of him.

She shut the door, started the car, gave him another smile and wave, and drove off.

Forgetting where he had parked, it took Billy twenty minutes wandering in a daze around the streets of Culver City to find his car.

THREE

Kari waited until she had cleared the theater's parking lot before calling her best friend.

"I'm so glad you couldn't make it to the play," she said without any preliminaries.

"Was it that bad?" Bianca Russell replied.

"No, no, the play was okay. It's that I don't think it would have happened if you were with me. I mean, not in the way it did."

"What happened?"

"I met this incredible guy. We could be made for each other. He loves all the same things I do and has a great imagination, even a little eccentric sense of humor. He laughed at my jokes."

"If he's like you, he's more than a little eccentric."

"I'm not that eccentric; it's just most people's normal is so lame. He's a writer too, just starting out like me. He was even wearing cowboy boots. I think I've found my kindred spirit."

"Now you're going to tell me he likes the old TV Westerns that you used to watch with your dad growing up?"

"Well, we didn't get quite that far, but he knows the words to

'Roy Rogers Is Riding Tonight'! And his email address is 'shoot the moon.'"

"No! What does he look like? There must be a catch."

"Yeah, he's a real dog—no, not really— Wait, there's a cop. I have to put my phone down."

After the patrol car passed, she resumed. "No, he's beautiful: tall, with olive skin and light-blue eyes, and light-brown hair, at least what I could see of it—he was wearing a Seahawks football cap. He grew up down here in the beach cities but went to college in Seattle. After he dropped out, he lived in Hawaii for a year, then came back here to be a writer. His only flaw—and it's not really a flaw, 'cause it's cute—is he's got a gold tooth and maybe a slightly broken nose 'cause he used to play rugby."

"I thought you hated the Seahawks?"

"Well, not this Seahawk. I didn't bring up that I'm a Patriots fan. Besides, one shouldn't judge a book by its cover—or a guy by his hat. Anyway, he asked me for my number."

It took Kari about fifteen minutes to drive back to her little one-bedroom home in Venice Beach, about eight miles away. For the last two years since she came to California, she had been renting the back unit of a bungalow duplex from a kind old widow.

As soon as she got home, she spent the next twenty minutes online trying to find someone with *shootthemoon* in his username that might be Billy. Unsuccessful, she quit, worried that her search might alert a government agency and make them think she was some kind of wacko planning mayhem in the atmosphere.

>»———▶

Billy wanted to play it a little cool, not too excited, even though he was going out of his mind. He waited till he got to his apartment in the Hollywood foothills to call his best friend, Byron West.

"Dude, what are you calling for? It's eleven forty-seven, and I'm sick in bed," Byron said. A bit of a hypochondriac, he thought he felt the flu coming and already planned to call in sick Monday morning. Byron was a junior lawyer in his father's law firm, and he was not very happy with the research task he had been given.

"You aren't going to believe what happened."

"I might, do tell."

"There was this person there."

"Yes? I hope there was more than one. Let me guess: You think you might be in love."

"This girl really is pretty amazing. I think I'm kind of seriously interested in her."

"What did she look like?"

"I think she's about twenty-six; she graduated from college four years ago. She's gorgeous, but you know there's lots of good-looking women around."

"That's what you always say."

"But she's smart and funny, and she's a writer, and she likes a lot of the same things I do."

"Yeah, if someone agrees with you, you always say how smart they are."

"She even laughed at my jokes. She's got eyes that sparkle like the diamonds in a queen's necklace."

"You've used that line before."

"Maybe it's been waiting for her."

"Were you looking at her chest or her eyes?"

"Her eyes. Dude, they're light blue like mine. We have a lot in common."

"How do you know? You hardly know her."

"I can tell."

"Does she have a friend?"

"What about you and Camille?"

"I broke up with her."

"You mean she broke up with you."

"It was mutual. Find out if she's got a friend."

"She was by herself. But maybe. She gave me her number and drew a little heart with it."

After the call, Billy spent about an hour wording and rewording a text message to Kari. He might be blocked on ideas for the story he was writing, but he was getting barraged with ideas for the text, which was just as bad as having no ideas at all. He wanted to let her know that he enjoyed meeting her and was interested in getting to know her better and, at the same time, wanted to suggest—without coming right out and saying it—that he was a little more than just "interested." Instead of sending out something then, he decided to sleep on it.

He woke before seven to work on it some more. Not wanting to seem too excited, he waited until nine fifteen to text her: "Great getting to know you last night. OK to call you later today? Billy."

It was the second day of Kari's four days off. On off days she liked to put in three hours of writing in the morning and go to the gym afterward. She was at her desk writing when Billy's text came. It took her twenty-one minutes to respond. She didn't want to seem too excited. She texted back, "Free today after 4:00. Kari."

They went out the next Friday night to an Italian restaurant in Venice Beach. At dinner they each had a glass of Chianti, and Kari ordered a Caesar salad—no croutons—with grilled wild salmon. Billy ordered the same. They were so engrossed with talking and laughing that they finished less than half their meals and passed on dessert.

After dinner they went to a small music venue in the back of a famous guitar store in Santa Monica. They stayed for just one set from a young woman from Wimberley, Texas. She sang a decent soprano, accompanying herself on fingerstyle guitar and playing mostly traditional Americana. Kari wondered if she knew "Heartstrings." Billy requested it for her, and the Texan pulled it off reasonably well.

After the show, they talked outside Kari's bungalow in Billy's old Volvo convertible with the top down for over an hour. He had planned not to try to kiss her good night, thought that it would be best to play it cool and go for an affectionate hug. After walking her to her door, they did have an affectionate hug, but one that somehow morphed into a flaming-hot good-night kiss.

FOUR

For their second date, Billy did something extravagant to impress Kari. As she was relatively new to the Los Angeles area, he took her for dinner at an exclusive but not-so-well-known restaurant up in the Santa Monica Mountains above Malibu. Back in Hollywood's heyday, it had been a hunting lodge for studio moguls and A-list movie stars.

The driving was slow most of the way up the curvy two-lane mountain roads, which gave them plenty of time to talk. They were both good at asking questions. Each wanted to know about the other more than they wanted to talk about themselves.

"Your last name—Porter—it's English, right?" Billy asked.

"Yeah, my dad's English and my mom's Boston Irish, an O'Conner. From my dad's side, I get a trace of Native American—Mohican. So, there's at least a couple of us still around." Billy liked the reference to the book.

"Do you have siblings?" he asked.

"A sister three years younger and a brother who's at Boston College on a hockey scholarship. I played volleyball and lacrosse in high school and maybe could have been a setter in college, but even back then I wanted to be a writer. My dad's a dentist, and my mom was a hygienist until she started having kids. Now that we're all out of the house, she manages my dad's office."

"I guess that's why you noticed my gold tooth: You come from a family of teeth people," Billy quipped. "Honestly, I haven't had any cavities in years." Billy paused, letting a thought pass without saying anything, but he did chuckle to himself.

"Okay, what's so funny," Kari said.

"Oh, I was just thinking about how, in the old days, when someone was buying a horse, they'd open its mouth and check out its teeth. Good thing mine are in decent shape."

"That's pretty good," Kari laughed. "Your teeth are fine."

Billy looked over at her, giving her a close-lipped smile.

"It was the first thing I checked out, back at the play—no, not really. I'm kidding. I mean, I don't go around checking people's teeth out. I used to get teased a lot about being the child of a dentist. If I floss twice a week, I'm lucky, and I was terrible in science."

Billy just laughed but was glad his grandmother had made him go through two painful years of braces. "So, you were a world lit major? I wasn't so great in science either—or math, except geometry."

"Yeah, with a minor in Italian. I got to spend a semester in Florence learning the language and studying Petrarch and Dante. My Italian helped me get my flight attendant job, though I hardly ever get to use it. Because of seniority, I almost never fly international."

"If you're from Boston, and your brother is a big hockey player," Billy said, "you must be a big Bruins fan and probably a Red Sox fan too." He didn't want to bring up the archenemy of his Seattle Seahawks, the New England Patriots.

"Are you kidding? From the cradle! My dad has season tickets to the Bruins." She decided it wasn't the time for her to unveil her equal passion for the Patriots, so she changed the subject. "I was actually born in Brighton, but we moved out to Lexington, one of Boston's suburbs, when I was five. I had a fairly normal middle-class upbringing. Was a bit of a bookworm. What about you?"

"I grew up mostly with my grandparents in Palos Verdes." Billy knew he was going to have to talk about losing his parents and wanted to do it in such a way as to not dampen the mood of their talk. "My parents died in a car wreck on the way to Mammoth for skiing. I was three, so it didn't have much of an impact on me. They were both writers: My dad was a fairly big-time journalist who covered the first Gulf War, and my mom wrote for *Mademoiselle*. So maybe I got my writer's bug from them. My grandparents, who I'm still real close to, stepped up and took me in. Growing up, it was pretty much the same as if they were my real parents."

"I'm sorry about your parents," Kari said, doing her best to convey an expression that was sympathetic while realizing it would be impossible for her to understand what losing one's parents would be like. "Seems like your grandparents did a pretty okay job." She offered a warm look that made Billy forget what he was talking about for a moment.

"My grandparents were maybe a little old-school in their parenting," Billy went on, focusing on the road not because he was driving but because her smile could be disconcerting. "Especially my grandmother—but it was probably good for me. They're actually pretty cool, though my grandmother can be annoying at times."

"Are either of them writers?" Kari asked.

"Yeah, my grandmother, when she was younger—published a book of fairy stories."

"Way cool. My grandfather was a fighter pilot in Vietnam and published a novel about it. It got optioned for a movie, but it never got made. Maybe we have inherited our desires to write."

"Yeah, though sometimes when you're stuck it feels like a disease," said Billy, "but when it's going well, you're on top of the world." Lately, Billy seemed to be coming out of his writer's block. He had been mulling over some ideas about how he could make his story darker, and a couple of them had possibilities he was excited about. But at the moment, what he was most excited about was the possibility sitting next to him in the car.

They were so immersed in conversation that before they knew it, they were at the restaurant's parking lot. It was a relief to Billy as talking about his parents brought too heavy a tone to their conversation. He didn't like talking about himself anyway.

>>>———→

The restaurant's interior had retained and embellished its hunting-lodge ambience. The elk antler chandeliers provided some dimmed overhead lighting. More light came from small rustic lanterns on the dining tables, of which there were about twenty. The walls were of dark wood and ornamented with all sorts of game heads: elk, boars, a few whole ducks, as well as armory, rifles, shotguns, pistols, and an old blunderbuss. There were also autographed pictures of Gary Cooper, Errol Flynn, Clark Gable, Bogie, John Ford, Michael Curtiz, Elia Kazan, and others. Though old English folk music played in the background, raucous sounds of careless people enjoying good food, lots of drink, and loud conversation almost drowned it out.

The menu was unique, a few notable items being roasted buffalo bone marrow, New Zealand elk venison, Faroe Islands wild salmon, Israeli lamb curry, and raw buffalo hump. A caramel ice cream sundae made from goat's milk and organic Tahitian cane sugar, a black gold mud pie, and a hand-rolled Carnielli cannoli were a few of the dessert offerings. The bar had liquor, liqueurs, wines, and beers from all over the world.

Kari ordered a blistered asparagus salad with sunny-side-up egg atop and a combo meat offering of salmon and a rack of lamb served with Moroccan couscous. Billy ordered an appetizer to share: oysters from the south of Spain with jalapeño dust—after making sure Kari liked things a little spicy. For his salad, he had the avocado boar-bacon wedge; and for his entrée, the combo of elk and wild boar pork chops with branzino, even though he didn't know what branzino was and didn't want to ask the waiter. For drinks, they started with glasses of cava; with their meals, they shared a bottle of Cabernet Franc.

They were taken up in the festive mood of the place. The time passed quickly as they ate, sharing tastes of their dishes and laughing and telling funny, self-effacing stories of childhood and schools and friends. They declined on dessert and almost had to be asked to leave. They left with hefty doggie bags and second cappuccinos to go.

On the drive home, they talked but were pleasantly mellowed. Billy felt like taking her hand but didn't, only because he wanted to keep both hands on the wheel while driving the dark, curvy mountain roads. They didn't get back to Kari's place till almost 1:00 a.m., and as Kari was flying the next morning, Billy didn't linger long on Kari's porch. But they did have a good-night kiss that kept with them both into the next day.

FIVE

Late in the afternoon of the next day, Billy's grandmother saw his number come up on her cellphone. She hadn't heard from him since Arthur had sent him the tickets for the Shakespeare play. She let it ring a few times, wondering how she should answer. It would be crass for her to say, "What are you in need of now?" too motherly to say, "We've been so worried about you," and too intrusive to directly jump into criticizing him for breaking up with Jennifer.

Finally, she picked up and greeted him with, "Why, hello, stranger. When are you coming up for dinner? It's been almost three weeks since we've talked. I want to hear what's going on in your life."

"Yeah, sorry, Nana. Been real busy. Just wanted to see how things are going with you and Pops."

This sounded fishy. "We're doing fine, William, and how are you doing?" She'd play along a bit to see if there was some ulterior motive for the call.

"Good. Oh, yeah, I wanted to thank you and Pops for the Shakespeare tickets. Interesting place, that little theater."

"So, you did end up going, even without a date?"

"Yeah, but I sort of met someone there who kind of got my attention."

To get information from him about his dating life, she usually had to pry it out. This someone must have gotten more than his attention. "Please tell me about her."

"She's from the Boston area, and she's been out here a couple of years."

"Oh?"

"She has a younger sister and brother, and her dad is a dentist. Her mom's an oral hygienist."

"Well, that's an assurance she has good teeth. What does she do for a living?"

"She's an aspiring writer too and studied literature and Italian at Boston College and in Italy. She's smart and has a sophisticated sense of humor like mine. For her day job, she's a part-time flight attendant."

Gwen tried a few more questions but didn't get anything more than surface details. The more she tried to get a feel for if this might be a serious relationship, the more he obfuscated or clammed up. She finally said, "When do I get to meet her?"

"Way too early for that," Billy said. "But I think you'll like her."

She couldn't remember Billy ever saying that he thought she would like one of his girlfriends. "Okay," she said.

"I just wanted to thank you and Pops for the tickets."

"Come up to lunch or dinner any time and do keep me posted. Oh, you didn't tell me her name."

"Her name is Kari, short for Kathrine."

"Kathrine?" Gwen said, wanting to hear him say it again.

"Yes, Kathrine. She was named after an aunt who wrote some plays."

Maybe Gwen was imagining it, but she thought there was something dreamy in the way he said her name.

》———◆

Billy was back in his writer's block, and at the moment, it was severe. This was one of the reasons he had called his grandmother—anything to procrastinate. Working on his story, he had thought he had found a way to turn it darker, but his agent said that it wasn't enough. This was only one of the contributors to his malaise. He also couldn't quit thinking about Kari.

Knowing she was on a two-night work trip, he texted, "Are you interested Wednesday when you get back in going for a bike ride on the Strand and watching the sunset and grabbing a bite afterward?"

Late that night, she texted back, "Love to but I probably won't be back in time to watch the sunset. Maybe some other time we could do the bike ride, but pretty sure I could make an 8:30 dinner, if we did it close to Venice."

Billy didn't see the text until morning. Remembering she had said she loved Chinese food, he texted, "I know a great Chinese place close to your house, Lung's Dragon. Meet you there at 8:30, unless you get delayed?"

About two hours later, she texted back, "In between flights. I love Lung's Dragon. I'll be there Wednesday 'with rings on my fingers and bells on my toes.' Can't wait."

Billy texted, "Me too."

>———➤

A little after the lunch hour on Wednesday, Billy drove over to Lung's Dragon. He had eaten there often and was friendly with Thomas, the manager and head waiter. The restaurant had mostly cleared out after the lunch rush.

Thomas saw Billy enter and greeted him. "Billy, so nice to see you. Please sit anywhere."

"I'm not eating now, but I wonder if you could do me a big favor?" Billy asked.

"I try my best; what you want me to do?"

"I've got this new girlfriend that I'm trying to impress. You remember that joke we played on my friends last year?"

Thomas gave Billy a knowing and excited smile. "Yes, no problem, I remember, know just what you looking for. It will not be my first rodeo."

"Excellent." Billy and Thomas sat down at a table and went over the details of Billy's plan.

———»———➤

Billy arrived at the restaurant a few minutes before eight thirty, and Kari not long after. A young Asian hostess seated them, and a busboy brought them water and menus.

"So, you've eaten here before?" Billy said as they were studying their menus.

"A few times," Kari answered, though she had eaten there more than just a few.

"Have you tried their *chao nian gao* or their Peking duck? Both are excellent."

"Everything looks wonderful," Kari said. "It's hard to choose."

"Do any of the appetizers look interesting?"

"Their 'crispy veggie spring rolls' look good," Kari said.

"Great, I like them too."

Kari pondered for a moment. "I think I'm going to go with the chao nian gao. It's a mouthful, pardon the pun."

"Nice one." Billy smiled. "And good choice. I'm going to go with the Mongolian lobster. Would you like me to order for you?"

"Sure," she said with a smile. "I'll just have green tea to drink."

"Okay."

After a couple of minutes, Thomas came over to the table, holding an order pad. Speaking in Mandarin Chinese, he said, "*Měnggǔ lóngxiā pèi zǐ mǐ hé lǎbā gū.*"

"He says," Billy interpreted, "the special tonight is the Mongolian lobster over forbidden grain rice and trumpet mushrooms." Billy looked up at Kari with an air of casual complacency on his face. With his left hand, he picked up the menu. With his right hand, he pointed to the items that he and Kari wanted to order and babbled a cacophony of *niang*s, *xiao*s, *yuan*s, and other single-syllable diphthonged sounds that possibly sounded something like the words Thomas had tried to teach him earlier that day. To Thomas, it was complete gibberish, but he nodded as if he understood perfectly. He responded in real Chinese.

Billy continued his impression and finished with, "*Zǎoshang hǎo, xīwàng nǐ yǒu měihǎo de yītiān*," the one phrase he'd managed to somewhat master. Translated, it means, "Good morning, I hope you have a nice day."

Thomas jotted down the order on his pad and left the table.

Kari said, "Wow!"

"When I lived in Hawaii, a bunch of my friends were Chinese, and I picked up some of the language," Billy said matter-of-factly.

"Oh, how interesting. You must have a gift for languages."

Before long, the crispy spring rolls came, which were wonderfully crunchy and not that oily. After eating one, Kari excused herself to go to the ladies' room and was gone for about five minutes.

Just after she returned, the main dishes came. As they served themselves, she asked him more about his experience in Hawaii.

"Well, you know I went to the University of Washington, and maybe could have done okay in football there, but even back then, I wanted to write. So I didn't play, though sometimes I regret it. I wanted to concentrate on studying the great writers and learn how to do it myself. But by the beginning of my third year, I got so depressed with the whole process. What most of the professors were teaching wasn't what I hoped to get out of literature. It was more about how to deconstruct it, take all the life out of it, and misinterpret it according to whatever was the latest wacky trend in interpretation. Eventually, I just dropped out and decided to go surfing and kind of find myself in Maui. Ticked off my grandparents quite a bit."

"And that's where you learned Chinese?"

"Yeah—and did a lot of reading and surfing."

Kari talked about her semester in Italy and some of her travels. She'd gone to the Caribbean a couple of times when she wanted sun and beach. She had also been to Key West to check out where Hemingway did some of his writing.

When they were done eating, a busboy came and cleared their plates. Thomas followed shortly after, holding the check.

As he reached the table, Kari reached for the check and made a bunch of sounds that seemed to Billy very much like the gibberish he had used. Yet Thomas seemed to understand Kari perfectly and replied back in Mandarin. They continued in a short conversation before Thomas handed her the check.

Billy looked at her quizzically, then to Thomas, then back to her. His look turned to an embarrassed smiling frown with his eyebrows furled.

"My good friend Bianca is half Chinese. I'm very close to her and her family—that's where I picked it up," she said, trying to keep a straight face.

"Really? How interesting," he said. This girl didn't stop amazing him. It was like he'd been bested by a worthy opponent.

They sat and stared at each other. Smiles slowly grew on their faces. Then they broke out laughing for about ten seconds, Billy sheepishly shaking his head, grinning from ear to ear; Kari with a huge smile also, though raising her eyebrows, hoping she didn't embarrass him too much. Across the table, she took his hand.

Thomas came back and deposited on the table two large grocery bags full of cartons of Chinese delicacies, one for each of them. He picked up the check and crumpled it. "I am so sorry, Billy, but Kari my good friend too. Dinner on the house tonight. You both poor students, need much work on your pronunciation."

"No, no, no," said Billy, trying to give Thomas his credit card. Thomas wouldn't think of it.

When they left, Billy stood up and, leaning across the table, planted a big, long smack of a kiss on Kari's grinning lips. "Well played," he said.

"My dad did the same thing to my mom on an early date, and she married him anyway," Kari said with a laugh.

"My grandfather pulled it on me and some guys on my little league team after we lost an important game," Billy replied. "I guess he thought it would cheer us up. Some of those kids still think he knows Chinese."

Gathering their stuffed grocery bags, they departed the restaurant, Billy leaving a fifty-dollar tip.

SIX

The Saturday morning after Kari and Billy's date at Lung's Dragon, Kari met Bianca and her other best friend, Amanda Hall, at Ariel's for a late breakfast. The outdoor café on the Strand in Venice Beach was not only known for its view of the ocean but also for their healthy breakfasts. Billy had told Kari that one of his friends wanted to know if she had any unattached friends of her own. She responded that she had two who had come out to California a little before her. After a little maneuvering, she and Billy managed to set up Billy's friends, Byron and Jackson, with hers, Bianca and Amanda, on a blind double date.

Kari had been friends with Bianca and Amanda since high school. They had gone to Boston College together and had even roomed together their last two years. Bianca—half Irish, half Chinese, short, petite, and according to Kari, adorable—had been a nationally ranked college gymnast and had come west to get her master's degree in dance at UCLA. She'd had a few auditions for commercials and taught dance at Santa Monica City College as an adjunct professor. Amanda—who was half Swedish, a quarter Haitian, and a quarter a few other things—was tall and thin and a head-turner with both men and women when she walked into any room. She had come west to take acting lessons while continuing her moderately successful modeling career.

It was a beautiful sunshiny morning that matched Kari's mood. The light marine layer of fog had lifted. The ocean was calm and glassy and crystal blue. Walkers, joggers, and rollerbladers were already cruising the boardwalk.

After they had been seated with a nice view of the ocean, Kari asked, "Well, how did it go?" directing the question to both of them. Kari was eager to hear about their dates, but even more so to gush about what was happening with her and Billy.

Bianca and Amanda looked at each other and smiled reservedly, though they were smiles. After a moment, Bianca said, "Interesting. Byron's really into cycling, so he's athletic and fit, and he's a lawyer."

"A definite maybe, maybe," Amanda said. "Jackson's fairly good looking, has a great bod. He has something to do with financial planning, is really into karaoke, and wants to take acting lessons and be a stand-up comedian."

"Are you going to see them again?"

"Byron texted me later that night," Bianca said. "He invited me to a Rams game tomorrow. When he asked me if I liked football, I told him a lot of professional cheerleaders had studied dance. It's only a preseason game, but he says he has season tickets."

"Did you tell him that you were a cheerleader in high school?" asked Kari.

"I told him you and I both were and that Amanda was on the flag team."

"They were both asking questions about you," Bianca said to Kari, "wanting to know who this woman was who had slain—that was the word Byron used—their friend."

"Jackson—and it's *Jackson*, not *Jack*—waited to text me till this morning," Amanda said. "He asked if I wanted to go on a sunset sail on his father's yacht this Thursday. I haven't responded yet, but I'm thinking I might go."

"She's going," Bianca said to Kari. "They look like they could be a match, physically at least. He's tall like her, and he's well built—at least his upper body; it looked like he has skinny legs. He's reasonably good looking, not the equivalent of Amanda's looks, but he's okay." Bianca didn't say that he also appeared to be a little too aware of his good looks.

"What do you mean, he's just 'okay,'" Amanda protested. "He's gorgeous, way better than my 'equivalent looks,' as you call them."

"She's being humble again," said Bianca. Amanda did have statuesque looks, with curves in the right places, and had nice blond hair, though it was a little thin.

"What about you?" Amanda asked Kari.

"Yeah, what about you?" said Bianca.

"I'm sure your guy was exaggerating, calling Billy 'slain,'" Kari said.

"He didn't seem like he was exaggerating," Bianca said.

"I'm sure he was, but anyway, we've gone out three times." She filled them in on the details, including how she'd conspired with Thomas at Lung's Dragon to turn Billy's trick back on him.

"That could have been embarrassing for him," said Amanda. "Are you sure he took it okay?"

"He sure seemed to. I mean, I think he took it okay." Some doubt crept in. "He didn't seem offended. He was just a great sport about it. I think I'm starting to like him. He's growing on me."

"Sounds like she's more than 'starting' to like this guy," Bianca said to Amanda.

"Sounds like she's finally over that bastard Richard," Amanda said.

SEVEN

Billy and Kari got together the next Tuesday to watch the sunset on the Strand in Redondo Beach. After the sun went down, they strolled out on the marina, looking at the boats and yachts. Billy pointed out a few that his company had worked on. When they came to his grandfather's forty-three-foot racer, on which he and his grandfather had been sailing early that morning, they hopped aboard. He opened it up and gave her a quick tour. The cabin wasn't very big, but it was well equipped and had a nice foldaway dining table.

"Sometimes when I really need a change," Billy said, "I come here to write. It usually works." Kari could have been imagining it, but he did seem a little weary.

"I know what you mean. Sometimes a change of place helps—coffee shops, libraries, even the dealership when I'm waiting to get my car serviced. But this place is perfect," Kari said, "especially if you're writing about sea dogs, shivering timbers, and Davy Jones's locker."

Billy laughed. Worn out as he was, that feeling of delightful longing was coming on him again.

He responded, "Yeah, you have to search for the right word like you're searching for buried doubloons and pieces of eight."

"And if you don't stay focused on your writing, they make you walk the plank," Kari added, frowning and trying to sound grim.

Billy grrred like a sea dog. "Let's go get some rum at Captain Kidd's."

They did go next to Captain Kidd's, though they drank Pellegrino rather than rum. The quaint fresh-fish market on the pier next to the marina had been there since before Billy was born. Relatively small glass-enclosed displays showed the catches of the day. Customers could make their choice from the offerings and either take it home or have it grilled in the kitchen behind the counter and served with coleslaw or a chowder and fried potatoes. They ordered shrimp cocktails and clam chowder with the sparkling waters, then sat at a picnic table in the back area with a view of the marina.

After eating, they were going to walk the bike path for a while, but as it was clouding up, it gave Billy an excuse to suggest that they head back to Kari's bungalow.

"Can you come in for a bit?" Kari said as they pulled into her driveway. It was still relatively early. "I don't have to be at the airport till nine tomorrow, and I've got a pretty decent bottle of Chianti we could try." And then, though she didn't mean for her tone to sound more serious, she added, "There's something I've been meaning to talk with you about."

"Sure, that sounds good," he said, wondering what was coming.

It was his first time entering her house, and the first thing he noticed was a large light-brown furry thing lounging in a corner of her couch. It stirred and lifted its big, ominous, dark eyes to Billy. Billy stared back at the pointy-eared fur ball. It investigated him and then seemed to determine him of little consequence.

The feeling wasn't mutual. As far as Billy knew, he was allergic to only two things in the world—camels and cats. Some breeds didn't affect him as much, but he couldn't tell what kind this one was.

After a moment, the cat languidly slid off the couch and moseyed over to Kari.

"This is Mac, my roommate." Kari picked her up, cradling her and giving her a kiss.

"Pretty cat," Billy said, trying not to show concern. "I didn't know you had one."

"Oh, she and I go way back to when I was a senior in college."

"Isn't it hard to have one with all the traveling you do?"

"Mrs. Martin, who lives in the front unit, loves Mac and takes care of her when I'm gone. And Mac likes her. It's like her second home. Make yourself comfortable, and I'll get the wine." Kari, carrying the cat, pushed through a swinging door into the kitchen.

Billy sat on the corner of the couch opposite where the cat had been camped.

Kari returned a few minutes later with two glasses of wine and a small plate of sliced Asiago cheese, balancing the plate atop one of the glasses. The cat arrogantly pranced after her.

Billy took the cheese plate and set it on the coffee table in front of him, then accepted one of the glasses of wine.

Kari sat down about two feet away from him, the distance suggesting seriousness. She didn't put on any music. Mac strayed over and started rubbing herself against Billy's jeans-covered shins.

"She likes you," Kari said as she picked up her glass.

As it appeared that Kari wasn't going to offer a toast, Billy didn't either. He took a sip—the Chianti was noticeably better than even the mid-priced stuff he got at Trader Joe's.

Kari took a sip to stiffen herself for what she was going to say.

Billy was concerned, but he was just as concerned with that cat, who continued rubbing against his legs. He could feel his eyes starting to itch.

Kari put her glass down. "There is something I thought you should know." She said this with an air of self-reproach and a frown that was directed at herself.

This got his attention off the cat—for the moment.

"You know how I told you I used to live in Boston? Well, back then I worked full-time and was flying out of Logan. When I had been there about a year, they needed someone to fill in for a flight to Rome, and they called me. I rarely got international trips, but I spoke Italian, so . . . Anyway, on the trip, I got to know this pilot who flew out of Logan too, and when we got back in the States, we started dating."

Billy was listening but wasn't that concerned. He had dated plenty of women before he had met Kari.

"To be honest, at first I was somewhat interested in him and thought I would give it a chance. But that faded fast, and it became obvious to me that he was way more serious about our relationship than I was. I tried to break it off, but he was uncomfortably persistent and wouldn't let up."

Billy had had similar experiences. He'd maybe get infatuated with a woman, but it was short lived. Then the woman wouldn't let go. In a way, this could be another thing she and he had in common. He could have almost smiled, which would have been inappropriate at that moment.

The cat decided to lie on his feet.

"Bianca and Amanda—my good friends from college, the ones we set up with your friends—had moved out here. So, to get away from him, I transferred to a position out here, even though I would lose the little senior-ity I had, and it would only be part-time." Though it was painful to her, she was being very vulnerable and honest. She looked at Billy with a humble, hopeful smile, hoping he was getting the subtext of what she was saying: There was no baggage in her past relationships that might get in their way.

Billy was a sensitive person who tried to be observant and read and care for the feelings and emotions of others. It was part of the internal makeup that real writers are gifted with. He heard her words and ap-preciated her openness. However, he was distracted by the cat still lying on his shoes. He was trying to wiggle his toes and rotate his ankles to get her off. Mac seemed to be enjoying the massage.

Kari looked at him and tried to gauge how he was responding.

He took another sip of wine and realized he needed to say some-thing. Trying to be kind and understanding, he said, "Thanks for sharing that." And then dully, "I can relate."

Kari wasn't exactly wounded by Billy's response; she was just expect-ing much more. Something tender and encouraging. She tried to blow it off, but in her current state of vulnerability, that wasn't easy.

Then she thought about the words he had just said—"I can relate." What did that mean? And why did his eyes look red? Was he upset by what she had said? Had she triggered some deeply painful memory?

She took another sip of wine, and seeing that both their glasses were almost empty, she said, "Do you have time for another glass?" Maybe he wanted to open up about it.

The itch in Billy's eyes had progressed to burning, and the last thing he wanted was to release the explosive series of sneezes he'd been holding back. He had to get out of there. He took another sip of his wine, almost finishing it off, and said, "Kari, I really appreciate you sharing. But you know, I ought to let you get some sleep. I'm kind of beat too."

"Oh. Okay." Kari did not at all know how to interpret this and tried to hide how much it hurt.

She walked him out to the porch. Billy kissed her, holding it only for a second. She accepted it passively. He hurried off.

EIGHT

True artists and poets don't necessarily display "artistic tempera-ments." They may look quite normal on the outside. But under that exterior facade is a seething brain, almost always a kind of hypersen-sitivity and a churning intensity that wants release. This intensity can sometimes produce art; sometimes it flares out in an action or overre-action, like a cat inexplicably springing up in the air from its repose. It's almost like the true artist can read unsaid signals coming from other people. Sometimes, depending on the depth of the artist's insight, he or she will read the signals correctly. But at times, even the most bril-liant will totally misread them. The results can be unfortunate, if not disastrous.

On the way home, after Billy had a good rub on his eye sock-ets and the rest of his feline reactions began to subside, a barrage of thoughts hit him. One was, If Kari had to choose between him and Mac, who would it be? Another was, Why did she bring up the thing with the pilot? Was she telling him he was coming on too strong like the pilot did, and he needed to back off a little? A third was, If he had to choose between losing Kari and taking allergy pills for the rest of his life, what would he choose?

>>————➤

Kari, also a born artist, tried to be observant and sensitive to the moods and feelings of others as well. It's unfortunate but understandable that Kari misread what she considered Billy's insensitive response to her vulnerable confession.

All the rest of that evening and through the next day, on her short flights to Boise, then Bozeman, and back to Boise to spend the night, she was miserable. She was so disconcerted on the Boise-to-Bozeman leg that she was late handing out the pretzels.

Was he mad that she had gotten even a little close to another guy? No, he couldn't be that possessive, could he? It was okay to be a little possessive. On their second date, she had told him that she'd once dyed her hair red, and he mentioned that he had gone out with a girl with red hair a few times in high school. She didn't like his response and had become suspicious of redheads ever since.

Maybe it was just the wrong time to tell him about Richard, the pilot she had a relationship with. Maybe she hadn't needed to mention it at all. No, she felt she needed to. Could he have thought she was trying to make him jealous? Could she possibly have come across that way? If he was going to be that kind of crazy jealous type, that was a red flag. No, she refused to believe that. But she had put herself way out on a limb, and it felt like he had just chopped the limb off.

She stewed over thoughts like these in her hotel room in Boise that night. Finally, she recalled some counsel an older flight attendant had given her about relationships: "It's not always wise to make unconfirmed assumptions. If you have concerns, it's usually best to communicate them." That sounded like good advice. But she had been vulnerable and attempted to communicate, hadn't she? Maybe it would be best to let their relationship cool off just a little. Yes, that's what she would do—she would back off a little and see what his next move would be.

A few minutes after she determined this, her phone buzzed. She saw Billy had sent her a text. She hesitated to read it.

➤

Billy's thoughts since "the night of the cat" were still as tangled as hair with gum stuck in it. *Why does the girl I*—he caught himself almost thinking the "L-word"—*the girl I like so much have to have a cat?* A cat she was, apparently, really devoted to. Almost simultaneously, he derided himself for being such a wimp. So what if he had allergies? It wasn't that bad having to take the pills, and in the past, most of the time they worked fairly well. Though the pills made him sleepy, and that wasn't good for his writing.

Should he have told her right then about his issue with cats? If he had, how would she have responded? It hardly seemed the right time, as she wanted to talk about her old boyfriend. And she was so serious. Why did she think it was so important to bring him up anyway? Was she giving him a hint, telling him how that guy came on too strong because she didn't want him to do the same?

Maybe the allergy medicine they had now was more advanced than when he took it as a kid? Maybe shots worked better than pills? Or was there some kind of naturopathic cure he could find?

Wait a minute—he hardly knew her. This thing was going way too fast, way too fast. Maybe that's what she was trying to tell him, and maybe she wasn't wrong. He should cool this thing down a little.

So, he'd waited till the evening after their date to text her—he knew she was flying and would be busy during the day anyway. That could be interpreted as cooling things off, right? Whether asking her to go out on Friday to see the Royal Shakespeare Company's production of *Murder on the Orient Express* at the Dorothy Chandler Pavilion, probably the most expensive venue in Los Angeles, was playing it cool was up for debate. But she'd said it was one of her favorite Agatha Christie stories. A chance to see the renowned British company put it on would be a treat. If she accepted the offer, he could still play it cool and be somewhat restrained on the date.

———➤

Kari held off for about twenty seconds before she read Billy's text. She had planned, the next time he asked her out, to make some excuse. That resolve vanished about eleven seconds after she read the text asking her out to see the play.

She tried to wait ten minutes before answering but only lasted nine and a half before texting back, "Love to!" She resolved that on the date, she would be reserved and not so familiar.

NINE

The weather on the night of *The Orient Express* was warm but overcast. All over the South Bay and into downtown, the clouds hung low and threatening. It was fortunate that Billy had picked Kari up early, for the traffic was worse than usual. Farther north in the San Joaquin and Sacramento Valleys, they were having one of those "tule fogs," where visibility can be limited to a few feet in front of you, and which have caused fifteen-car pileups on the freeway.

On the ride to the play, Kari was cordial but more reticent than usual. Billy noticed this and asked if she was feeling okay.

"I'm a little tired," she said. "My flight home last night was three hours delayed. Do you think we could stop and get an espresso? I really do want to see this play. It was quite thoughtful of you remembering how much I like Agatha Christie."

"Sure," said Billy, "I could use one too." He had been crewing that day on his grandfather's sailboat, and he still felt the rolling of the ocean, even after taking a nap. Before they got on the freeway, they stopped and got cappuccinos.

The play was excellent. Most of it took place in a few first-class railroad cars. The art deco set designs of deep greens and burgundies, soft grays, and blues overlaid with silver geometric patterns evoked not only the pre–World War II era but also an air of mystery. The costumes and first-class dining car props added to the overall mood and ambience. The acting was brilliant, though the famous detective Hercule Poirot, who had added a soul patch and a spade goatee to his upturned mustache, overdid his faux Belgian accent.

On the way back, they discussed the play, both liking it but disagreeing about a few insignificant features. The mood in the car, like the weather outside, was gloomy.

When they pulled into Kari's driveway, Billy shut off the car. He turned to look at her. "Is everything all right?" he said, almost pleading.

"I'm just a little tired," she said, not raising her eyes. She wanted to say something but was hoping for something more from Billy. She didn't get out of the car.

"Are you sure?"

"Yes, I am okay."

"It doesn't seem like everything's okay."

"I'll be all right."

Billy knew he had to address the issue, even though he didn't know for sure what the issue was. "I'm really sorry if I was curt with you the other night," he said. "I'm really sorry," he repeated. "Would you forgive me?" He looked into her eyes as if asking for mercy.

"Why did you leave so fast?" Kari said. "Was it something I said?"

"No, no," Billy insisted. "I just wasn't feeling well." He didn't feel the timing was right to bring up the cat. Maybe he should have, but he didn't want to make an excuse for his rude behavior and blame it on something else, much less her cat.

"I thought I had made you mad, talking about my creepy old boyfriend."

Billy almost laughed because it was so far from the truth, amazed at how sometimes people can misread each other. "No, I just had gotten up really early that morning and was beat." He did end up making an excuse. He reached for her hand, which she let him take, and moved closer to her, bumping against the parking brake.

"Really? Is that all?"

"Yeah. But that boyfriend of yours came on to you so heavy and strong—I don't want to be like that."

She scooted closer to him. "It's true we haven't known each other that long, but I think we're going about the right pace."

"I agree," Billy said. "We're getting to know each other. I don't have any papers on you, and you don't have any papers on me."

"What does that mean?" She scooted back.

Billy immediately realized that he had said the wrong thing. What he meant to imply was he didn't want her to feel obligated to him. It didn't come out that way at all.

"Oh, it's just the lines from a song I heard." He was in a hole now and had to dig fast. "What I think it means, or what I'm trying to say, is that I want you to feel really free with me." This still didn't cut it.

"What do you mean, 'free'?"

"Oh, all those old guys on my grandfather's boat listen to all these old songs, and I don't know what they mean. I just want you to know that I care very much for you and think about you all the time and want you to be happy. If you think ditching me is what you want, then . . ."

"Then what?"

"Well, I'd rather you didn't."

She scooted back closer to him.

Their talk went better after this. They did agree that they didn't want things to flame out, but—though they didn't use these words—they still wanted to keep putting wood on the fire.

"I better go in," Kari said at last. "I'll call you tomorrow night from Montana. Thanks for a wonderful evening and for being so understanding."

After a good-night kiss, she hopped out and hurried to her porch. Billy waited till she had gone into her house before he drove off.

>>———▶

Over the next two weeks, Billy and Kari saw each other three times. They talked or texted every other day. As far as Kari was concerned, they had worked through their misunderstanding well, and her feelings for him were growing even stronger. They had agreed that they might have been moving a little fast at first, but now they were going at just about the right speed.

Billy had determined that he was going to do his best to put up with Mac. He hadn't said anything about the cat because he didn't want to put pressure on Kari to choose between him and it. Some medieval stories of knights who made great sacrifices wooing their ladies came back to him. At the moment, it didn't seem so ridiculous to him. He renewed his prescription for allergy pills and made sure he had taken one an hour before he went over to Kari's house. The pills only worked okay. But Billy and Kari also started spending time at Billy's apartment. As long as his health could handle it, he would make the sacrifice. He wasn't ready to commit to anything yet, but he'd never felt like this with any woman before.

TEN

Billy was having a hard time putting off his grandmother's requests to meet his new flame. Gwen didn't give up easily. She was impatient to make her own assessment of Kathrine and how things were going firsthand. Though Billy loved and appreciated his grandparents dearly, sometimes his relationship with them—particularly his grandmother—could be challenging, even annoying. And to the friends and girlfriends he had brought up to meet her, she could be intimidating.

Again, she hadn't heard from Billy in what she considered too long. She sensed that some information she "deserved" was being withheld. Either he had been rejected, which was unusual for him, and he didn't want to share this, or he was smitten and desirous of this young woman to a degree she had not seen before.

After leaving three messages in one day for Billy, she finally received a call.

"Is everything all right?" she answered. "You haven't returned my calls. I thought you might have drowned scraping barnacles off the bottom of a yacht."

"No, Nana, my guys do most of that work for me nowadays," Billy said, "as they have for the last two years. And all of them are just fine."

"Is everything else fine?"

"Yes, everything is going fairly well. I've got some good new ideas on where to take my novel."

"I think your agent is full of baloney. You should get a new one."

"It's not that easy to get an agent, at least not one with cred. At this point, I need to try to do what he suggests."

"You should follow your own instincts and not someone else's cred, whatever that is. You have a wonderful imagination."

"It's credibility with the publishers, and that is exactly what he has. He has been very encouraging."

"Whatever. Now, what is happening with you and Kathrine?"

"*Kari* and I are doing fine."

"If you're still seeing her, when are we going to meet her?"

"Yes, I'm still seeing her."

"Do you think I'll like her?"

"I'd like you to like her, but it doesn't matter if you like her, because *I* like her."

That's something, Nana thought, *saying that he likes her and sticking up for her. Maybe this one is different.* "Does she have any brains?" she asked.

"Yes, she has brains. We're passionate about a lot of the same things. She's a writer too."

"You told me that before. Passion is good if it is toward the right things. You need a woman who is affectionate and capable of deep feelings. Writers generally are. When do I get to meet her?"

"At the right time."

"What does she write?"

"She's done some children's stories, but not fairy stories like you used to write. She's working on something more mature now."

"Every story is a fairy story. What does 'mature' mean? You don't think fairy stories can be mature? They can say a lot more than so-called realistic fiction."

"She's writing some humorous detective things, kind of like a Christie flavored with P. G. Wodehouse."

"That could be interesting."

"Yes, she's pretty cool."

"I guess that means you like her quite a lot. When do we get to meet her?"

"Soon."

"Bring her to dinner this weekend."

"Too formal."

"What about lunch then?"

Billy thought about it. It was still a risky step to bring a girlfriend up to meet his grandparents. Their stately old house with its magnificent view atop the peninsula could be intimidating. More so could his grandmother. But they were his only family, and at some point, if it looked like there was any possibility in the relationship, he had to introduce Kari to them.

Nana, as anxious as she was for him to find someone, had a rather high romantic ideal for his relationships. Based on her and his grandfather's courtship, which was wonderful if not quite ordinary, and their subsequent fifty-year love affair, she wanted the same thing for her grandson. She thought she could tell the difference between a doting infatuation and the real thing. But they were his only family, and at some point, if it looked like there was any possibility in the relationship, he had to introduce Kari to them.

"Are you still there?" Gwen asked.

"How about a casual little lunch party Saturday?" Billy finally replied. "Nothing too fancy. Byron and Jackson are seeing two of her friends. They're relatively new to the area. I'll invite them too." Billy's friends, whom he had known since junior high school, knew his grandparents well, having survived the adventures and misadventures of growing up with Billy. He thought a larger gathering would make it seem that it wasn't one of those "meet the parents" meetings. With the other girls there, Gwen, who was conscientious in her manners, would have to share some of her attention with them. And his grandfather, always affable and amusing on these kinds of occasions, would try to change the subject if Nana started prying too much.

"*Very* casual," Billy emphasized. "Okay?"

"Of course, darling," Gwen replied.

>>———▶

The lunch went better than Billy had expected—almost. To make it seem even more casual and less like a date, Billy, Byron, and Jackson drove up together a little early, and the girls arrived later.

Gwen did try to make it informal and relaxed. She dressed casually—for her anyway—in a baby-blue cotton shift, navy-blue flats, and an old pair of good-luck diamond earrings Arthur had given her before they were married. The luncheon table was not set with her most elegant china but with her favorite casual ware that had a theme of cherubs in pink and white hovering on the lips of the light-blue plates and saucers and the sides of the cups. The light blue was close to the same shade as her shift, which was spangled with tiny white, green, and red starbursts. She used her second-best silverware, set out with crisply folded white linen napkins that had the family escutcheon embroidered in the corner. Gwen, who loved to cook and was good at it, made her version of a Nicoise salad with avocado, broiled tuna, and quinoa, in case anyone was gluten-free. Her maid, Crystal, helped with the preparations and served.

Kari was not overawed by the stately old house and its furnishings. She was much impressed, however, with its views spanning the South Bay coast up past Malibu to the northwest, down to the megalopolis of Los Angeles, and to the mountains beyond the massive city to the east. One of the things Kari loved back home in New England was that from the hill on which she lived, she could see off in the distance, for miles and miles, the rolling wooded hills. Kari wasn't intimidated by Billy's grandmother either. She was comfortably respectful and confident without being smug or brash.

Gwen seemed to take a liking to her immediately. But she went out of her way not to pay too much attention to her and to show an appropriate amount instead to Bianca and Amanda, Byron and Jackson's dates.

Arthur didn't need to go out of his way to be casual and charming. He dressed in jeans—though Gwen made sure they were ironed with a crease down the legs—Sperry boat shoes, and a navy-blue polo shirt. He was on the alert to keep the atmosphere light and restrain Gwen from seeming to interrogate Kari.

As suggested, writers tend to be, or ought to be, observant and even sensitive to situations and people they meet. With the gifted ones, it is more than just an impersonal interest but a kind of empathetic engagement. Kari was captivated by Nana. There was almost a kind of magic about her or at least a kind of fairy godmother quality. And Kari wanted to know more about her. While the dessert of strawberries and whipped cream was being served, Kari said to her, "Billy said that you've written a book of children's stories."

"Yes, I dabbled at that in my youth, and wrote a few things. I was always intrigued by the old legends and folktales. You know, in those old stories, as I've tried to show William, there are timeless truths that need to be retold. I tried to mold some of them into a few stories. The difficulty is getting what one sees so clearly in one's imagination out and down on the page in some kind of coherent and intelligible fashion. I guess I was meant to be more a connoisseur than a creator."

Yes, Billy thought, *and now she wants to connoisseur me.* But he didn't say it.

Kari smiled and thought she had expressed the writer's dilemma well but didn't mention her own writing. She only said, "I'd love to see some of it."

"Oh, it's been long out of print, but I might have something or other lying around somewhere."

"You aren't writing at all anymore?" Kari asked.

"Oh, I scribble a few things now and then, just thoughts and ideas. But there is something based on the place where Arthur and I met that I plan to do someday."

Billy reacted in horror at the direction the conversation had just turned. He had heard the story about the lodge up in the mountains, where his grandparents fell in love, a hundred times. He feared the talk would stray into the territory of the "M-word." He looked over to Arthur, desperately trying to catch his eye.

ELEVEN

"Billy, why don't you tell the girls your famous bobcat story," Arthur suggested.

Billy was relieved Arthur had headed Gwen off from the direction she had been going but not so relieved that he had brought up the bobcat. His grandfather loved the story not only for its humor but also for the way he could get a brag in about his grandson's athletic accomplishments.

"I witnessed it. It was awesome," said Byron.

Billy groaned.

"Tell it," Kari said, and the other girls insisted as well.

Billy acquiesced. "Well, in high school, football—"

"Billy was quite good, you know," Nana interrupted. "He was all-state."

"I wasn't all-state, Nana. California doesn't have an all-state team."

"Whatever. He was all-half-of-the-state," she allowed.

"It's called CIF—California Interscholastic Foundation," Arthur clarified. Arthur had been quite a football player himself and later a rugby player.

"Anyway," Billy went on, "at PV High, a couple of weeks before school started, we would have these grueling two-a-day practices. It would be late in the summer and usually really hot and smoggy. But they would give us Sundays off, and one of those Sundays, a few of my teammates and I went down to the beach in Portuguese Bend. If you walk down there past the tide pools, there's a bunch of old caves that you can swim back into. Between the caves, there're these little canals, or more like shoots of ocean, that you have to swim across to get from one cave to the next. The sides of the shoots are covered in gnarly coral and rocks.

"Climbing up out of the water onto one of these, I scraped my right hand pretty good on the coral and my right thigh too—you can still see a trace of the scars on my hand." Billy showed three parallel little lines, about three inches long, on the back of his hand that contrasted with the darker shade of his skin. "The cuts weren't that deep, but they did bleed for a while, like cuts in the ocean do.

"The next day, before practice, it was really hot and smoggy, so I showed them to the coach and suggested I probably ought to take it easy at practice that day."

"I was on the team too," Byron interrupted, "and Billy more than 'suggested' it; he was trying to not even have to suit up. When the coach asked him what happened, Billy told him that he was out trapping red-tailed hawks in Peacock Canyon and a bobcat attacked him. And fighting it off was how he got clawed up."

"Is that true?" Kari asked.

"Yeah, pretty much. The scratches did look like I could have gotten clawed by a big cat. Coach put some ointment and bandages on them and made me practice anyway."

The girls gave out something between an amused shock and an admiring laugh. "I love it," Kari said. "More proof you're a born story-teller." She didn't mention the prank he had tried to play on her at the Chinese restaurant that didn't turn out quite so well.

"But here's the rub of the story," Byron said. "I was in a chemistry class that Coach taught the next semester when football season was over—Billy had been in it too but dropped out the first day he learned we were going to have to memorize the periodic table—and after the class one day, Coach asks me, 'How's Billy doing? Has he had any more encounters with bobcats?' And I said, 'What? You believed that story? Those cuts weren't from a bobcat. He scraped himself on some coral down at the Portuguese Bend caves.' Coach had been totally taken in."

"Did he get mad?" Kari said.

"Oh, no," Byron said. "He just laughed and laughed. He thought it was great."

"Yeah, Byron really busted me. It's a good thing I was a senior because I'm sure he would have gotten even with me next year in practice. After that, whenever he'd see me, he'd call me Bobcat."

"What a great story," Kari said.

"There's a little more to it," Gwen interjected. "When he came home all scratched up, he also told *me* it was from a bobcat, and I almost had a heart attack."

"Darling, it wasn't quite a heart attack," Arthur gently corrected her.

"Well, I was quite alarmed. With those open wounds and his cat allergies, he could have had some kind of dangerous reaction. It wasn't until I was going to rush him to the hospital that he came clean with what really happened."

Kari tried to force a smile.

"That was terrible of you, worrying your grandmother like that," Bianca said. After this, Billy managed to get the conversation off himself and onto the others.

When the dessert plates were cleared, the group went out onto one of three terraces, where they were served coffee and the Cognac that Byron had brought as a gift. The mood for the rest of the time continued to be genial, and the guests departed soon after with warm adieus.

»———▶

"Well, what do you think?" Gwen said to Arthur. Billy and his friends were barely out the door.

"About what, my dear?" Arthur said.

"Don't be difficult, you know about what."

"The Cognac Byron brought was excellent; no doubt he raided his father's cellar."

"Arthur!"

"It was fine, my dear. The lunch was beautiful, though we might have eaten out on the terrace."

"Would you stop it?" They walked out of the entry hall and into the living room. "Now, sit down and tell me what you think."

He did sit—and sent the question back to her: "What did *you* think?"

"I asked you first. I liked almost everything about her."

"She had nice table manners, and so did her friends."

"Yes, go on."

"Appears to come from good salt-of-the-earth people, not too moneyed or unmoneyed."

"Yes, like us. I hope she doesn't think just because we have this house . . ."

"No, I think you make it perfectly clear that we are on the verge of poverty."

"Well, it's true that if we were just starting out, we'd never be able to afford this place."

"Do you really want to know what I liked about her?"

"Yes."

"She's funny. She and Billy have compatible senses of humor."

"Yes, I saw that. And that's important. That's all?"

"I like the way she looks at Billy and he looks at her; the way they give each other knowing looks and smiles; the way he seemed to be being physically drawn close to her and then backed off a bit, seeing it wasn't the time and place; and that they didn't seem to worry a bit what either of us thought of them."

"Oh, Arthur, you are describing what it was like with us."

"It still is, darling."

"Are they really smitten? Do you think it is really happening?"

"Time will tell," Arthur said.

"There was one thing, maybe of concern. I hope it's not insur-mountable."

"What might that be?"

"Did you see her reaction when I said Billy was allergic to cats? I think she might be a cat person."

TWELVE

Kari spent the afternoon after the lunch at Billy's grandparents' brooding over why Billy hadn't told her about his allergy. It continued to bother her into the next day. So, this was why he never picked Mac up, and when Mac would rub against his legs, he would only pet her with his sock-covered feet. She didn't want to take this the wrong way. But didn't he trust her enough to talk about it? Could it be that Billy was just being noble and really did care for her so much that he was willing to suffer being around Mac for her? What if it came down to Mac or Billy? Kari didn't even want to think about that. She decided that the next time she and Billy got together, she was going to bring up the subject. Yes, that's what she would do. She went over to pick up Mac for a comforting snuggle, but the cat, who had been acting strangely lately, struggled free and went to lie down off in the corner.

Billy called her later that evening and asked her out for Wednesday night.

"I'm flying Wednesday through Friday," she told him, "but Saturday would work, and after that, I'm free for a whole week." They agreed on the upcoming Saturday for a bike ride on the Strand and dinner watching the sunset. She had thought about how and when to bring up the subject weighing on her mind. Saturday, when they got together in person, would be the time.

>>———▶

Billy picked up Kari for their Saturday date at 4:00 p.m. The plan was to rent bikes at the Manhattan Beach pier and then cruise down as far as Torrance Beach and back, a total ride of a little over ten miles. Then they'd have dinner at a restaurant just up from the pier that had a great view of the sunset. Kari's plan was to have the talk over dinner.

While they were returning their rental bikes to the vendor, Kari's cellphone woke up with the opening lines of a classical guitar version of Bach's Cantata 147.

Kari saw that the call was from Mrs. Martin, the lady who lived in the bungalow in front of her. Mrs. Martin did occasionally call Kari just to chat but not frequently, and she had just visited with Kari earlier that day. The phone played only a couple of bars of the piece before Kari answered it.

"Hi, Mary," Kari said, "I hope everything is all right?"

"Oh, Kathrine, I'm so sorry to bother you, but when I went over to check on Mac just now, she didn't look well at all."

"Yes, she's been a bit off lately, but I think she's okay."

"I'm not so sure. She didn't want to get out of her bed, and she's regurgitated on the floor in front of it."

Kari walked a few steps farther away from where Billy was paying for the rentals. "She has thrown up a couple of times lately, including this morning. I think it's just something in her diet that disagrees with her. She likes to sneak food she shouldn't, even though she can be sensitive to it."

"Well, I cleaned it up, but I think there was blood in it."

"Blood?" This was concerning. "Okay, thank you for letting me know. I'll come back as soon as I can."

As she and Billy were walking back to his car, she was torn about how she should handle what might be a crisis. She needed for them to have the discussion about Mac and Billy's allergy. But to bring up the subject while Mac was sick would be inappropriate or even seem manipulative.

"Billy, I don't feel much like dinner," she said. "Do you think we could call it a night?"

"Oh, sure, okay," Billy said. "Is everything all right?"

"Yeah, I'm just not that hungry."

"It doesn't look like there's going to be much of a sunset anyway," Billy said. Clouds were gathering over the ocean.

"Sorry you're not feeling well," he said as they drove back to her house. He had raised the top in his Volvo, hoping it would be more conducive to talking, but she seemed preoccupied. He had never seen her like this before. She didn't talk that much on the bike either, but they had been peddling pretty fast.

He pulled up in front of her apartment and turned the engine off. "Well, I hope you feel better soon."

"I'll be okay. I just need a little time."

He got out of the car and started to go round to open the door for her. But she had already let herself out.

"I'm sorry, I really have to go," she said. "I'll give you a call." She turned and ran off to her bungalow. There was no good-night kiss, not even a hug.

"Wow," Billy said out loud once he was back in his car. "That was weird. Wonder what I said?"

>>———→

Kari entered her house and rushed into the laundry room. Mac was sprawled out listlessly on her fluffy cotton-lined cat bed. Mac merely raised her eyes to Kari. To the side of the bed, her bowl of water was almost full except for a little that had been spilled on the floor. There was blood in the water and on the floor. She had barely touched her organic no-hormones–no-antibiotics canned cat food. Kari reached out to pet her on her side—Mac snapped at her.

Kari didn't know what to do. She hadn't been in Southern California long enough to need to take Mac to a veterinarian. She searched the internet for one that was open on Saturday nights. She couldn't find one.

Finally, she found an emergency animal clinic that was on call twenty-four seven. The problem was it was in the hills of Ventura County, ninety minutes away. She made an appointment with the answering service to meet the vet there in two hours anyway. It was going to cost her a mint.

After making a bed for Mac on the passenger seat of her VW bug, moving her there, and gently and loosely fastening the seat belt for her, they took off for Ojai, eighty-seven miles away. Mac was unhappy the whole way, especially at any minor bump in the road or jostle.

Kari considered calling Billy and explaining the situation. He was a caring and sensitive person. But he was also allergic to Mac and must dislike, if not hate, cats. He might think her neurotic, driving all the way to Ojai late at night just because her cat vomited, even if there was blood in it. Maybe she should just wait and see how Mac was doing in the morning. But what if Mac died? She tried to put away the thought. She didn't want to think of Mac dying. She would figure out what was wrong with Mac before she talked to Billy about it. She'd call him tomorrow and explain everything.

THIRTEEN

The veterinarian didn't show up at the clinic at all that night. After numerous calls, Kari got through to someone at the answering service again and was told that someone would be at the clinic at ten the next morning. Kari asked if the doctor would come even though it would be a Sunday. The answering service confirmed.

Kari stopped at a supermarket for a few essentials for herself and Mac, then got a room at a motel a few miles from the clinic. She arranged for a late checkout in case her appointment ran past eleven o'clock. On the floor next to her bed, she made a bed for Mac. At least Mac slept well and only threw up once early in the morning.

Someone did meet Kari and Mac the next morning at the clinic—but not at ten. The weather had cooled and clouded up, and there was a forecast of squalls coming in from the ocean. It started to drizzle while she and Mac waited in her car. Remembering she owed Billy a call, she texted him: "Sorry I didn't get back with you last night. I'm tied up now, but I'll connect with you later."

A white Ford Ranger pickup truck with oversized tires pulled up at

10:37. A young man wearing a cowboy hat and boots got out and approached her VW. She got out of her car.

"Morning," he said. "I'm Dr. Luke. I hear you got a sick feline." He was tall, husky, and nice looking despite his fledgling attempt at a Pancho Villa mustache that still wouldn't have kept him from getting ID'd at bars.

"I'm Kari," she said. She pointed in toward the passenger seat. "That's Mac. We drove up from Venice Beach."

He looked in and simply grunted, "Hum."

"I don't mean to be rude, but are you a full-on veterinarian, or is your doctorate in something else?"

"No offense taken, ma'am. I'm an accredited DVM from UC Davis and have been for almost a year and a half now."

As the look on Kari's face suggested that she didn't know what a DVM was, he clarified: "Doctor of veterinary medicine."

"Oh, okay. I hope you can help. She's very important to me."

"I understand, ma'am. Let's take a look at her."

They walked around to the other side of the car. Kari picked up Mac from her pillow bed, and Dr. Luke led them into the clinic.

The vet hustled through a door in the front office and returned with a gurney, the size of which could have held a calf. Kari set Mac on the gurney, and Mac snapped and growled at the vet as he tried to strap her down. Per his request, Kari did the strapping. The vet, with Kari following, rolled the patient into the exam room behind the front office.

He first tried to take Mac's anal temperature. She writhed and would have bitten him if she were not bound down. "That's nothing compared to taking the temperature of a sick goat. But maybe it's best we give her a little something to calm her."

"I'd rather not, unless you think it's absolutely necessary," Kari said.

"Then how about just a small dose of nitrous oxide? It will help her relax. I'm afraid she won't let me examine her without it."

"As in laughing gas?"

"Yes, dentists frequently use it."

"I know. My father's one. Well, okay, if you have to."

Dr. Luke rolled over a large tank that had some rubber hoses running from it. From a cabinet, he chose the smallest mask available, made of leather, and attached its narrow end to one of the hoses. "If you could just hold her down for a moment, this shouldn't take long." He offered the mask to Kari.

Kari moved back, half appalled, half amused.

"Just kidding," he said, "but it would help you to relax. You know, tension hurts one's performance. That's what they teach the sprinters. I took a course in kinesiology and sports medicine, and—"

"Yes, I know," Kari cut him off and was glad he didn't take a few hits on the gas himself before starting his examination.

He twisted one of the knobs on the tank. Kari put one hand on Mac's shoulder and one on the back of her head and held her down as the vet put the mask over Mac's nose and mouth. Mac squirmed for about five seconds, then let out a purr or two and mellowed. The vet then took her temperature. Next, with a tiny flashlight, he checked her now dilated eyes. He carefully looked inside her mouth using flat wooden tongue depressors, keeping his fingers clear. With his hands, he delicately felt around her stomach.

"She's got a bit of a bulge here," he commented.

With a stethoscope, he listened to Mac's heart and lungs and then around the protrusion. "So, you say she's been lethargic, vomiting, and irritable?"

"Yes, for maybe a week now."

He went off to a desk with a computer terminal on it and began typing on the keyboard. Kari stayed with Mac and couldn't quite see what was coming up on the screen. After about five minutes, he got up and walked over to Kari.

"We would have to wait till Dr. Streeter gets in tomorrow for a formal diagnosis," he said. "My informal one is—and please don't be alarmed—Mac either has some kind of growth, possibly malignant, or as she has many of the symptoms, she could be pregnant."

"Pregnant! She can't be pregnant. She's been spayed—I was told so anyway."

"Medical diagnosis is not quite an exact science," he said.

Kari wasn't sure if he was referring to the science in general or the diagnosis he just made. "What do you mean, we need to wait? I thought you were a certified DVM."

"I am, but I primarily work with large animals—horses, cows, sheep—not so much cats."

Kari was annoyed he hadn't said so earlier. "What do you advise then?"

"I could be wrong, but if she is pregnant, the long drive, especially if it's raining hard, could set her in labor. If I were you, I would stay over and let Dr. Streeter, who is certified and experienced with small animals, see her tomorrow."

"Are you sure the one who treats cats will be here?"

"I'll give her a call and make sure she will—she's my mom."

It didn't take long for Kari to make up her mind. Sure, she could head home and hope to find another vet, but it was Sunday, and she might not get in to see one till Monday. And she didn't want to risk another long car ride without knowing what was wrong, especially given how cranky Mac had been on the drive up.

While at the clinic, the clouds had gotten thicker and darker. Before escorting her and Mac out to her car with an umbrella, the young vet offered, as she wasn't familiar with Ojai, to show her around and grab a bite later.

"Thanks so much for the offer, but I think staying close to Mac would be best."

"You're probably right," the vet said. "A herd of cats could be coming any time."

"I think it's called a clowder," Kari said.

"That's right. You know your cats," he said. "I'll drop by the clinic tomorrow to see how things are going."

Before returning to the motel, Kari googled for a drive-through that served some kind of salad. An El Pollo Loco was not too far away. She found it and ordered a taco salad with pulled chicken and avocado.

On the drive from the restaurant, thunder rumbled, and the rain turned from a drizzle into pellets splattering against her windshield. A strange feeling came upon her, and she almost ran a red light. She tried to concentrate on her driving the rest of the way to the motel.

Once she got back into her room, the feeling returned. It was intense, but it wasn't easy to describe. Something hurt and ached. But it was an ache that she wanted more of. It had been there before, but she had been holding it down, suppressing it. She didn't understand what was going on inside her, but she wanted Billy to be with her. Being with him was an adventure; even *this* could be an adventure.

Was it just her loneliness, tiredness, and vulnerability causing such thoughts?

Then the dreadful idea came that she might be losing him. Was she going to have to make a choice between him and Mac? If Mac had something terminal, like cancer, she wouldn't have to decide. But she didn't like thinking about Mac dying.

Did true love have to make hard sacrifices? Did love get tested like this?

Billy would need to sacrifice too. No, that thought wasn't right; love didn't make demands like that. But if Billy loved her, he would. But wasn't he already? What were his true feelings? Wasn't he still seeing her even though he couldn't stand her cat? Yes, he was still seeing her. But didn't it seem like he was backing off some? But then, she had deliberately, for the sake of keeping their relationship sizzling, cooled it off a little too. On the surface, that didn't make a lot of sense, did it? Could he possibly care for her in the way . . . She let slip for a second what she was suppressing: the incredible, deep, wonderful wound she had for him. *Maybe* had. No, *knew* she had. No, *could possibly* have. Was she going insane? Or was she in love? Why was all of this so hard to understand?

She almost called Billy right then but didn't know what she would say—she was trying to figure out what she was feeling. She texted him: "Billy, we really need to talk F2F. I can't tomorrow, how does your Tuesday look?"

FOURTEEN

Early that same Sunday morning, Billy met his grandfather at his sailboat in the King Harbor marina. Billy had committed to go sailing with him earlier in the week. It was something they used to do regularly and now served as an excuse to get together. It was also a much more subtle way than his wife used to try to get Billy to talk more freely about what was happening in his life.

The storm that was brewing a hundred miles to the north had been picking up force down there. They were drinking coffee in the boat's cabin, deciding whether to go out despite the rough sea warnings.

"You look like you had a tough night," Arthur said. "You need a little spice in your coffee?"

"Nah, I'm okay. Just didn't sleep so well."

Arthur read that statement to mean Billy was hurting and might have something he was willing to talk about but needed coaxing.

Billy was hurting—intensely. He feared he was losing the love of his life.

"Well, how about it?" Arthur said. "It's barely twenty knots, the wind in our faces, a little adventure on the boisterous ocean? Get our minds off our troubles."

"You know, that sounds great," Billy said.

They motored out through the slip, and Billy, at the mast, hoisted the mainsail halyard before leaving the marina's breakwater. By the time they had entered the open sea, the wind had picked up to twenty-six knots, which was still below the thirty-four to forty-seven knots for gale warnings. Twenty-six knots was nothing for experienced sailors like them, though hoisting sails in that wind can be tricky. Billy unfurled the jib while Arthur kept the boat at just the perfect angle into the wind. Their teamwork was precise. Going farther out past the tip of the Palos Verdes Peninsula, they sailed, close hauled and heeled, into the southwest wind. They had sailed so much together that tacking communication was barely needed.

Before long the wind picked up to thirty-three knots; the rain increased, seeming almost to be falling sideways; and the ocean's whitecaps rose to five-foot swells. To Arthur, it was a joy to watch his grandson's sure movements and sailing skills. To Billy, the wind, the rain, and the waves were exhilarating. At least for the moment, his thoughts were not on Kari.

Out over the ocean, a long, jagged bolt of lightning flashed, followed almost instantly by another. Four seconds later, thunder cracked and roared. It started raining even harder.

Billy turned and frowned at Arthur, who frowned back. Sailing in stormy seas was one thing, but sailing in lightning was, on a boat with aluminum and carbon fiber masts and metal riggings, not advised. As it was, Gwen was probably going to reprove Arthur for going out in any storm, let alone one with lightning. Arthur shrugged and gave a slight flick of his head to turn back. They did turn to go back, but not exactly straight back. First, they would have some major fun. Billy hoisted the spinnaker, furled the jib, and they almost flew back to the marina, sailing crosswind.

>>———▶

Entering the marina, Arthur turned into the wind, Billy dropped the spinnaker and the mainsail, and they motored back to the slip. After putting away the lines and cleaning and closing up the boat, they hustled to the yacht club bar and restaurant. A late breakfast / early lunch was called for. At the bar, they ordered Irish coffees before setting up at a cozy table close to the fireplace, which was burning real wood. They had gotten wetter from the scamper to the club than from sailing. Their "foulies" kept them mostly dry but hadn't wholly kept out the chill. The warmth of the fire and their spiked coffees were a delight after their wet and wild morning on the sea.

"That was awesome, Gramps," Billy said. "Just what I needed."

"Don't tell your grandmother we stayed out so long."

"Don't worry, she'd probably get mad at me for letting you." But as they sat warming by the fire with their drinks, Billy started thinking about Kari again. It was weird the way she had cut off their date the night before. Arthur noticed Billy sinking back into his gloom.

A waitress whom Arthur knew well and who also knew Billy came and took their meal orders. Arthur had his regular: ham and eggs with hash browns—crispy—instead of homestyle potatoes. Billy didn't feel much like eating but ordered a steak, medium rare, and eggs over easy with hash browns, also crispy. If he didn't eat all the steak, he could take it home. Crispy hash brown potatoes were a tradition he and his grandfather shared.

Not feeling like eating made Billy think even more about Kari. Then he remembered he hadn't checked his cellphone in hours. He reached into his right jeans pocket for it. It wasn't there. He tried his left pocket, his rear pockets. Horror!

Arthur noticed. "I saw you put it in the cup holders above the sink. I didn't think of it till now. Sorry."

Relieved, Billy said, "I need to run and get it. Bet my keys are in there too."

Arthur smiled. Something really was going on with him. He handed Billy his keys, and Billy hurried off.

➤

Billy came back about eight minutes later, walking much more slowly than he had left. He had received two text messages from Kari. One said, "Sorry I didn't get back with you last night. I'm tied up now, but I'll connect with you later." The other said, "Billy, we really need to talk F2F. I can't tomorrow, how does your Tuesday look?"

Just after he sat down, the waitress arrived with their orders. Billy ordered another Irish coffee. She noticed Billy's countenance and shot a quick look at Arthur. Arthur acknowledged the look. After she left and a few moments of silence had passed between them, Arthur said, "You want to talk about it?"

"Ah, it's nothing," Billy said.

"Girl problems?"

"How'd you guess?"

"They sometimes can be a difficult species to understand."

"I'm having a hard enough time understanding myself."

Arthur gave a short chuckle.

"What's so funny?"

"Oh, I was just remembering some of the best advice about relationships I ever heard."

"Yeah? Please tell me."

"It's from an old Motown song that was popular when I was growing up. Sometimes those old songs got it right."

"I'm all ears."

"I don't remember all the words, but it goes something like, 'You can't hurry love, sometimes you just have to wait.'"

"Easier said than done." Billy didn't add, *especially when your heart feels like it's breaking into a million pieces.*

"Forcing it can make it worse. If it's meant to happen, it will. And if not, there's someone even better for you. That's my experience anyway."

"Yep, you're right. Thanks for the advice." Billy took a long drink of his coffee, mixed a dollop of ketchup into his hash browns, and ate a few bites.

In his car, before driving home, he considered texting Kari back but didn't. She said they needed to talk face-to-face. How was he supposed to interpret that? He needed some time to think. On his cellphone, however, on Spotify, he did find an old song by the Supremes: "You Can't Hurry Love."

FIFTEEN

Kari was going crazy in her motel room. Billy still hadn't replied to either of her texts. She couldn't work on the story she was writing because she hadn't brought her laptop. Even if she had, she couldn't have concentrated. She hadn't thought to bring a book to read either. She'd tried flipping through the channels on the TV. There wasn't anything that even slightly interested her. Mac was being lethargic on the bed she had made for her on the floor, ignoring any attention she tried to give her.

Great, so now my cat is rejecting me too. She needed to talk to a human being.

She speed-dialed Bianca, the person, other than her mother, she could be the most honest and unguarded with. Bianca didn't pick up; Kari didn't leave a message.

Twenty minutes later, Bianca called back.

"Hey, I saw I missed your call?"

"Yeah, hi. Seems like forever since we talked."

"We had lunch last Thursday."

"Seems longer. Anyway, how are things going with you and Byron?"

"We're doing okay. He's not your typical lawyer; he's kind of a lovable, dorky child and likes to have fun. What he really wants to do is cycle, which he's pretty good at, and write and direct plays. He's working on one called *Law and Disorder*. He says he went through a goth stage in college until his parents threatened to cut him off. Anyway, we'll see. I'm going out with him again tonight. How are you doing? What about you and Billy boy?"

"Oh, I don't know." This was a prompt for Bianca to inquire more. When Bianca didn't immediately, Kari said, "You'll never guess where I am."

"You and Billy eloping?"

"Hardly. No, I'm in a motel up in Ojai." She was still trying to figure out what she was going to say about Billy.

"Where's Ojai?" It sounded like Bianca was trying to softly chew something. She was always eating to maintain her blood sugar, and it was frustrating to her friends that she could eat so often and still stay so trim.

"It's up in the hills above Ventura. Mac got really sick, and the only clinic I could find that was supposed to be open twenty-four seven was up here."

"Is Mac all right? What's the matter with her?" She tried to sound sympathetic, but she was a dog person, and her Maltese didn't get along with Mac.

"The only vet we've seen so far is a horse-and-cow vet. He's not sure, but she's got this growth that he says could be cancerous. Or he says she has many of the symptoms of being pregnant."

"What! I thought she was spayed."

"So did I. But he says sometimes it's hard to tell."

"He's a horse-and-cow vet?"

"Yeah, he's kind of cute, he looks like he's about seventeen. The cat vet is coming in tomorrow. He doesn't think it's a good idea to drive back with Mac in her condition."

"He's probably hitting on you. Anyway, what about you and Billy?"

Kari didn't reply for about five seconds. Bianca stopped chewing and said, "Kari, are you there?"

"Yeah, I'm here. I'm just going a little crazy. There's a lot going on."

"Okay, what's happening?"

"I don't know. I mean, I'm not sure how I feel about him anymore."

"A week ago, you were madly in love."

"Did I really use that word?"

"How do you think he feels about you?"

Silence again on Kari's part.

"So, you think you might be losing him?"

"It seems like he might be cooling off." She didn't mention that she had backed off a little too.

"Do you think that maybe you came on too strong?"

"He came on strong too. Are we going to be one of those crazy couples that just flame out?"

"Relax, sister, this is just early in the match. You're extra vulnerable with what's going on with Mac. We've all been—" A little shock of static crackled on over Bianca's phone.

"We've all been what? Your phone cut out."

"It's really stormy down here. I said we've all been through it."

"It's stormy up here too. I haven't been through anything like this before."

"That's because you've never met a guy like him before. If he's playing it cool, then you need to too. He needs to know you aren't so easy a catch."

"I'm not into playing those games."

"It's not playing games; it's tit for tat. If he's cooling some, then you cool some. When you make it too easy for a guy, he loses interest. For them it's the conquest. My mother told me that a long time ago."

If Kari had been thinking clearly, she might have observed that tit for tat very much sounded like a game. "I don't know," she said.

"Didn't some poet say, 'Men prize the thing ungained more than gained.'"

"Something like that, but you're probably taking it out of context."

"Plus, that way you'll find out if he really cares. And you'll save that tender heart of yours a lot of pain." Bianca was truly trying to protect her friend. But what she was suggesting had some risk to it—sometimes with risk comes reward, sometimes calamity.

The lights in Kari's room flickered and went off, followed by a loud crack of thunder, then came back on. "So, you don't think I should at least give him a hint about how I feel?" The lights flickered again.

"Personally, I would wait to figure out how he feels. And if he comes back on strong again, it doesn't hurt to make him suffer a little."

"That sounds mean."

"Might seem that way, but I've never seen you like this before. Like I said, this isn't a game you're playing. It's war."

>>———▶

Billy was at his apartment after his drive home from the marina. As he tried to take a nap, that song he had listened to on the way home was lingering in his mind. Not hurrying love may be good advice. It sounded like the general principle of not forcing things, which he had learned from some hard lessons. As he was trying to sleep, he thought of a painful experience he had while still in high school.

The summer before his senior year, he wanted to buy this older VW van. He saw it as the perfect thing to take him and his friends on a surfing trip down in Mexico. But he would have had to almost completely drain his bank account to buy it. His grandparents were strongly against it. The mechanic who looked at it for him wasn't wild about it either and said the engine was old and didn't look like it had been well taken care of. He said better deals came around all the time.

But Billy had this vision of him and his friends camping out in it for a week down at Rincon de Baja, surfing perfect waves. Billy went for the van anyway. The engine blew up around K38. A garage eighteen miles to the south, in Ensenada, said it would cost 27,000 pesos to tow it and fix it. Back then, that was about $1,800 US, which was more than Billy had paid for the van. They ended up having to call one of his friends' older brothers to come down in his mom's minivan to pick them up. Billy gave his van to the garage in exchange for letting him and his friends leave their surfboards and stuff there and sleep one night on the floor of the garage's office until their ride came. While they waited, they did, however, get to hang out and drink beer at Hussong's Cantina, which was some compensation for the seventeen-year-olds.

The principle sounded applicable enough to relationships. But how was he supposed to apply it? Especially if it looked like Kari was either doing the same thing or not even trying at all. Drained after his vigorous morning sail, he fell asleep wondering what he was going to do.

SIXTEEN

Billy woke and needed to talk to someone. He called Byron to ask if he wanted to go to happy hour at the Charthouse. Byron said they didn't have happy hour at the Charthouse on Sunday, and he was going out that night with Bianca anyway. Drinks before wouldn't do, as he needed to be his sharpest around her. He thought he might be beginning to like her, but she had a sharp wit and he needed to be on his game.

Billy tried Jackson. He was up for it. They decided to meet at four at the Fog Cutter in Marina Del Rey. It did have a Sunday happy hour.

"You look miserable," Jackson said. Billy indeed needed more than slightly discounted beers and appetizers to make him feel better. They had taken a seat at a table by a window that looked out over the docked boats and the stormy sea beyond. The rain had let up, though the dark clouds remained.

"I got up early to go sailing," Billy said.

"That must have been radical," Jackson said. "This storm's a southwester from a typhoon off the Marianas. There's going to be waves in Mexico, son."

Jackson had been a geek in most every sport except surfing until after college, when he got into bodybuilding—if bodybuilding is a sport. His family had a sailing yacht, and he wasn't very good at sailing, either, and once almost capsized it. He changed majors in college three times before settling on theater arts with a focus on acting and improv comedy. His desire to be an actor was why he got into bodybuilding. He was tall and blond, his upper body was well built, and women considered him handsome. So far in his professional acting career, he had only landed a few commercials and a twenty-nine-second, three-sentence spot on a soap opera. He was still taking acting classes and was currently studying Stanislavski. But what he really wanted to do was stand-up comedy.

"I haven't been surfing for weeks," Billy said.

"That could be contributing to your malaise," said Jackson, "but I discern something more existential." One of the majors that he had tried was philosophy. "Is she dumping you, my son?"

"Would you get off this 'my son' bit? Are you in character or something?"

"I am getting ready for an audition, playing a kindly old father who's going out of his mind."

"You don't have to get into someone else's character for that."

"So, are you having trouble with Kari?" Jackson said. "She would not be a bad catch. Excuse the fishing metaphor and the cliché."

"It's vivid enough for me not to be a cliché. I don't want to get into one of our philological debates."

"Well, are you?"

"I don't know. We both might be losing interest in each other."

"You should know if you're losing interest in her; why do you think she's losing interest in you?"

"First of all, lately, I'm not sure about my feelings for her." Billy knew this was untrue, though he would try to adjust his feelings if he knew her feelings had changed toward him. "And second, a number of things—like she split on me early during a date the other night. She was supposed to call me back and didn't. I've just sensed a coolness in her lately. And she says she wants to talk to me but only face-to-face. And not till Tuesday."

"Hmm," said Jackson, like a scientist analyzing a germ under a microscope.

"And I've gone way out of my way trying to show her I care. Like putting up with her very conceited cat."

"Hmm," Jackson said again, and took a sip of his margarita. He got up, went to the table where the free appetizers were, and came back with a plate of blue, green, and yellow tortilla chips and guacamole.

"As I recall, you don't like cats," Jackson said, sitting back down and putting the plate on the table.

"Yes, I have to take an allergy pill whenever I'm going over to her house." Billy grabbed a big blue chip, scooped up a glob of guacamole, and ate it.

"You seem bitter, my child."

"I'm not bitter." This was true.

"You are a reactionary," Jackson said. This was a term that he had heard but not understood in a political science class. But it sounded clinical and applicable.

"I mean, I'm trying to figure out how I feel and what to do." Billy crunched another guac-dipped chip and washed it down with a sip of beer.

"Have you talked to anyone else about this?" Jackson held a chip like a pen he was about to write a note with.

"No, only my grandfather."

"What did he say?"

"He basically said, 'Don't force it, but hang in there.'"

"What do you think that means?" Jackson said like a psychiatrist might.

"I don't know. All I know is if she doesn't want me, I guess I'll just back off."

"It is wise to heed the words of the aged. There are other women out there, you know. Like Amanda, for instance."

"Yes, I know." Billy took another chip. "I'm not hungry, but I can't stop eating these. How are you and she doing anyway?"

"She's almost as tall as me. Her skin is amazing. She looks like

Nathalie Emmanuel, only better. She's going somewhere. We're talking about taking an improv class together."

"I don't know who Nathalie Emmanuel is. But Amanda is pretty."

"She was Daenerys's gorgeous assistant in *Game of Thrones*, and Ramsey in *Fast X*. She's going somewhere."

"I haven't seen either, but it sounds like she already is somewhere."

"I think we've found each other. But I'm playing it cool. I think she's crazy about me. She wants me to come to watch her model on Tuesday, but if the storm is done, I'm going surfing in San Diego. Why don't you come? It would do you good."

"I'm going to wait to hear what Kari has to say. If she says she wants to call it off, I'll be good with it." Billy had come to the conclusion that that's what she was going to do.

Sometimes artists like Billy and Kari can be a little too sensitive, to the point of bordering on paranoia. Because their intuitions are right once in a while, they think they're right all the time. When these misreadings happen in romantic relationships, it can be especially problematic. Like Othello's misreading of Desdemona, which didn't turn out well.

"If she does give me walking papers, then it'll just fuel my writing," said Billy, trying to spin the situation positively. "She's a distraction anyway."

"So, do you think you'll want to go to San Diego?"

"Who knows? The way I'm feeling, the howling wastes of lower Baja sound better."

SEVENTEEN

At 9:00 a.m. sharp, Kari and Mac were back at the clinic. In the early morning, the storm had moved on to the east. The sky was brilliantly clear, and the air was cool and crisp. Kari got out of her car and waited. The freshness of the morning almost compensated for how she was feeling.

Twenty minutes later, a white Ford Ranger without oversized tires pulled into the parking lot. A pleasant-looking fortysomething lady hopped out. Tall and neither fat nor skinny, she was wearing tight-fitting blue jeans, cowboy boots, and a light-brown Carhartt jacket and had a brunette ponytail falling from the back of a cap with a jumping trout insignia on it. Her looks were reminiscent of the young man Kari had met with yesterday, or vice versa.

"You must be Kari and Mac," she said, offering her hand. "I'm Maggie. I can see why Luke wants to make sure I take good care of—" She paused for a moment and smiled. "—of your cat. Why don't you grab your little friend and follow me inside." Kari immediately felt comfortable with the lady.

In the examination room, after washing her hands, the vet put on a lab coat and latex gloves and donned a pair of glasses that had been hanging from a leather strap around her neck. She looked Mac's protrusion over, staying clear of her jaws. Without asking Kari's permission, she gave Mac a shot in the lower hip. Mac went to sleep. The vet then did multiple tests and took X-rays.

"You want the good news first or the bad news?" she said, taking off her glasses and smiling.

Her tone and smile confused Kari. "I don't know. I guess the good news."

"Mac doesn't have cancer."

"Oh, that's wonderful." Bracing herself, she said, "What's the bad news?"

"She's not pregnant. I don't know how that dolt of a son of mine could have thought that. Mac is about as unable to have babies anymore as Methuselah's wife. She's not only spayed but past her time."

This news wasn't altogether bad news to Kari. In her present circumstances, a clowder of cats wouldn't be convenient. "Well, what's wrong with her then?"

"I figured it out the moment I examined that bulge Luke called a protrusion. I think he was trying to sound doctorly. But I wanted the X-rays to make sure. Ole Mac has swallowed herself a heteromyid and didn't bother chewing it."

"A what?"

"A heteromyid. They're also called pocket mice. They can get up to about two and a half inches, but this one's maybe only two. Some of the beaches down there are infested with them and other rodents."

"Is it dangerous? What do you suggest we do?"

"There could be side effects that are dangerous. It could take weeks for her to digest it, and she could get even more miserable. But it's a simple operation for me to go in, take it out, and sew her up."

"Oh, this is good news. Thanks so much. How long do you think the operation would take?"

"Well, the other day I had to get a golf ball out of a Labrador retriever, and the operation itself only took about twenty minutes. But we should watch her in recovery for a few hours. If you really do need to get back, I could give her a sedative for the drive home, and you could be out of here by midafternoon. I'd take Highway 1 rather than the 405—a lot less traffic that time of day. Mac will need to take it easy for a while. The stitches will dissolve in a week, and she should be as good as new."

After asking how much it would cost—about half what a city vet would have charged—Kari gave the go-ahead. Even though she was a writer and craved new experiences, she declined the opportunity to watch the operation. But she did ask to see the mouse.

While Kari waited alone in the lobby, her phone rang.

"Hi, Amanda," Kari answered.

"I heard about Mac. So sorry. Is she going to be okay?"

"It looks like it was a false alarm. She swallowed a mouse."

"Yuck. I also heard about you and Billy."

"What did you hear about me and Billy?"

"That he's being a creep. Listen, you can have any guy you want."

"That's not true, and what if I want *him*?"

"Well, you can't let him know you want him that much so soon."

"Is that working with you and Jackson?"

"Are you kidding? He's totally into me."

A cute young girl, maybe fourteen, walked into the clinic. She was dressed similarly to Maggie and had similar features too, though her hair was blond. She said a quick, uninterested hi, set her backpack behind the counter, and walked through the door leading to the examination room but soon came out and took a seat behind the office counter.

"I have to go; I'm still at the vet," Kari said on the phone. "Thanks for calling. I should be back later today; I'll call you then."

"Okay, be strong," Amanda said and hung up.

"Luke is such a nerd," the girl behind the counter said while scrolling through her cellphone. She looked up. "I could have told you your cat wasn't pregnant. I think he's got a crush on you. His last girlfriend was named Kate too. I'm Annie. Just think, you and I could be sisters. You are pretty."

"My name's Kari, not Kate," Kari said, half amused. Though she wasn't interested in the young vet, it felt good that she had gotten at least someone's attention.

"Just like him," Annie said. "When he comes, don't tell him. Just let him go on calling you Kate. Then I'll say, 'Her name is Kari,' and he'll get all embarrassed."

"Shouldn't you be in school?"

"I'm office manager Mondays and Wednesdays after school, and as it's teacher training or something and no school today, I came in early."

An older man entered the office. He nodded at Kari as he took his cap off, revealing close-cropped gray hair. He hung his cap and jacket on a rack by the door and winked at Annie. As he went off into the back of the clinic, he took another glance at Kari.

"That's my grandfather," Annie said. "He's a vet too but mostly retired. He's got a sick alpaca in the stables out back."

"Wow, this is a real family affair," Kari said. "Is your father a vet too?"

"Yeah, but he's out of town at a horse conference in Tennessee. We're a little shorthanded at the moment."

A few minutes later, Luke arrived carrying a pizza box and two grocery bags, which he set on the counter.

"Hi, Kari. So glad Mac is going to be just fine. I was just being super cautious with my diagnosis. Guess I need to take some cat classes."

Hearing Luke get her name right, Kari smirked at Annie. Annie grimaced, flaring her nostrils, then shook it off.

Luke, not noticing any of this, said, "Lunch in the conference room in five minutes. The pizzas are half pepperoni-and-olive and half veggie, and I got salads too. Annie thinks she's a vegetarian, except when she's not." He went off to fetch Maggie and their grandfather.

EIGHTEEN

The lunch and the conversation were a nice diversion from how Kari had been feeling. Maggie said the operation went as smooth as a baby's rump. She let Kari view something like a baby monitor she had brought into the room, which showed Mac sleeping real-time in a crib.

They were a close, fun, and interesting family. They asked all sorts of questions about her, and she about them. With these characters, Kari thought she might have the makings of a short story.

As they were eating the dessert of homemade rhubarb pie that Luke's grandma had sent, music from Kari's phone started playing.

"I'm so sorry. I have to take this; it's my work," she said. To be polite and show how much she appreciated the meal, she took another bite of pie before she left the conference room.

By the time she got out to the parking lot, the call had dropped. A text message arrived a few seconds later: "Please call Livia King ASAP, important." Livia King was her supervisor's manager.

She dialed and was transferred to Ms. King after getting screened by her assistant.

"Thanks for calling, Kari," Ms. King said. "We're having a bit of an emergency, and we need your help. The Italian-speaking attendant for tomorrow's eleven fifty-five p.m. from Newark to Rome got in a serious car accident and is in the hospital. We need you to come through for us. Your file shows your passport is current, you're fluent in Italian, and certified on Dreamliners."

"Well, yes," Kari said, "but I haven't flown international or been on a Dreamliner for over a year." She didn't want to go, especially in her current circumstances. Though Mrs. Martin could take care of Mac, her relationship with Billy needed attention. But it didn't sound like Ms. King was asking, even though there were union rules that applied in situations like this.

"You know I'm in California?" Kari said.

"Yes, we know. We've already reserved a seat for you on tomorrow's eight a.m. LAX direct to Newark, business class. You'll be there in plenty of time."

They're really in trouble if they're offering me business class, Kari thought, but didn't immediately answer.

"Can we count on you?"

"Would it be okay if I called you back in about fifteen minutes? I'm at the veterinarian's for my cat."

"All right, fifteen minutes. I can see from your file that we have made special considerations for your transfer to California and for your limited hours. So please understand this is important to us and to your career. And you'll be getting special-duty compensation."

Kari didn't go right back inside after ending the call. This couldn't be happening at a worse time. She just ached for Billy, but she didn't know what to do. It would be totally inappropriate to have the conversation they needed to have over the phone. She didn't even know what she wanted to say. She cared for him so much, but maybe telling him so was the worst thing she could do. That's what her friends implied anyway. And if his feelings had cooled off, it would be humiliating. Maybe putting off meeting him was a good thing—to see how he would react. If he really cared for her, wouldn't he do something?

Kari went back into the conference room, not having made up her mind about whether she would go. She took a bite of her pie.

"Is everything all right?" Maggie asked.

"It's just work. They want me to fly to Italy tomorrow."

"How cool," said Annie. "I want to be a flight attendant."

"I thought you wanted to be Taylor Swift," Luke said.

"If you're concerned about Mac," Maggie said, "Annie would love to take care of her for you."

"I would. I could keep her in my room," Annie said.

"You'd have to move your hamsters," Luke said.

"Thanks so much," Kari said. "That's not it. I have a neighbor who takes good care of her when I'm gone. It's just that I had other plans."

Annie turned to Luke, who was sitting next to her, and whispered, "I told you she must have a boyfriend." The whisper was loud enough for all to hear.

"Can't you just say no?" said Maggie.

"They've done me a lot of favors and just reminded me of them."

"I'm sure everything will work out fine," said their grandfather.

"I guess I'm going to have to go," Kari said, in one way relieved that at least she had made up her mind.

Luke didn't say anything but thought, *If it means trouble with her boyfriend, she ought to obey her boss.* He tried to look sympathetic.

"You probably need to get going soon, then," Maggie said. She stood and started cleaning up the paper plates and leftovers. "Mac should be waking up any minute. She should rest for another hour or so"—she looked at her watch—"say till two, and if all's well, you can get going."

As they were cleaning up, Kari's phone rang again. She took the call in the lobby. It was Ms. King calling her directly. "Are you going to be able to help us, young lady?" she said. The condescending tone was extremely irritating.

"If I take it, when would I be able to get back?"

"Back to LA Friday by noon."

"Would I be working the flight back?"

"Yes, we'd need you on that too."

"And no more, without regular notice?"

"Yes, we just screwed up on our scheduling."

"Double pay on the way back too."

"Okay."

"And two confirmed business-class round-trip tickets to Maui for me and my boyfriend. If I take this, I'm going to have some making up to do."

"If I do it, you'll go?"

"Yes, I'll do it."

All was well with Mac. Maggie gave her a shot of something that would make her docile and pain-free on the way home. She also gave Kari some pills that Mac should take for the next week for pain from the incision and stitches. Kari paid her bill, which was a pittance compared to what she was expecting, and after warm goodbyes and hugs, Kari and Mac started off.

"I bet you didn't even get her phone number," Annie said when Luke came back into the office after helping load Mac into Kari's car.

"You don't know anything. She's a writer; I got her social handle."

Billy was at his desk in his apartment, working on his novel. He wasn't making good progress. If he had been using a typewriter to write, he would have chucked eleven partially typed pages into the garbage basket on the other side of the room.

His agent had given him Capote's *In Cold Blood*. The paperback lay on his writing table, four ominous eyes staring out of the cover over the book's title. Billy hadn't read much of it, only the part where Capote starts going to the jail to interview the murderers. It was plenty bleak so far.

He was trying to add something maybe a little less gruesome, but it was hard getting his thoughts off Kari. Those thoughts were not dark, but the thought of losing her was worse than gruesome and confused and painful. If she was going to tell him in their meeting tomorrow that her feelings weren't aligned with his, what should he do? Maybe she was only going to say they should continue cooling off a bit and not break things off altogether. Maybe he had come on too strong.

His phone buzzed, and he glanced down at a text from Kari.

"I'm so sorry, but something came up with work. I have to go to Italy and can't meet Tuesday. How does Saturday look for coffee?"

Italy? To see her pilot boyfriend? was Billy's first deduction.

And why did she only want to have coffee?

Maybe he should say he had other plans.

He phoned Jackson. They decided to leave on Thursday night for a four-day weekend surfing trip to Baja.

He waited a few hours to text her back: "I can't make it on Saturday, I'll be out of town."

NINETEEN

"I was expecting Kari to come here with you," Billy's grandmother said to him. It was Saturday at lunchtime, two weeks since the last time Billy had seen Kari, when she had cut short their date. "You did invite her, didn't you?" He had barely seated himself in an azure velvet-lined Victorian armchair across from where Gwen sat in a similar chair.

The table in front of them was set for three with a tea set decorated with pink and white cherubs hovering in a background of baby blue. Sterling silver teaspoons, salad forks, and butter knives; linen napkins; and a plate of cucumber sandwiches cut into fours completed the setting.

Billy didn't answer.

Gwen leaned over, poured a cup of tea, and almost thrust it at him, spilling a few drops on the saucer. "What is going on with you and Kari?" she asked, sterner than usual.

"It's complicated," Billy finally said.

"I have a feeling about that girl," she said. "And please take your sunglasses off. I like looking into your eyes when we speak." Even in her current mood, her elocution had an elegance that went well with her erect posture and her black silk pants and beige cashmere sweater.

"Sorry, I forgot I had them on." He took off his Costa sunglasses. "Driving up the hill, the sun was in my eyes."

"Those are the same kind I got your grandfather; they're supposed to be the best for sensitive blue eyes."

"It is a beautiful day down there," Billy said, hoping Nana wasn't going to get back to her initial question. He turned his head slightly to look out through the three large picture windows that made up most of the northern wall of the room. There was no fog and little smog, and the large white letters of the Hollywood sign sang its siren song in the middle of the view.

"If you insist on all that late-night reading, you must take care of your eyes."

"If I'm going to be a writer," he said, looking back to her, "I need to read everything I can and experience everything I can. And as meaningful experience is somewhat limited these days"—this last phrase he said with a frown—"reading is the best way to get it. That's what Faulkner said, or something like that."

"Well, you don't want to end up like Milton, do you?"

"You know, we do have electricity down in Hollywood, and the lighting in my study is quite good. And we have audiobooks now, so if I go blind, I won't need my daughter to read Greek to me."

"At the rate you're now going, you're never going to get married and have a daughter. Now, what about you and Kari? I even liked her friends, especially Bianca. Did you know that all three of them sent me thank-you notes? You know, you can tell a lot about a person by her friends."

Billy started to get up.

"Please sit down and tell me what is going on between you and that wonderful girl. You know I think the world of her. She could be perfect for you."

"You've only met her once."

"I even had a dream about you and her." Gwen didn't mention that she and Kari had also traded a few letters.

Billy sat back down.

"So, what's the problem? Last month, you said you couldn't sleep or eat because you were so smitten. And I know she's very fond of you."

The problem was that Billy didn't think this was still the case. "To be honest, I'm not feeling much of anything anymore." He wasn't being close to honest.

"I highly doubt that. I have some experience with things of the heart, you know. Your grandfather and I have been crazy about each other since the day we met. And I have a feeling about you two."

"Yes, I know: love at first sight and all and that place in the mountains you're always talking about."

"It wasn't quite at first sight, but when it happened, it was like a thunderbolt. You said something like that happened the moment you saw her."

"I said it took a couple of minutes," he corrected her. "There's a difference between infatuation and real love. You told me that. I've been saved from that before."

"It's obvious you still care for her. What do you know about infatuation anyway? Infatuation and love are complex, mysterious, even magical things—at least *real* love is. Your grandfather and I are not always infatuated with each other but always in love. Infatuation is a tricky thing. If you want something to write about, you should learn about those kinds of things."

"She's become a distraction." This last phrase did have some truth about it. His heart so perpetually ached for her that he could hardly keep his mind on anything else.

"A distraction from what?"

"Well, from my writing and studying and, most of all, from life. I'm twenty-nine, and what have I done? Napoleon conquered Egypt when he was twenty-nine. If I'm going to write anything great, I need to get experiences and get deep into the bowels of life."

"You should be more selective with your metaphors."

"Okay, into the sinews and the heart of things. The heart of reality is what I'm shooting for."

"The reality of the heart is what you ought to be shooting for, which, for your information, happens to be the heart of reality. Those are the experiences and the reality to write about."

"I'm sorry, Nana, I just don't have time for anything else right now."

Gwen got up, walked over to the middle picture window, and looked out on the bay.

After a few moments, without turning, she said, "Dear William, you know you are playing the fool. She's perfect for you."

She turned and walked over to a table behind Billy's chair that was set with numerous framed pictures of her and her husband. She picked up a twelve-by-eight-inch picture of a young woman and man in a lush pastoral setting. To one side of them, a tree-lined stream ran through a grassy meadow. Down by the stream, a shepherd sat on a rock, piping to a shepherdess while sheep frolicked about them. On the other side was a large old lodge. From the angle of the picture, the only words that could be seen on the sign above the entrance were "the Bow." Also visible on the sign was about two-thirds of the plump-cheeked face of a cherubic child. Gwen set the picture back, turned, and asked, "Have you told her?"

"Well, I haven't—I haven't exactly told her yet."

"You haven't told her? You better not leave that girl hanging."

"It's not that easy—but I'm going to."

A few hours later, Gwen and Arthur sat on one of their balconies, sipping sparkling wine, watching the sun's departure and the latest version of pinks and blues and purples it was leaving in its wake.

"I just don't approve," Gwen said.

"Of what—the sunset or the wine?"

"Don't be mean. You know what I'm concerned about."

"Worrying, dear, never helped anything."

"He's going to break off his relationship with that darling girl we think so highly of. They seem so much a match, have so much in common but also complement each other nicely."

"*Complement* with an *e*, not an *i*, I assume you mean, as in 'completes or fills up what the other is lacking'?"

"With an *e*—like us. But he says he has higher priorities."

"I'm sure it's more complicated than that."

"Did he talk about her when you went sailing?"

"He'll figure things out." Arthur didn't give much detail when it came to his private talks with Billy.

"But he was smitten. The way he was acting before—he had that joyous, agonizing madness." She smiled as memories and images of their romance through the years floated back to her.

"Well, he did seem fairly wounded. I don't know about joyous."

"Wounds do sometimes hurt. I so want him to know even a little of what we have. I want him to know what it is to be so madly and deeply in love that time stops. I wish there was something we could do." Gwen shifted closer to her husband.

"Now, darling, matchmaking is tricky business; much can go wrong. We should probably stay out of that line and let nature take its course."

"Maybe there's just a little something? There's that place up in the mountains."

"Yes, where I made such a fool of myself."

"So did I. But that's what happens when it happens."

"You'd think I'd get tired of being a fool after fifty years."

"It's fifty-one," Gwen corrected him, loving what he'd said.

"I guess anyone who falls in love," Arthur said, "has to be a bit off his rocker."

"Yes, we're all crazy," Gwen said matter-of-factly. "There's been an epidemic of it since the world began. Now, if we could only get Billy and Kari up there."

"Didn't we just agree we weren't going to meddle?"

"I didn't actually agree."

TWENTY

Fifteen days had passed since Billy and Kari's abbreviated date. Their last communication, either by email, text, WhatsApp, or any of the other options in the modern "world electronic," had been Billy's blunt text ten days ago: "I can't make it on Saturday, I'll be out of town."

They both were dying to know what was going on in the other's mind. Billy figured it was Kari's turn to respond as he had sent the last text. Kari thought Billy needed to say something more than just that he couldn't make it. They, unfortunately, were acting as many mortals do when confused about the status of their romantic relationship—they were not being forthcoming, which basically means chicken.

For almost three months they had been dating and were—or had been—crazy about each other. Their relationship had seemed so right and easy. But now they had both backed off. And both for the same wrong reasons: One, because they thought it would keep their relationship from flaming out. Apparently, to overly sensitive artistic types this makes sense. And two, they both thought the other's backing off was more than mere backing off. It was a sign that he or she was about to get dumped. And thus, though they might not have been consciously aware of what they were doing, it was protection from the looming threat of a heartbreaking rejection.

It was now early September, the second Sunday of the football season, and Billy's favorite team, the Seattle Seahawks, was facing Kari's favorite team, the New England Patriots. It would be an understatement to say that it was an uncomfortable moment when they noticed each other sitting at the same dark and crowded bar in Santa Monica.

As Billy and Kari were trying to avoid dealing with the matter, their running into each other at a sports bar could have been a coincidence. But strange and portentous things sometimes happen amid the tinsel of Southern California. It also could have been that they—as could-be, would-be lovers often do—did appreciate many similar things. And one of these was American football.

Billy saw her first. At the far end of the bar, he noticed a tall man wearing a business suit standing between a couple of the barstools, ordering a drink. There was a young woman sitting on the stool to the man's left, and he was blocking from view whoever was sitting to his right. He saw the man's head turn to say something to this person.

Billy turned his attention back to the big screen on the wall behind the bar counter. Soon an annoying commercial about sports gambling came on. Disgusted by the commercial, as well as by the score of the game, he leaned back on his stool and looked to his right again. The man who had been ordering left with his drink, revealing a very attractive young woman with golden-brown hair wearing a New England Patriots jersey. A moment or two later, the young woman looked down the bar to her left and saw a handsome, olive-skinned young man wearing a Seattle Seahawks cap. Their eyes met. They quickly looked away.

They slowly looked back. Billy tried to smile, more or less; Kari smiled, less than more. Both their hearts pounded, and their stomachs churned. Billy realized he had to do something. He took a deep breath, got up, and walked over to her.

"Come to watch the game?" he said.

"Yes, and my Pats are winning."

"The Hawks are a fourth-quarter team," Billy said.

"Yeah, they did great in the 2013 Super Bowl fourth quarter."

"That was a long time ago, and Brady was a cheater."

"He's retired. Didn't cheat anyway. Another right-wing conspiracy."

The young woman sitting next to Kari got up and left.

"This game's not over," Billy said.

"Just as good as."

"I've been meaning to talk to you anyway," Billy said. It was almost halftime, and the game did look like it was going to be a blowout. "I'm glad you're here."

"I'm glad you're here too," Kari said. "I've wanted to talk with you as well."

"Let's go outside, it's too noisy in here," Billy said.

"We'll miss the game," Kari said.

"It's too painful to watch."

"Okay, I do need to talk to you." Kari got up.

"Hold my card," Billy said to the bartender after downing the rest of his beer. "And you can put hers on my tab. I'll be back."

"I paid cash," Kari said, and put a cardboard coaster over the top of her unfinished glass of Chardonnay.

They walked outside and went into a coffee shop two doors away and sat down at a table.

"Okay, what did you want to say?" Billy asked, trying to brace himself for the blow he thought was coming.

"No, you go first," Kari said, not really wanting to hear what she thought was coming either.

"Ladies first," Billy said, peeking into the big blue-green eyes that still entranced him.

"I'll kill you if you say that again," Kari said. Sometimes a good offense is the best defense.

"Okay," said Billy, taking a couple of napkins from the holder on the table. "Write what you want to say on a napkin, and I will too, and we'll turn them over at the same time."

Instead, she pulled a couple of sheets of paper from the notebook in her purse and handed one to Billy. She also grabbed a pen from her purse. She took a deep breath and said, "Okay, go," and started writing.

It took her about three minutes to compose her message. Billy watched, wondering what he did to lose the most wonderful girl in the world and how she was going to lower the boom on him.

"What are you waiting for?" she said, looking up at Billy when she had finished writing.

"I don't have a pen."

"You're a writer and you don't have a pen?" She loaned him hers and thought how adorable he looked when he tried to be humble.

Though prone to writer's block, when he got going, Billy had to restrain his verbosity; he took about five minutes to write his note. He wanted to get it just right.

He had been mulling over what he was going to say to her ever since he had come to the conclusion that she was going to break up with him. He wanted to say something that would soften the blow, something that would suggest that although he kind of liked her, he wasn't *that* into her and, at the same time, wouldn't totally cut off the possibility of them getting back together someday. He also wanted it to be dramatic.

An idea had been percolating and taking shape after his meeting with his grandmother. His agent's input to write darker had planted the seed. "Experience," he had told his grandmother, was what he was lacking. This was also the best thing he had come away with from his literary studies at the University of Washington nine years ago. Most of his professors were promoting the latest critical theories. These bored Billy. He had come to college hoping to learn what made—and how to make—great literature, not how to shred it. But there was one professor, Dr. Friedman, who had studied at Oxford. His idea was that the hyper-analytical approach to literature eviscerated it. He emphasized that one can't analyze something and experience it at the same time; one can't bask in a lover's kiss while dissecting anatomically what is happening in one's labial membranes. Billy didn't fully understand the example, but this was the genesis of his wanting "meaningful experience" to be at the core of his writing. Experience was what was in, and communicated by, real literature. It was what Hemingway got and communicated in war and what Capote got and communicated from his relationship with Perry Smith in jail. It was what he needed to get and achieve in his writing.

In his note to Kari, he needed to write something that would not only *not* cut off his chances with her in the future but might also even draw him a little sympathy.

"Well," Kari said.

Billy was starting to panic and still hadn't started writing. As necessity is the mother of invention—at a table in a Hollywood coffee shop, in his whirling, seething brain—he remembered those ominous eyes from the book on his writing table, and the seeds that had been germinating in his subconscious blossomed, if that is the right word, into an idea. A plan took shape. Without taking time to think it through, he wrote.

"On the count of three, we hand them over," Billy said when he finished.

"Okay," Kari said. "One, two, three."

"I am quite fond of you, Billy," he read from her paper, "but I'm just not ready for a committed relationship. It's not you, it's me. To be quite honest, I've had a lot of things to deal with lately and just can't handle any distractions right now."

She had tried to put it in a way that would not cut off the possibility of them rebounding if Billy's feelings ever changed. It was not that original. But it's not easy prevaricating about one's true feelings. And there was some truth to it, given what she had gone through with her cat.

What Kari read from Billy's paper was, "Dear Kari, there's just a lot of stuff going on in my life right now. You really are terrific, and we do have a lot in common, but with what I'm going through right now, I just don't think you would want a relationship with me—I'm going to jail."

TWENTY-ONE

Most everything Billy had said in his note to Kari was at least partially true, or at least he was going to try to get sent to jail. William D. Spiers was a determined young man. Though he wasn't that young, his thirtieth birthday being just three months away. But the number of one's years was not important. What was important was how much of the raw marrow of life one had sucked out of those years. What he had determined he needed was to peel off the veneer and tap into the "real" of reality, into its pulsating heart.

But those thoughts had, in turn, depressed him. He had not fought in any wars or been an ambulance driver in one, nor had he been a communist spy in MI6 or a spy hunter in the State Department. He had not been to a jail to interview a blood-splotched criminal to get a story, as in the book his agent had given him. But that had given him his idea: What was better than interviewing someone in jail? How about a day or two in jail! That would be an experience as full and dark and sordid as any modern publisher could ask for. It could also serve multiple purposes in his relationship with Kari.

But as determined as he was, he also tried to be circumspect. He wanted to make sure he would get out after a day or two. So, that night, after Billy had run into Kari, he consulted his lawyer, who also happened to be his best friend, Byron.

Byron had become a lawyer for practical reasons; his father was the principal in an important Los Angeles firm. But law wasn't where his passions lay. His early college "goth" stage had evolved into a passion for avant-garde drama. His other passion was cycling, which he was pretty good at. The law firm wasn't giving him a lot to do other than research and traffic and parking ticket cases. He had a lot of time for cycling and to work on his one-act play.

Byron answered Billy's call: "You owe me eight hundred and eighty-four dollars. I got the tickets for the seminar."

"Great, but I thought it was going to be eight hundred."

"Tax. Eight hundred for two nights, a single room, and the honor of hearing his professorly highness, Dr. Fulkles, and ten point five percent more for your government. I sure hope this is worth it."

"In person, he's supposed to be amazing. We're lucky we get a chance to see him. His whole thing is creating creativity. From what I've read, I think he's on to something." The seminar, the weekend after next, along with his new plan, could maybe let loose the smoldering creativity he felt cramped inside him.

"Jackson's already paid up."

"I'll Venmo you after we get off the phone. But there's something else I want to talk to you about."

"What's that?"

"I need to get thrown into LA County Jail."

"William," Byron said after a few seconds, wanting to sound lawyerly, "LA County Jail is one of the most dangerous and sordid places for anybody to be incarcerated, much less a white boy, even one with olive skin."

"That's just what I'm looking for," Billy responded, "as long as you can get me out after a few hours."

"That depends on what law you are going to break."

"Theft. I'm going to steal your new twenty-four-speed."

This didn't go over well at first. "You are not stealing my new bike."

"How about your old ten-speed? I'm only just going to borrow it."

"I don't have a ten-speed anymore. My least expensive bike is a sixteen-speed."

"Can I steal that? You'll get it back."

"I'll let you borrow my old sixteen-speed." Byron was getting the idea that this was going to let him do a little real lawyering.

"Okay, that should be good enough. I'm working on the plan. I'm targeting this coming Friday night. Let's talk tomorrow."

◆━━━━▶

The next day, they worked out the details for the "job," as Billy called it. There would be a minimum of bodily harm to him and no damage to Byron's property. The morning after, Byron would come down to the police station, drop any charges, and claim the whole thing was a misunderstanding. Byron liked the idea and fully bought in.

◆━━━━▶

Late Friday night, Billy dressed in a black turtleneck, black jeans, and a black stocking cap. At exactly 10:50 p.m., he stealthily entered Byron's house. The one-bedroom California bungalow his father had bought for him lay on a quiet street a mile up from the beach in Venice. The front door had been left unlocked, and the bike was in the front hall. Byron could see the hall from the living room, where he was sitting with a volume of Beckett's plays. Ever the critic, he thought Billy was overdoing it by wearing the turtleneck and all.

At 10:53 Byron called 911. They presumed that it would take the cops (they liked using the term for its noir nuance) ten minutes to get there. Billy would wait in the doorway, foot on pedal, until he saw the patrol car approaching. He'd then take off down the street, at less than full speed, for an attempted getaway and chase.

Not analyzing one's presumptions is unwise. With modern

technology, the police are quite efficient these days. The black-and-white pulled up in five minutes and twenty seconds.

Billy made a dash for it anyway. He didn't get his getaway chase. He slammed into the patrol car, denting the rear passenger-side door, smashing the bike's thin front wheel, and launching himself over the handlebars and into the car door's window. As he staggered to his feet, he was thrown to the ground and ungently handcuffed.

TWENTY-TWO

The Venice police annex, where Billy was initially held, was one of the far-outreaching tentacles of the monstrous LA County jail system. Nestled in a strip mall, it was about as far away from the ocean as it could be and still be in the city of Venice Beach. It could formerly have been a 31 Flavors ice cream store or a Starbucks. Inside, the office was walled off from an iron-barred cell in the back—really an eighteen-by-eighteen-foot cage.

After the arresting officers deposited Billy at the annex, the officer there searched Billy again and took his wallet, belt, watch, shoelaces, pocket-sized Moleskine notepad, and pen. Old, white, and rotund, this officer strained the buttons on his duty shirt. He had Billy remove his turtleneck and handed him an oversized bright orange T-shirt.

While Billy sat on a chair, hands cuffed in front of him, the officer hunted and pecked Billy's name, address, and other particulars from his driver's license into a computer. He also entered all the items he had taken from Billy into the computer and stuffed them in a clear plastic bag. He didn't say more than ten words to Billy, other than explaining that the reason he had taken his turtleneck, belt, and shoelaces was so he wouldn't hang himself.

He then took Billy through a door to the rear of the facility and into the cage and locked him in. He had Billy stick his hands back through an opening in the bars and removed his handcuffs. The officer then returned to the outer office, slamming the metal door with an echoing clang.

Not designed for comfort, the cell's only furniture was a coverless, seatless, stainless-steel toilet set against the far wall and a stainless-steel water fountain a few feet to the left of it. The cell's concrete floor was cold and bare and somewhat clean except for a splotch of dried blood in front of the water fountain.

After fifteen minutes, Billy, tired of standing, chose what looked like a clean spot on the floor and slid down against the cold iron bars next to the cell's sliding door, which was more like a big, barred iron gate.

"Hey!" Billy called out to the outer office after a few more minutes. "Do you think while I wait I could have my pen and notepad?"

"A pen is a dangerous weapon," came the reply, "and paper is a fire hazard."

"Who am I going to stab?" He was using imprecise grammar on purpose.

"Suicide."

"That's ridiculous. Why would I kill myself? I'm not going to be in here much longer." Thinking about the jailer's response, Billy saw the unintended irony—pens could be dangerous weapons. Maybe his would be one, someday.

But after this pleasant thought, his mind turned toward Kari. How did he mess things up so badly with her? Here, in the loneliness of the cell and after the drama of his arrest, he turned nostalgic, and his heart ached for her. Their relationship was so great for a time. There was no one else with whom he could have what they had. There was no one else he would ever care about. Maybe he would go and join the French Foreign Legion—isn't that what brokenhearted lovers used to do? He sighed and banged the back of his head against the bars—harder than he had meant to.

"Don't do that," came a warning from the front office. Billy hadn't noticed the video camera that peered into the cell.

After what seemed longer but was only about twenty minutes, he called out again. "Any word about my case yet?"

Through the thin wall that separated the office from the cell, Billy heard, "Relax."

After another fifteen minutes, he called out again. "Listen, don't I get a phone call or something?"

This time, there was no response.

After another twenty minutes or so, the door from the outer office opened and a different officer, who was tall and Latin and fit, took a few steps into the room and held the door open. Then another Latin officer, also tall and even more well built, escorted yet another Latin man into the room. This one was definitely not an officer. Midsize, muscled, and extremely tattooed, his hands were cuffed behind his back. His hair was just long enough to have been in a ponytail but was disheveled, as if he had just been through some exertion. He was maybe in his early forties.

Billy rose, stepped away from the door, and faced them as they approached the cell.

The first officer removed the new prisoner's handcuffs outside the cell while the other officer stood guard. He then locked him in with Billy.

"Sir," Billy said, trying to get either of their attentions before they left, "do you know when I'm going to be booked or charged or whatever they are going to do to me? And when am I going to get a phone call?"

"Chill out, dude," was the response in Latino-accented English. It didn't come from one of the officers but from Billy's new cellmate.

After contemplating Billy for a few moments, the cellmate growled, "Whitesauce, you know you were sitting in a bunch of dried piss?"

As first impressions go, this was not comforting. Billy moved a few steps, looking down at where he had been sitting. "It didn't look like dried piss."

"Everything in here's dried piss. What you in here for?"

"I should be getting out any minute."

"Yeah? Why you looking so glum, man, if you getting out so soon?"

"It's complicated."

"Oh, trouble with your old lady, huh?"

"She's younger than I am."

"Your *woman*, Sauce."

"It's nothing, I'll get over it."

"Yeah, just what I figured. But it's inevitable, Sauce. We all go through it. I'm having an issue with my old old lady again too."

"How old is she anyway?" Billy said. "She rich or something?"

"It ain't that she's old, Sauce, it's just that she's my old lady, but at the moment, she don't know it anymore, so it's like she's my *old* old lady, but she's still my old lady, 'cause I'll destroy anyone who tries to move in on her like I did to Julio Bocardo, which is why I'm in here now. Just like she thinks, at the moment, I'm her old old man, but really, I'm her old man and always will be her old man. I'd feel sorry for the woman who'd try to take me away from her. I know it's all counter-itner—" He paused, trying to find the word.

"I think *counterintuitive* is what you're looking for," Billy said. "I don't know if it is any kind of intuitive."

"Cool gold tooth. Your old lady give you that?"

"I used to play rugby."

"Whatever, Sauce, but if you got problems with your old lady, I mean, I'm like the one the homies go to. I got deep experience in matters of the heart."

"I just need to get out of here," Billy said, not appreciating where their conversation was going. "They haven't even given me my phone call yet."

"Whitesauce, what they charge you with anyway?"

"They haven't charged me with anything yet; there's been a huge misunderstanding."

"Yeah," grunted or chuckled the cellmate, Billy couldn't tell which. "That's what they all say."

"They haven't told me anything. Aren't I supposed to get a phone call?"

"You don't look too good. You more worried about jail or your old lady?"

"I was just borrowing my friend's bike."

"You ever been in jail before?"

"Well, no. As I said, there's been a misunderstanding."

"Where you from?"

"Hollywood. The bike I borrowed was in Venice Beach."

"If you from Hollywood, what you doing down here?"

"I'm a writer; I'm just trying to get some detail for something I'm working on."

On hearing this, the cellmate's chin lifted, his eyes opened wider, and a grin rose at the left corner of his mouth.

"Marty!" the cellmate called out. "What's Whitesauce in here for?"

Through the closed door that separated the cell from the booking office, a voice called back, "GT, resisting arrest, fleeing the scene of a crime, reckless endangerment, and damaging government property."

"Homestone, that don't sound like just some 'misunderstanding,'" the cellmate said.

"That's crazy. They can't be serious!"

"Damn, where you're going, Hollywood"—he studied Billy for a beat before going on—"where you're going, you're going to need some friends. I'm Rogero, but the homies call me Elrond." He offered Billy his right fist to pop. Billy cautiously returned the pop. The back of Elrond's hand was tattooed with an elaborate multicolored curved sword with some kind of script on its blade.

TWENTY-THREE

"It ain't really piss you were standing in," Elrond said to Billy, trying to cheer him up. "I was just messing with you, homestone. They clean this place daily at six p.m., getting ready for the nighttime rush."

"Thanks, that's good to know." Not all that relieved, Billy slid back down against a wall of the cell several feet away from where he had initially sat, onto a place that did look somewhat clean.

Elrond slid down next to him. "You're going to need to know some other stuff where you're going to. But listen, Hollywood, I'm a writer too. I got some great stuff for you. I mean real meat. I get into the guts of things, you know—the real, real stuff, from the hood. I took McKee's class twice, man. Me and you could team up. I also got poems, not some rap shit either, real iambic pentameter. What I'm working on now is real dope—matters of the heart, of love, treachery, and bloodshed."

"Yeah, I'd love to look at what you have," Billy said, actually a little interested, "once I get out of here."

"I'll have Marty put my email address with your stuff. Depending where they put you, they give you email privileges, and you can check it out. I've copyrighted it."

"I was just borrowing my friend's bike. I really need to have that phone call."

"You don't get your call or to see your lawyer till after you're booked, and they got till noon tomorrow to do that. And even if GT is dropped, you got all that other stuff—resisting, fleeing, reckless endangerment, and damaging government property. That's worse than GT."

"What's GT?"

"Grand theft—anything over nine hundred fifty dollars—and it can be a felony."

"But this is my first offense."

"You white, Sauce, so won't help. Probably hurt. They like to stick it to rich white boys."

"I'm not rich."

"If you ain't got bail, from here you going to the 'Dungeon' in Van Nuys, where you'll suffer until Monday sometime, when you'll get your bail hearing. From there, it's to the 'Hole' downtown, where you'll die . . . or worse."

Billy was silent.

"If you have a rich *mamacita*, at least you could raise bail," Elrond continued. "It might keep you out the Hole, but you still got at least till Monday in the Dungeon. They don't do bail hearings on the weekends."

"My lawyer friend didn't tell me that. How much do you think my bail would be?"

"Hundred large or so. Then, if your lawyer's good, he might be able to string out your trials for a couple of years and then maybe get you only nine months. You say your friend is a lawyer—what kind?"

"Something to do with family trusts."

"That ain't so good, Whitesauce," Elrond laughed.

"Why do they call it the Dungeon?"

"'Cause the jail is in Van Nuys, and it's underground 'cause the air in the Valley sucks. A few years ago, they found a couple of skulls under some white dude's bunk. Downtown's the Hole 'cause, you know, black holes, those weird stars. Sometimes they forget you're in there, and you just seem to disappear. I did astronomy in junior college—it was a hard class; they graded on a curve."

"I need to get out of here soon."

"I've gotta give this some thought." Elrond got up and paced the cell, his left hand alternating between rubbing his goatee and the balding spot on the top of his head. After a few moments, he stopped pacing and said, "Yeah, I need to get out and back to my old lady too. As I said, I got experience. I know women. A lot of cats your age just don't know what they're doing anymore. You gotta be bold, man. You know what I'm saying? Chicks don't like mealymouthed wimps. But you can't be too bold either. You gotta not take the whole business so seriously. Know what I'm saying?"

"Yes, I think I know what you're saying," Billy answered, not really knowing what he was saying.

Deep in his thoughts, Elrond went on, half speaking to himself. "It's true—at the moment, things could be better with me and Vivian, and then there's Julio Bocardo trying to move in." He let out a slight groan. "Viv might be a one-of-a-kind. Problem is, most of the time they're all kinda one-of-a-kind."

Changing the subject with barely a pause, Elrond continued. "Anyway, even if you can raise bail, it's the Dungeon for you—at least till Monday and maybe longer. Parts of it are less bad than the Hole. Depends on if you're in minimum, medium, or maximum security. Maximum is okay 'cause you're isolated, all by yourself. Minimum is for unpaid traffic tickets and is usually not too dangerous. Medium is the worst. That's where all the blood gets spilled."

"And you think my bail will be a hundred K, even though this is my first offense?"

"Yeah. They like to slam first-time white boys, scare the chorizo out of 'em. It's politics too. If you was brown or black, you'd be out O.R. tomorrow. But you're a honky. And where you're going, you don't want to be a honky."

"That's bad?"

"It's a numbers game, homestone. You're outnumbered: by the brothers, two to one; by the homies, three to one."

"You mean gangs?"

"Tribes and territories, Sauce! In the Hole, even in the Dungeon, it's rule by tribes, and if you ain't got protection, you're ground meat. The whites don't stand just for any white boy unless there's somethin' in it for them. They're too outnumbered. And if you stand alone, you might end up one of those skulls buried under the floor."

This was not at all going according to plan. Byron had not even considered that he was going to need bail. And $100,000! Billy had been trying to suppress thoughts that were tending toward his grandmother. Now, he could no longer hold them back. "I have to get free soon," he said. "I've got important stuff going on."

"What you got that so important?"

"I have a chance to hear this guy that only a few people ever get to hear. Supposedly, he knows how to unlock your creativity, like what made Shakespeare so great. I've paid a thousand bucks to hear him next weekend." Here, Billy embellished, rounding the figure up.

"What's the dude's name?"

"Professor Sydney Fulkles."

"You getting to hear Sydney Fulkles?" This got Elrond thinking. He had already taken a liking to Billy because of his Hollywood connection and because, despite what he said, he thought having a lawyer friend who did trusts seemed to suggest that Billy had access to money. Cash money can open a lot of doors in the LA County jail system, figuratively as well as literally. And now Billy was going to get to hear this great teacher about the secret of creativity.

Elrond paced some more, fingering his goatee. Billy's imagination was far from silent.

"Sauce," Elrond said after a minute or so of silence. He stopped pacing and walked up to Billy, staring at him. "You ain't *that* white!"

"I'm not. I mean, I'm only half white." Which was somewhat accurate, depending on how you define ethnicity. "My mother was . . ." Billy almost said *Italian*, wondering if being one-quarter Italian (as well as one-quarter Jewish) qualified her as Italian. "She is Latin," Billy said. "I'm actually half Latin. That's where I get my coloring from."

"Where she from?"

Billy had to think fast. He'd read something recently about a Cuban major league baseball player getting a walk-off home run.

"Cuba," he said.

"She a pinko? The tribes ain't no Communists, Sauce—we into freedom, man."

"No, she's American, middle of the road."

"Huh, might do. Now listen, homestone, you pay attention and do what I say. And you remember your old homie when the time comes."

"I will. I promise. If anything I write ever gets made into a movie, I'll fight for you to work on the screenplay."

"Okay, okay. And if you do get out before the weekend, you gonna share the secret with your old homestone, yeah?"

"Yeah, for sure," though what secret Elrond was talking about didn't immediately register. "Oh, you mean from the seminar."

"But if you don't get out, you're going to be in good and with me and my homies and have all the protection you'll need, unless something bad happens. Okay, okay, first of all, what's your name?"

"Billy."

"No, no, your name ain't Billy. You be . . ." Elrond thought for a moment. "Damn, you ain't got no tats. Ah, we can get around that: Your mama is a JW." And then, after another pause, Elrond announced, "You gonna be Lando."

"You mean like Lando Calrissian . . . in *Star Wars*?"

"No, Sauce, like short for Orlando, Elrond's homestone from Visalia."

TWENTY-FOUR

A little after nine fifteen, the morning after the heist, Billy was taken out of the holding cell to undergo formal booking. This included having his *Miranda* rights reread, getting fingerprinted, having his mugshot taken, and a few other unpleasantries. After this, he was allowed a phone call. The call wasn't that pleasant either.

"This is Attorney Byron West." Seeing that it was a restricted number calling his cellphone, Byron was careful to sound professional in case it was someone from the jail.

"Byron?"

"Billy!" Byron changed his tone. "Are you all right?"

"No, I'm not all right." Billy was more than a little agitated. "This is not going at all according to the plan."

"Well, I hope you're getting some good things for your writing."

"If you don't get me out of here soon, they're going to send me to some really bad place. You have to do something fast."

"Yes, but it does seem there is a problem."

"Are you going to be able to get me out of here or not?"

"I've told them I'm not going to press charges for my bike, which, by the way, you really messed up ramming the police car. But the cops are claiming you resisted arrest and fled the scene of the crime, and a few other things—they're really pissed you dented their car. Now they have to do all this paperwork. It looks like you might be stuck there until Monday at the earliest, when your bail is set.

"Are you still there?" Byron said, after about ten seconds of silence on Billy's end.

"Is there any way that the bail can be set earlier?" Billy finally responded.

"I called one of the lawyers from the office who does criminal cases. He says that, ordinarily, judges don't come in on Saturdays. It is possible, on rare occasions, to get a judge to do something special, but even then, you'd have to come up with a lot of cash."

"Do you know how much? This guy in the cell with me says a hundred K."

"It could be that high."

On the other end of the phone, Billy was silent again.

"I would lend you money," Byron went on, "but you know my monthly isn't close to that, and I don't get access to my trust fund till I get married. And that's not in the immediate future. Bianca and I are having issues. She's very hardheaded and opinionated."

"If I can't get bail, I could be locked up for weeks—if I survive that long."

"And we have that seminar Friday with Professor Fulkles," Byron said, "and there's no refunds."

"Yes, I know, but you need to get me out. You're going to have to go to my grandmother for me, and it's going to cost me big-time."

"No. Why don't *you* just call her?"

"It would be too much of a shock and needs too much explanation. I only get a couple of calls, and they're only supposed to last five minutes. You have to come through for me."

"Why me? Why not Jackson?"

"You know her a lot better than he does. She kind of likes you anyway, ever since you got your neck tattoo lasered off." Byron's dad had exercised his financial leverage to help him out of his goth experiment.

"Bummer," Byron said.

"You have to see her today, like soon. I don't know if I'll survive in the next place they're sending me, and after that, it looks worse. See if Bianca will go with you. Nana likes her. They're kicking me off. I'm counting on you."

»———▶

At about the same time that Saturday morning, Kari sat at a table at Ariel's Café on the Strand in Venice Beach. The marine layer of fog had not yet lifted. The ocean was calm, and many surfers were out in the water as there were four-foot swells. There was some kind of race going on, and number-wearing participants were running by on the Strand.

Waiting for her two best friends to arrive, Kari had ordered a glass of wheatgrass. She didn't like the taste of it but had placed the order for the nutrients—and to torture herself. What had she done? Why did she have to be such a fool? She reached into her purse for that stupid note she had written for Billy at the coffee shop. Looking at it again, she scrunched it up, then tried to tear it up but didn't make much progress, because tearing a balled-up wad of paper is difficult. She wished she could take it back or had written something else.

She had taken off right after they had read their notes with scarcely another word between them. She didn't return to the bar to watch the rest of the game and finish her wine. And before she got home, she knew she had not been honest with herself. She was crazy about him. She had lost the only guy she had ever cared about this way.

She took another sip of her wheatgrass. It gave her the trembles; it was repulsive—no, *she* was repulsive. Why did she have to be such a fool? She took another drink, this time a gulp, and as she was grimacing from the taste, Bianca and Amanda walked up and took seats.

"What's the matter, girlfriend?" Amanda said. "You look like you swallowed a mouse—just kidding."

"It's the wheatgrass. It tastes awful, but it's supposed to be good for you."

"Are you sure that's all?" Amanda said. "Your eyes are swollen."

"My allergies."

"You don't have allergies," Bianca said. Her mother was a Johns Hopkins–trained MD. Bianca, perhaps being a little rebellious, was into naturopathy. "What's happening between you and Billy?"

A waitress came over with menus and, noticing Amanda's French-girl bangs and chocolate lowlights, said, "Love your do."

"Oh, thanks." Amanda tried to blush, but she was used to compliments. "I have an audition later today."

The waitress gave the girls the menus and asked what they wanted to drink. Bianca and Amanda ordered nonfat lattes with sugar-free vanilla. Kari said she would have one too and asked her to take away the wheatgrass.

"He broke up with me," Kari said, her lips quivering. "Well, kind of."

"What? I thought you said you broke up with him?" said Bianca.

"I did, but he broke up with me too. I mean, we kind of broke up with each other."

"You kind of broke up with each other," Amanda said. "What does that mean?"

"I don't know, but I'm not happy." Kari dabbed her eyes with her napkin. "I mean, I think we did," she went on, taking the napkin away. "I just said he was a distraction—and he *is* a distraction 'cause all I do is think about him."

"What did he say to you?" Amanda asked.

"That's the problem. It's like he didn't really say he didn't like me anymore—he said I was okay. But I called him a distraction."

The waitress delivered the lattes. All three girls ordered egg-white spinach omelets with fruit in place of potatoes and gluten-free toast.

"Well, what did he say?" Bianca asked, after the waitress had left.

"He said he couldn't see me any longer 'cause he was going to jail. He didn't even bother to give me a decent excuse."

"At least it was creative," Bianca replied. "I beat Byron to the punch. I just came out and told him I wasn't putting up with his dallying anymore."

"You think he's been dallying on you?" Amanda asked.

"No, not that kind of dallying; I'm just tired of him waiting around.

His response, the chump, was that he wasn't ready to get serious and needed to get his theater career going first."

"But do you still like him?" Kari asked.

"I can't help it," Bianca said. "Maybe telling him to get lost will make him wake up."

"Well, I've basically told Jackson to take a hike too," Amanda said. "I just got off the phone with him. Do they have Irish coffees here?"

"What happened now?" asked Kari.

"I hadn't heard from him in almost a week, then he calls and says he thinks we need to take a week or two off," Amanda said. "He had gone off surfing in Mexico and hadn't even told me. I told him we should take a decade off and hung up on him."

"At least he was straightforward," Kari said. "A lot better than the lame excuse Billy gave me."

"There's a lot of other fish in the sea," said Amanda.

From their seats at the café, they had a good view of the beach and the ocean, and though they couldn't see any fish, there were quite a few surfers out in the water.

"There are," Kari said, trying to be resolute.

"So, you think him going to jail was just an excuse?" Amanda asked.

"I don't care," Kari said, now determined. "He's probably got an unpaid parking ticket or something. He ought to be in jail, as far as I'm concerned." She took a deep breath. "I need to be over him."

"I'm with you, sister. I'm over Byron too," Bianca said.

"Me too," Amanda said. "I'm going to be over Jackson, the chump."

Just then, Bianca's cellphone buzzed. She saw it was Byron and killed the call. The phone buzzed again. "It's Byron," she said, and killed the call again. It buzzed a third time. She looked at her friends. "I better take it. Maybe the dork has had an accident."

She got up and walked out on the bike path, away from the noise of the restaurant. She came back after about five minutes, sat down, and said, "Billy really is in jail."

Amanda gasped and covered her mouth with her hand. Kari spilled her latte.

TWENTY-FIVE

After Billy's booking and phone call, he was taken back to the holding cell. He was told to wait; his transportation to Van Nuys was on its way. Sometimes a fertile imagination can be unpleasant. The names and descriptions of the places where Elrond said he was headed stirred up gruesome scenes of cruelty and torture from old penal movies like *Papillon*, *The Count of Monte Cristo*, and *The Man in the Iron Mask*.

But Elrond had given him strict and hopeful instructions. Once he was admitted to the Dungeon, he was immediately to seek out Renaldo, the homies' main man in the Dungeon when Elrond wasn't there. The homies easily outnumbered the other gangs. "Tell him you're Lando, Elrond's cousin from Visalia," Elrond instructed, "who I've told him about before. He'll take *bueno* care of you."

"How will I recognize him?" asked Billy.

"Easy. He's a tall, red-haired homie with freckles—like Viv, but she's better looking, though she can be just as mean."

"Viv, your old old lady?"

"They're half Irish. But don't call him Red—he's killed people for calling him that. You can call him Fin."

"Why do you call him Fin?"

"Two reasons: 'cause his dad couldn't hold his liquor, and he used to sleep in a barrel, and 'cause if you fight with Fin, you're finished—you know, *fin*, like short for *finished*."

"I'll make sure to not call him Red," Billy said.

"Good. Now you got any money with you?"

"I had about eighty dollars when they brought me in."

"Good, they'll credit that to you at the Dungeon commissary. Use it for buying stuff for Fin and his main men—soap, smokes, candy, whatever."

"Okay, I think I follow."

"Oh, one other thing: If you see Julio Bocardo in there, tell him to keep his hands off Vivian. You'll recognize him 'cause he only has half a left ear. I did like a Tyson-to-Holyfield on him. Tasted bad."

"I thought she was your old old lady?"

"It's complicated."

As Billy was wishing his Moleskine and pen hadn't been taken away, Elrond pulled from his back pocket a three-inch pad and a pencil.

"Why'd they let you bring that in?"

"It ain't always *what* you know, but *who*," Elrond said. Writing on the pad without looking up, he said, "*Lees español?*"

Billy looked at him blankly.

"Guess your Cuban mom didn't speak a lot of Spanish at home," Elrond said as he kept on writing.

Billy had to think for a moment. "Yeah, she wanted us to learn American."

Elrond tore the page from his notebook and folded it into a two-inch square. He turned so his back was to the video camera up against the far wall, as if to block what was in front of him from the camera. He looked around as if someone else might be able to see them. He unfolded the piece of paper and looked it over.

"You and me are homies now, right?"

"Yes. I really do appreciate the help you're giving me."

"Good. Then if you get free before I do, take this to the Phoenix in Pedro and give it to Vivian, the woman with red hair."

"Pedro? San Pedro?"

"You got it, Sauce. You be doing me a big favor." Elrond folded the piece of paper back up into its little square. He handed it to Billy and told him to put it in his sock. "Remember, give it to the redhead at the Phoenix."

TWENTY-SIX

Even though they were having trouble, Byron still considered Bianca his girlfriend, and Bianca hadn't yet given up all hope on Byron. After she finally took his call, Byron explained Billy's dire situation. She made him plead for a while and then agreed to help. She was Kari's friend and knew Kari still cared for Billy.

A little before 2:00 p.m., Byron and Bianca arrived at Billy's grandparents' estate high in the Palos Verdes hills. The September afternoon sun had burned off the morning fog, and the light onshore breeze had turned into a wind. The glassy ocean from the morning was now rough with white-capped swells. The wind had made the view from the top of the peninsula even more striking; one could see up past Point Mugu deep into Ventura County and past downtown to San Gorgonio Mountain.

Byron had called Mrs. Spiers after Bianca had agreed to come, telling her that he and Bianca were going to be in the area, and asked if they could drop by. She replied that she would be happy to see them and to please come for tea at three. The gate that ordinarily closed off the private driveway was open.

She greeted them at the door and noticed right away that Byron was dressed more formally, in khaki pants and a blue button-up shirt, than usual for an early Saturday afternoon. Bianca, the former gymnast, wore a cotton skirt—light blue, Nana's favorite color—and a white satin blouse. Nana first apologized that Mr. Spiers wouldn't be joining them as he had a previous obligation. She led them to the den with the striking view of the South Bay below. On a coffee table, tea for three and cookies had already been served.

Seated, there was a moment of silence, with Grandma Spiers comfortably smiling at Byron and Bianca, waiting for one of them to say something. Byron looked at Bianca. Bianca, with her ankles crossed and her hands on her lap, finally got the hint.

But as Bianca started to speak, Nana said, "I am aware of the reason you are here." She said it pleasantly and with a smile.

"You are?" Byron said.

"Yes, I am well versed in the situation, and it is very thoughtful and loyal for you to come up here and do the dirty work for your friend."

"But how?" Byron asked.

"And Bianca," Nana said, "I can imagine what a sacrifice it is for you to come up here with Byron, considering the difficulties you two are having."

"It's a delight to see you, again, Ms. Spiers," Bianca said. In response to an invitation Nana had sent for her and Byron to come visit again, Bianca had mentioned that they were having issues. "But I am Billy's friend too, and I'm concerned for him and want to help."

"I do think you two make such an interesting and beautiful couple. I wish there were something I could do for you."

"It's quite all right. Some things just aren't meant to be," Bianca said.

"But how do you know why we are here?" asked Byron. "It only happened last night."

"Have you forgotten that your father is our lawyer?"

"I guess I did talk to him about it."

"After I heard from him this morning, I talked with Mayor Argus, whom Arthur and I have known for years. Please try one of these cookies; Crystal cooked them just this morning." Nana took one for herself.

"So, do you think you will be able to help?" Byron asked, also taking a cookie.

"Crystal's special recipe—oatmeal, raisins, and coconut—Arthur's and my favorite," Nana said, after taking a dainty bite.

"At first, I thought the bail was going to be a hundred thousand," Byron said, after taking a bite of his cookie. "Hmm, these are good." He took another bite and followed it with a sip of his tea.

Bianca sipped the tea also.

"But I found out that it's probably only going to be around fifty—the bail, I mean."

"It would be so amazing if there was something you were able to do," said Bianca.

"How could you let such a gem as this young lady slip away?" Nana said to Byron, shaking her head.

"Oh, please don't trouble yourself," Bianca said, looking at Byron. "He's not the only fish in the sea."

"I believe there is a special catch for each one of us," Nana said.

"Byron says that if Billy doesn't raise bail, he's going to be in a very unwholesome situation."

"I am aware of the situation, and the amount needed. You know that I am currently quite disappointed with that grandson of mine. That blockhead has gone and broken off his relationship with your wonderful friend. I thought she was just perfect for him."

"But according to Kari, it was mutual," Bianca said.

"According to Billy, he broke it off with her," Byron said.

"In a breakup, everyone claims to be the one who initiated it," said Nana. "My hope is that it is only temporary."

"Well, I started ours," Bianca said to Byron.

"What do you mean?" said Byron. "All I said was we ought to take a little break."

"Well, you'll get more than a little break."

"I would help him if I could," Byron said, trying to get back to the main subject, "but I won't have that kind of money till I get married, and that's not on the horizon." Byron took a quick glance at Bianca.

"I'll say," said Bianca.

"That was wise of your father, holding off your funds until you get married," Nana said.

"Will you be able to help him?" pleaded Byron.

Nana got up, walked to the table that held the many pictures, and stared down at the one of her and her husband in front of the mountain lodge. "There might be a possibility," she said, turning around to look at Byron and Bianca.

"A possibility?" asked Byron.

"Yes, a possibility. But he would have to commit absolutely to my requirements."

"I'm sure he would do anything," said Bianca. "You're his only hope."

"What would he have to do?" asked Byron.

"He will have to commit to staying for at least a weekend."

"In prison?"

"No, there's a place I have in mind. It's in a charming setting, has activities and a wonderful spa."

"I'm sure Billy would agree to that," Byron said.

"It would be this coming weekend," Nana said and smiled.

"Ah, that could be a problem," said Byron.

"Why would that be a problem?"

"Billy, Jackson, and I have signed up to go to a seminar this weekend."

"What's so important about this seminar?"

"It's about unleashing your creativity."

"Unleashing creativity?" Grandma Spiers said.

"This famous professor thinks he's discovered the secret that made Shakespeare so great."

"You know I support my grandson's ambitions to some degree. But if he thinks there is some sort of shortcut, he is going to be disappointed. To discover and capture the truth of human nature in words is the distiller's art, the moonshiner's magic, and only comes with hard work and practice and patience. The magic comes with the work. And the greatest truth about human nature and all its intricacies is what you fools are running away from, what you're afraid of or are too vain and proud to see. Or rather, you are not courageous enough to embrace its magical hilarity."

"Hilarity?" asked Bianca.

"Something like that anyway," Nana said. "One cannot take the mystery of romance seriously while taking oneself so seriously. You need to see and enjoy the wonderful silliness of the whole subject. It's when you quit taking yourself so seriously that love will seriously take you."

"That's interesting, Ms. Spiers," Bianca said. "Are you listening, Byron?"

"Is there any chance of some flexibility," Byron said, "on when Billy would have to do it?"

Grandmother Spiers walked over from the table with the photographs to the big picture window and peered out over the bay. From a table close to the window, she picked up a spyglass that looked like something a pirate captain might use and, after extending it, looked down at the windy ocean below. "If Arthur were sailing in that regatta, those lubbers wouldn't stand a chance."

She collapsed the spyglass, put it back on the table, and turned around. "No, no flexibility is possible. The person I want him to meet could be gone at any time."

"The seminar is very expensive, and we've already paid the full non-refundable tuition," Byron said.

"Where is this seminar being held, and what's this professor's name?"

"His name is Sydney Fulkles; he's left academia and only gives private lectures now. It's being held this Friday night and Saturday at the Landon in Palm Desert. Billy thinks it will be the answer to his writer's block. He was really excited about going. Jackson and I were planning on it too, until Billy's misfortune."

"Yes, Billy's misfortune. I can see you're learning lawyer's talk," said Nana. "But perhaps it wasn't so misfortunate after all."

Nana sat back down and took another cookie. There was silence for about thirty seconds. Bianca took a cookie too and, to break the silence, said, "These are wonderful. I have to get the recipe."

"Byron," Nana said, "you need to get down to where they are holding Billy right away. He will be needing a ride home. The situation has been dealt with."

TWENTY-SEVEN

Billy's exit paperwork had nearly been completed by the time Byron got to the Venice Beach lockup. He had first dropped Bianca off and then went straight there. He was glad he dressed up for the lunch. On the drive over, he called his father to ask what he knew about Billy's release. His father told him to go look up client-lawyer privileges and obligations in his law books.

As soon as they got into Byron's BMW, Billy said, "So, Nana came through?"

"She didn't actually say she was going to do it, she said it had been taken care of, but who else could it have been, your grandfather?"

"He'd never go around her back. They pretty much stick together on things like this."

"Well, it's going to cost you. It looks like you're going to have to miss hearing Professor Fulkles. I'll take notes for you."

"I'm hungry. Let's find an In-N-Out." Billy thought maybe a Double-Double Animal Style would make him feel better.

»———➤

Later that night, Billy got a text message from his grandmother's helper, Crystal. Nana was inviting him to tea the following afternoon. Byron and Jackson were at Billy's apartment when Billy received the message. "Looks like I'm going to have to face the music," Billy said.

"More like face the executioner," Jackson quipped. "It was Dr. Johnson who said, 'Nothing focuses the mind like being on your way to the hangman.' Maybe it will help your writer's block."

"It won't be that bad," Byron said. "Her bark's worse than her bite. She's a romantic. She's like your fairy godmother in this age of neorealism."

"More like her bite is worse than her bark," Billy said. "She never raises her voice."

"Well, you have to go," Byron said. "The way bail works, she could pull it at any time, and back you'd go."

>>———▶

Grandpa Arthur seemed to be holding back a grin when he met Billy at the front door of his and his wife's hilltop home. He escorted him out to one of the large balconies overlooking the bay. The afternoon was warm, and the balcony was sheltered from the breeze. Iced tea and finger food were set on a round wicker table with a grayish-blue marble tabletop. Arthur and Billy seated themselves on two of the three wicker chairs padded with floral seat cushions.

After a couple of minutes of talk about his grandfather's latest sailing cruise, Billy's grandmother made her entrance, graceful but not particularly like a fairy godmother alighting on the ground. As they both rose to greet her, out of the corner of his mouth, Grandpa whispered, "Good luck." She waved them down and took the seat between them.

Billy tried to look sullen and repentant; the best he could come up with was a toothy grimace that tried to suggest, "Oops! I made a big mistake." After a few moments of Grandma's scrutiny, she said, "Well, William, you did it this time."

"It was a total misunderstanding, a plan that went awfully awry— the best laid plans and all."

"Would you care to elaborate?"

"The idea was that by appearing to steal Byron's bike, I would get put in jail for a few hours, and this would give me a good experience to write about. You know, I told you my agent wants my stuff to be darker."

"Well, it has certainly given you something to write about. Maybe we should have left you in there longer?"

"No, no, I was in there long enough. I did meet some interesting people. But that's not the only reason I did it. And I do so much appreciate you getting me out."

"Go on."

"I thought it would be easier to break up with Kari that way before she broke up with me, and that maybe it wouldn't be a full breakup that way."

"You're not making any sense. Would you try speaking English?"

"Dear, these kinds of things can be confusing," Arthur said.

"You're telling me," Billy said.

"I can't believe her feelings for you have changed. So, instead of having the courage to talk about it with her, you came up with the idea of going to jail."

Arthur held back a laugh that came out as a muffled cough.

Grandma gave Grandpa a stern look. "Do you still have some interest in that girl?"

"She said I wasn't a priority for her. And I'm sure that it is even more true now, now that I'm a convict."

"I don't believe you have been convicted of anything yet," Arthur said.

"Yet," Nana echoed.

"Thank you again for bailing me out. I am eternally grateful."

"Are you aware of the terms?" Nana said.

"I can't leave the state and have to show up in court in a month."

"I wasn't speaking about those terms," Nana said. "Our terms."

"I'll pay you back, just give me a little time."

"Don't be ridiculous," she said. "Please tell him about the possible charges," Nana asked Arthur.

"Billy, if they don't get dropped, or at least significantly reduced, you're looking at some hard time as well as an ugly mark on your record."

"And extensive legal expenses," Nana said. "The charges are way beyond Byron's expertise."

"I realize now it was not good judgment on my part—but my motives were good, just not very wise." After a pause, he went on: "Why are relationships so hard?"

"Because the best ones are risky and cost something," Nana said.

"Did you know that Judge Rea is a sailor and has crewed with me on the King Harbor–to–Catalina race the last few years?" Arthur said. "Great fellow, I had a chat with him this morning."

Billy's eyes lit up.

"To get to the point, your grandfather and I are willing to see what we can do about the whole matter."

"What do I need to do? I'll do anything."

"There is no quid pro quo," Arthur said. "We don't believe in conditions in relationships with loved ones."

"It's not a quid pro quo," Nana said. "It's only a favor we ask."

Here it comes, thought Billy, wondering how what was coming would be different from a quid pro quo.

"We only ask," Nana went on, "that you don't miss that seminar you've been planning on attending and have a wonderful time there."

After taking a few moments for the shock to subside, Billy managed, "That's incredibly nice of you both. I thought I was going to have to miss it, and I really do want to go."

But this seemed more than a bit fishy. Something else was going on here. His grandparents were gracious, generous, and kind but usually not that tolerant when his behavior was questionable—at least not his grandmother. "Are you sure there's not something I need to do?"

"No," Arthur said, "we just want you to have a wonderful experience and become even more creative."

"By the way," said Grandma, after taking a sip of tea, "did you hear the location has been changed?"

PART 2

The Perils of Love

An adventure is only an inconvenience rightly considered. An inconvenience is only an adventure wrongly considered.

G. K. Chesterton

TWENTY-EIGHT

Early Thursday evening, as Billy was packing for the seminar, he remembered the note that Elrond had given him. Possibly the most interesting memory from his jail experience, other than the events themselves, was getting to know him. As nice as Elrond had been to him by trying to help him out, Billy felt he had an obligation to try to do what Elrond had asked of him. And it might be an experience too.

He looked around, trying to find where he had placed the note. Finally, he found it in his laundry basket, in a pocket of the black jeans he had worn the night of the heist. Fortunately, he had not washed the pants yet. He still hadn't unfolded it or tried to translate it.

He didn't have plans for dinner, so he looked up the Phoenix in San Pedro on the internet and found they served dinner, though it didn't show a menu. There's nothing like a good bar-food burger, so he figured he'd drive down to the Phoenix, grab a bite, and see if he could run across some Latin girl there with red hair. He was having a hard time remembering her name.

Fifty-five minutes later—the traffic is always miserable on the 405—Billy pulled up in front of a dingy bar in his Volvo convertible. An old neon sign blinked "The Phoenix," the first four letters of *Phoenix* stuttering intermittently. Three "hogs"—big black-and-chrome Harley-Davidson motorcycles—were parked on the curb in front of the entrance. Billy found a space two doors farther down and parked. He didn't bother to raise the roof of his old convertible. Nothing in it was worth stealing, and even if it were, he would rather they not cut into its top or break a window to get to it.

Walking up to the entrance, careful to stay clear of the Harleys, he heard the sound of the Ronettes' "Be My Baby" pulsing through the open door of the bar. The song reminded him of Kari. She loved listening to oldies. For the fun of it, and for the food, they had visited a couple of dive bars. She liked doing novel things like that. That caused him to think of the bar where they had painfully run into each other the day they broke up.

He remembered another night when they were having drinks at the top of a high-rise hotel overlooking downtown Los Angeles. Sitting shoulder to shoulder, they were giggling over quirky little things about other people in the bar and imagining funny scenarios about them. A young couple a few tables away were glomming all over each other.

Kari whispered to him, "How many dates have they been on?"

Billy thought for a moment. "They've been dating for three years, but she's got a tiger mom who doesn't like him and won't let them get married until she finishes law school and passes the bar."

"That's terrible," Kari said, pushing him on the shoulder but also laughing.

"Something like that happened to a friend of mine in Seattle. I admire parents that push their kids a little."

"Yes, so do I, but not *that* much."

Billy smiled and, after a moment, raised his sparkling wine. She raised hers and smiled, and looking into each other's eyes, they clinked their glasses. "But I'm not for long engagements," Billy said.

Kari's eyes opened wider, and for a moment, a wondering smile grew on her face.

Billy couldn't remember what he had said after that, but he did remember her blushing and looking away.

Was that the beginning of him frightening her away? Did he come on too strong? It didn't seem that way at the time. In the exhilaration he felt then, it was radical, but seemed perfectly suitable. He thought she enjoyed it. In his experience, most girls liked a man who was a little daring, though sometimes they wouldn't show it.

He usually loved the thrill of adventure, doing radical things, and taking risks, like he did with his skiing and surfing fairly big waves in Hawaii. But the risk of physical injury, he was coming to learn, was nothing compared to the risk and pain of a broken heart.

Coming back to the present, he walked through the open door of the Phoenix. He took a few steps inside, letting his eyes adjust to its darkness. It smelled of tobacco and was smokey despite city regulations against it. The lighting was mostly from neon beer signs hanging on the walls. In the rear, there were two pool tables. A large man wearing a sleeveless Levi's jacket leaned over one of the tables, aiming a shot, and another big man, holding a pool cue upright with the bottom of the stick on the floor, watched the shot. Two women in tank tops sat on chairs across from the table, talking to each other. Nearer, to Billy's left, the jukebox from which the music came glowed with red, blue, and green lights. Four wooden booths lined the wall down from the jukebox, and on the wall hung some neon beer signs and a large old LA Raiders poster.

Opposite these was the bar, old and made of dark wood, maybe sixteen feet long. A lamp, its shade tinted to look like stained glass, was fixed high on the back wall of the bar area. Two older black men sat at the far end of the bar on two of its eight stationary stools. Behind the bar, which had another Raiders poster on its back wall, leaning across the counter and talking to the two men, was a woman. In the dim light, Billy couldn't make out what color the hair falling to the middle of her back was.

The heads at the bar turned to Billy as he walked in. He looked toward them, then looked around, then back again. Wearing khaki shorts, a black polo shirt, and leather Top-Sider boat shoes, he didn't quite fit the mold of the place.

No one said anything.

The song on the jukebox ended, and there was a moment of silence as the next 45 flopped down onto the turntable. Suddenly, exploding out of the machine came "*Uno! Dos!* One, two, *tres, cuatro!*" followed by the driving beat of "Wooly Bully" by Sam the Sham and the Pharaohs. Billy couldn't help but relax a little—it was an oldies song the junior high garage band he was in had played at the one school dance where they had performed. Whether real or imagined, the mood in the place seemed to loosen up. Billy took a seat at the opposite end of the bar, leaving five seats between himself and the two other men.

From where she stood talking to the other customers, the bartender turned and looked at Billy. He thought she was going to ask him what he wanted to drink, but she just went back to talking. As his eyes adjusted to the darkness, he saw that she was dressed in frayed short-short jeans and a number 25 Seattle Seahawks jersey. Her arms were tattooed at least up to where the sleeves of her jersey hung just below her elbows. She was probably in her midthirties.

She turned and looked at Billy again as she opened a bottle of beer for one of the customers, then looked away. He still couldn't tell for sure what color her hair was, but he could make out that she had a few freckles dotting her upper cheeks. There was a strong attractive quality about her, and the freckles made it even more so. For a moment, the attraction fought with his aching unrequited love for Kari. But he soon came back to himself: A vivid image of Kari came to him—not only an image in his mind but a fragrance and even something like soft, comforting, and alluring music amid the blaring of the jukebox.

After a few moments, she walked toward him and stood there inspecting him, apparently knowing and enjoying that she was making him feel uncomfortable. Finally, she said, "What can I do for you, Whitesauce?"

TWENTY-NINE

She sounded a lot like Elrond but looked like an attractive female version of what Billy imagined Fin, the homie Elrond had told him about, would look like. He wasn't sure if it was natural or not, but she did have reddish-auburn hair. He realized he hadn't thought out what he was going to say once he found her.

When he still hadn't said anything, she said, "You gonna order something, or you just sit there staring?"

"What do you have on tap, and can I see a menu?"

"Only bottles and cans. There's the menu." Without turning her gaze from him, she thrust her thumb behind her to the chalkboard on the wall.

"What do you recommend?" The list on the board wasn't vast.

"The breakfast burritos are good, but we don't start serving them till two."

"It's past two," Billy said.

"Two in the morning."

"I'll have a Modelo Negra and a cheeseburger."

"Fries or chips?"

"Could I trade the fries for a small salad?"

She looked at him and smiled. "How 'bout some brussels sprouts? Hell no, Sauce, you can't have no salad. I'll take a quarter off if you don't want fries." She laughed. "Or guess you could have Beer Nuts."

"I'll take the chips."

She typed Billy's order into some kind of old computer/register, retrieved Billy's beer, and set it before him. Then she just stood there looking at him with her hand on the beer bottle.

"You want a glass?"

"The bottle's fine."

She took an opener from her cutoff jeans' left back pocket (her cellphone was in the other) and opened the bottle. She stayed there looking at him for another few moments, then said, "You ain't so bad lookin'."

When a woman whom a man is even slightly attracted to tells him he's something like that out of the blue, unless he is extremely conceited, it can rattle him. Billy became even more speechless. An image appeared in his mind of Elrond biting his ear off and pounding him to a painful death.

But a stronger thought overtook this one: He was so much in love with Kari that this red-haired woman hardly even tempted him. This thought startled him, though he wasn't sure where it came from. He thought he had loved Kari; did this mean he really did? The wonderful and dreadful ache and longing came on him again. It was wonderful because every thought of her was pleasant and peaceful, and dreadful because she was out of his reach forever.

Billy took a big slug of his beer, then said, "You a Seahawks fan? I went to school up there."

"Friend of mine from the hood played for them. Anything else I can do for you?"

"I'm looking for a woman with red hair," Billy said.

Just then, a young Latino entered the bar and took a seat two spots away from the black men and three seats from Billy. The bartender didn't acknowledge him. She said, "What does *this* look like?" She moved her head so that her hair swung around to the front of her face and back. She hadn't been pleased with Billy's lack of response to her earlier compliment. Those kinds of nonresponses tend to annoy women.

"It looks red, but I can't remember her name."

"Listen, Whitesauce," she said, taking a quick glance at the man who had just sat down, "you got a name?"

"My name's Billy."

"No, Sauce." She said this in a whisper, again glancing at the man three seats away.

Billy thought for a few moments. "Oh yeah, I'm—"

"Shhh," she hushed him. The new man had been listening but looked away.

"Lando. I'm Lando," he whispered.

"Okay, good, but you don't look like a cousin of Elrond's. I heard you was coming."

After this, Billy and Vivian—for that was her name—talked on in low tones. She told him she was Elrond's old old lady, which didn't mean she was old—she emphasized this—but simply that she wasn't his old lady anymore, at least not for the time being. The implication in the way she said this, and the smile that came with it, was something Billy didn't want to think about. What he did think about was getting pounded to a painful death.

"Now, I get bothered a lot."

"Is that what the guy who lost a chunk of his ear to Elrond did?" Billy hoped he wasn't bothering her.

"Shhh! Just a part of it. That's one of Julio's boys," she whispered, and motioned with her head down the bar. "El's the jealous type. They'll probably off each other one of these days. I still do stuff for El even though he ain't my old man anymore—'cause we're homies, and he and my brother are partners, and me and El are working on our projects together. Julio don't like that at all—he the jealous type too."

Billy hadn't finished his cheeseburger and chips, but his beer was running low; she brought him another, unsolicited. She leaned forward and whispered, "You got anything for me?"

"Oh, yeah." Billy took out of his pants pocket the note Elrond had given him.

She opened it, and when she had finished reading it, she made a noise, something between a laugh and a grunt. "You read this?" she asked Billy.

"I don't read other people's mail," Billy said.

"It's a note, not mail. So, you don't read Spanish—that makes sense: Lando from Visalia don't read Spanish."

Billy didn't know what to say, so he picked up a potato chip and ate it.

"So, Hotsauce, you're a hotshot writer from Hollywood," she said and, with a smile, added, "by way of Visalia."

"Is that what he says in the letter? Pretty creative of him."

"The chump is, but most of his good stuff he gets from me. El was in the Navy, a journalist in the PAO—the Public Affairs Office—E-6 petty officer first class till he got busted down to an E-5. El tends to get in fights. I was an E-6 in the PAO too. That's where we met. That's where we decided to be writers. We can use good grammar when needed. Go Navy."

"Being a creative writer can be brutal. Sometimes I have second thoughts about it."

"You don't think being a journalist is creative? So, you're going to see some big noise who's got the secret and lots of connections, huh?"

"Yeah, Professor Fulkles. It's a rare opportunity to get to hear him."

"That's where you're going this weekend? You want to take a date?"

"I'm going with two of my friends." This woman made him feel considerably uncomfortable.

"Just kidding—kind of."

"Well, I better be going. Could I have the check, please?"

She walked over to the register and printed out a bill that came out in two slips. She wrote something on one and took them to Billy. It was for $18.78. Billy put a twenty and a five on the counter; he didn't want to pay with a credit card. He took up the customer copy, and on it was written, under a smile, her phone number.

As Billy started out, Vivian followed from behind the counter and walked with him to the door. "You know, Sauce, I'm the one that El gets his ideas from—his muse, you know? He couldn't write jack without me. But I got stuff of my own too. Text me your email address and I'll send you a few things. Maybe we should collaborate."

"Sure," said Billy.

Vivian gave Billy a hug. His arms just dangled at his sides. Letting go, she said, "Hope to see you soon."

Billy's main thought was, *This woman is poison*. He gave her a half-hearted smile and fled.

THIRTY

At 1:00 p.m. the next day, Byron and Jackson met at Billy's apartment for the drive to their much-anticipated seminar. Rather than being held at a moderately priced, three-star resort in Palm Springs, it was now to be held at an exclusive lodge and spa up in the San Bernardino Mountains. Late Septembers in Southern California can still be warm, and spending the better part of two days in the mountains sounded better than spending them in the heat of the desert.

The traffic was better than expected coming out of the city on a Friday afternoon, and it took them only about an hour and a half before they exited the I-10 freeway to start up the mountain road. A little after three fifteen, Billy's GPS instructed them to turn off onto a narrow dirt road. A half mile up the road, the cellphone lost its signal. Billy kept going and slowed to minimize the dust his convertible was stirring up and to take it easy on his old Volvo.

"You say your grandparents met here?" Jackson asked from the back seat after a mile on the bumpy road. "How old is this place anyhow?" He had put his handkerchief over his mouth and nose to avoid breathing the dust and pulled his cap down tight to keep it out of his hair.

"I don't know, but my grandmother assured me it was an upgrade from the place in the desert," Billy said. "*Enchanting* was her word for it. My grandfather said, 'It should at least be amusing.'"

"I just hope they have running water and the internet," Byron said. He was used to the best of modern conveniences.

After another mile or so, the bumpy dirt road turned into an amber-colored cobblestone lane. Bordering its side were four-foot-high forest-green holly bushes blooming with red berries. On the left side of the lane, a squirrel chased another in and out of the hedges; on the right, a different pair scampered around. Behind the hedges rose lofty pines and graceful elms whose branches, like leafy arms, stretched arching out and over the lane, making something like a canopy. Songbirds flitted and sang among the trees. It was like they were driving in a large dome of various shades of green and brown. Beams of sunlight danced through the branches to the birdsong and rhythm of the car's tires pattering on the cobblestone. There was even a sweet scent of something like honeysuckle hanging in the air.

After maybe five minutes—it was hard to tell how long—the lush green canal opened to a broad meadow. To their left, the meadow sloped downward and past a stream until it reached a dense forest. Up ahead and to the right side of the lane was a small grass-covered parking lot that was nearly full.

Farther to the right, beyond the parking lot, the grassy ground sloped up the mountain and became more and more wooded. Ahead, the cobblestone lane was blocked by the gate on an old split-rail fence. The lane went on past the gate and up a hillock, then disappeared behind the rise. Next to the gate stood a sign with a picture of a plump-faced and plumper-bodied cherub aiming an arrow on a strung bow. The arrow pointed up the road.

"I don't know if this place is enchanted"—Billy had stopped for a moment before pulling into the parking lot—"but that lane we just drove through might be." The strange beauty of the flora and the way the sunlight shone through the trees had set off one of those mysterious feelings he'd been getting lately. It was like he had scented and was on the trail of some wonder. Something aesthetic often triggered the feeling: a song, a picture, a sunset, a line in a poem or a story, or even a single word in the right context. But it wasn't the thing itself so much that was the wonder; instead, it seemed to be the vague remembrance of something else the stimulus had stirred.

Or was it just a confused combination of nostalgia, melancholy, and sentimentality he was feeling? Or was he getting a glimpse of true beauty, with all its illusiveness, before it would coyly disappear? He didn't understand it, but he did realize something about it this time that he hadn't before: He desperately wanted to share the feeling with someone.

Did this have something to do with his passion to be a writer? To have such experiences and to distill them in words in such a way that would generate these feelings? And could it be that his unwillingness to commit himself to a woman was due to not having found one who could even partially relate to such aesthetic and emotional experiences? His desire for Kari came back suddenly and almost unbearably. He had found the one and had lost her.

"Are you going to park or are we going to sit in the middle of the road all night?" said Jackson.

"It's like we just drove into another country," Billy said. He pulled into the parking lot.

THIRTY-ONE

"I hope it's not into another century," Byron said. "I have an online race in the morning."

"Let's remember what we came here for." Billy tried to cheer himself with the thought of hearing Dr. Fulkles and getting inspired. "If they don't have internet, you can borrow my phone's hotspot."

Billy raised the top on his Volvo, and the boys gathered their luggage and started toward the gate. As they approached, they heard the clip-clopping of hooves and the rattling of wooden wheels on cobblestones. After a few moments, a horse pulling a coach of some sort clattered over the hillock. A young man, or old boy, was driving it. As it got closer, the coach appeared to be just a long wooden wagon painted in faded purple with curved poles holding up a curved and sloping roof. There were no doors, just two rows of seats with a driver's bench in front of them and an area behind the last row for luggage. Sitting next to the young man on the driver's seat was a dog, mostly black but with a white forehead and chest.

Jackson said, "They sent Cinderella's coach for us."

"Welcome to the Arrow," the young man said, and agilely hopped down from the driver's seat. The dog followed him. The driver was beardless and wore a straw hat a little like a cowboy's but with a round, flat brim. His dark hair hung down to the collar of a blue denim jacket. The collar was of white, fluffy wool and contrasted with the blue of the denim. His brown corduroy pants were tucked into calf-high leather boots, the tops of which were also fringed with white wool. His jacket was unbuttoned, and underneath it showed a light-blue calico shirt and red suspenders.

He opened the fence enough for Billy and his friends to walk through, pulling their roller bags. His dog stayed beside the coach, monitoring the situation, with his tongue lolling out.

"Thanks," said Billy. "I guess we're in the right place."

"I reckon you are," said the young man. "Three fancy young men from the city in a fancy European car. I'm Curdi. I'd offer you my hand, but I've been helping with a birthing ewe."

Even from six feet away, Billy had caught an odor that reminded him of wet wool and something else. "I'm Billy. That's Byron and Jackson."

"Glad to meet you, sirs." Curdi nodded to each of them.

"You were expecting us?" asked Byron.

"Colin"—the dog's ears perked up on hearing the name—"said to be on the lookout for a William and his friends coming up for some education. I do believe *Billy* is short for *William*."

"*Billy* is also what they call goats," said Byron.

Curdi chuckled to himself, thinking the same thing.

"This seminar we're here for got moved up from the desert on very short notice," said Byron. "You know anything about that?"

"I don't know much about your seminar," said Curdi. "Only something 'bout some famous poet or something. Colin makes poems himself, songs and stories too."

"So, who's this Colin guy?" Billy asked. "Is he the guy who runs the place? My grandmother talks about some real interesting old guy up here."

"Colin's kinda old, and he's interesting, but the place has other management too. He's been here for a while—way before my time. You might be talking about someone else though. He looks after the sheep and goats and cows and horses and ducks and geese and us and our dogs. We even have a few swans and a bear, but the bear don't come down from the forest much. Colin's like the chief herder of me and the other herds. Here, let me give you a hand with your bags."

"We can get them," said Billy.

"Okay then, just toss them in the back." Curdi and his dog hopped back up into the driver's seat.

The boys loaded their bags in the back and hopped into seats in the second row.

"You don't allow cars up at the lodge?" Byron asked.

"Not anymore," said Curdi. "Spooks the livestock, and th'aren't good for the sheep's coats. But there is a back road for deliveries." He turned the coach around, and they started back up the lane.

The horse clip-clopped over the hillock and farther up the lane. In a short time, out in the distance, the lodge and an expansive view of its grounds came into sight. What they could see of it suggested classical Greek architecture, with columns supporting a peaked roof. A semicircular drive-way curved directly in front of the building with a fountain in the center. Acres of meadow and pastureland stretched out in front and beyond.

Meandering down through the meadow was the stream they had seen earlier. Now, in places along the stream, groves of willows shaded its grassy banks. The frothy white of a cascade disturbed the clear water of the stream. A small flock of sheep fed on the nearby grass.

Close by to the flock, a crowd of youths dressed like Curdi, male and female, sat with their dogs at the base of an outcrop of rock. Atop the rock above them was another shepherd—hatless, with silver hair— piping a tune on a small wooden instrument. After a few moments, the tune, barely audible amid the clatter of the cart, ceased, but the atten- tion of the audience below remained fixed on him.

"What's happening down there?" Billy asked, as they continued along the lane.

"That's old Colin helping the young herds get ready for the games," Curdi said.

"Games? What games?" said Billy.

"It's an old tradition we keep. Toward the end of the season, we have our games—friendly competitions, though sometimes less than friendly—to hone our craft."

"Like sports?" said Byron.

"You could call them that, and frolics," said Curdi. "Skills a good shepherd boy or girl needs to have in caring for their sheep."

"Like what?" Billy still considered himself more than a fair athlete and, in certain things, was considerably competitive.

"In the olden days," Curdi said, "there used to be more, but here we mostly just focus on accuracy with the bow and sling, names and calls, course running, tunes on the pipe, and inditing stories to soothe the flock."

"What are names and calls?" Byron asked.

"A true shepherd is able to tell the sheep apart, and the sheep learn to recognize their shepherd's voice."

"Cool," said Billy. "What does the winner get?"

"Oh, he or she gets to be the lead under Colin, like me, and do what I get to do."

"You're the champion?" said Jackson.

"I don't like to boast—but three years running."

"Any of the stories funny?" said Jackson.

"He's a comic," said Billy. "He's always looking for new material."

"He could use some new material," said Byron.

"Good tales ought to do magic things, make us laugh and cry and the sort, and joined with pleasant piping can soothe the flock. A shepherd's pipe and voice can even call and warn his sheep. The tale needs to blend easily with the tune and the tune with the tale. And the sheep, though mostly they ain't that smart, do know a good yarn when they hear one. Colin is a master of it, with interludes on his pipe."

"That's what I'm hoping to be someday: a master storyteller. The speaker at this seminar is supposedly going to teach us the secret of true creativity."

"Yes sir, indeed Colin can spin a tale. Not sure about what you call creativity. Colin would say it ain't possible to create nothing out of nothing. Just combining and mixing up to get the right mix of what's already there."

"I'd love to hear some of his stories," said Billy. The two other boys agreed.

"He don't talk much to the visitors," said Curdi.

"Maybe you could put in a good word for us," Billy said.

"He don't take that kind of advice from us. But though I couldn't tell it like Colin would, I could tell you one of my favorites he's teaching me. Of course, it'd not be as good or all in verse and rhymes like he does."

"We'd love to hear what you have," Billy said.

"You sure? It can be a bit sad, depending on your point of view. Colin got it from some old swain called Ambrose something-or-other and a couple of other fellows."

"What's a swain?" Byron interrupted.

"It's a country boy," Billy said. "The opposite of you. And quit interrupting."

"Yes, yes," said Jackson, "do please get on with it."

"Well, okay, Colin calls it 'The Perils of Love.'"

THIRTY-TWO

Curdi began: "Once upon a time, there was a wise old shepherd greatly renowned for his large and contented flock and for the beauty and texture of its fleece, which was light as gossamer and soft as snow. But of even greater fame than his own was that of his maiden daughter. The old shepherd and his shepherdess wife had been childless till past their time, and they despaired of ever having an heir to leave the care of their lambs and ewes and rams to. Then, one day, a broken-down old woman came from out of the forest with a bundle in her arms. She unwrapped it, revealing a beautiful and perfect month-old baby girl. The child's father, a huntsman, had died on the chase of a wild boar a month before the child was born, and the mother had succumbed to the fever shortly after the birthing. As it was known how the old shepherd and shepherdess longed for a child, the old woman had brought it in the hope that they would take the babe and save its life.

"They accepted the child with joy, and very soon it was nursing on the fresh and wholesome milk of a recently delivered ewe. The shepherd and the shepherdess welcomed the old woman into their household and honored her with gifts and comforts. Though they treated her with much kindness and much effort to restore her health, the old woman passed within a month's span of having brought the child.

"The shepherds named the baby Kara for the joy she had brought to them, and the babe grew and thrived."

Billy was stunned by the similarity to Kari's name—was this some kind of strange destiny trying to torture him?

"Early on, Kara would accompany her adopted parents on their shepherding duties, and she took to the love and care of the flock as one born to it.

"One day, when Kara neared her twelfth birthday, she and her father were watering the flock at a pool near the forest. A baby lamb, not four weeks from the womb, had strayed from its mother to the edge of the forest. A red fox snuck out of the woods and, taking the lamb by the scruff of its neck, dashed off with it into the forest. Kara, who had been tending an old ewe at the pool, turned and saw the theft. As quick as thought, she took off into the woods after the wily thief.

"Now, foxes are extremely swift of paw, even with a treasure of living meat in their jaws, but Kara, like a flash of lightning across the sky, gained in the chase. In a clearing, after four furlongs, she closed within shot of the fox. Without breaking stride, from her shepherd's pouch she fitted a stone into her sling. Taking aim, she let it fly. The stone struck the fox at the top of its right foreleg. Yelping high and loud, it stumbled and dropped the baby lamb. Rapidly reloading and slinging another stone, Kara struck the fox behind the ear. The fox collapsed, dead. Kara retrieved the lamb in her arms and returned to the flock, dragging the fox back by the tail. Its pelt made a nice gift for her ailing adopted mother.

"With such feats and more, the young shepherdess's reputation grew. The country folk would call her Melangell for the way she excelled like an enchanted saint in the ways of the shepherd's craft.

"As her renown grew for the love of her lambs, more so it grew for her grace and beauty. Swains would come from afar to glimpse the maiden shepherd and, on sight, would fall in love with her. Even before she was fully of age, suitors came to the old shepherd, begging for his daughter's hand. And not only swains, but merchants, nobles, and even scribes, tax collectors, and hard-hearted lawyers.

"But having years before lost her adopted mother, she would have none of the thought to wed and part from her father and beloved flock.

"'Oh, daughter, my delight and strength,' pleaded her father, 'though I know there be not one in the land worthy of you, would we not have an heir? For what would become of our flock should some evil fortune befall you?'

"The young shepherdess finally agreed, but with a requisite—one she thought impossible to meet and would dissuade even the venture of an attempt. She would agree to wed the one who could best her in her choice of contest in the shepherd's craft. With the bow she could fell a vulture high on the wing, and with the sling she could down a wolf on the run at fifty cubits. But in these, perchance, a rare shot of luck might match her skill. And with the pipe, though there were none better at creating sweet and soothing airs, song of the pipe was an art for the flock to judge, not man. She chose the skill in which her prowess excelled all and in which she least feared losing—a race on foot through hills and vales of their pastureland. She would wed only one who could best her in the race.

"'Oh, father dear,' she said, 'the inconvenience of these venturing pests will be distractions from our sheep. Therefore, one boon more I ask of you to perhaps allay so many irritants.'

"Kara's father, rarely resisting her requests, agreed.

"'That the challenger who fails at besting me will have his eyes plucked out.'

"'Oh, daughter dear,' her father replied, 'is that not too severe? Though many would still assay the attempt, it would not be much sporting of you to them.'"

Byron interrupted the story, "I agree. It does sound harsh."

"Ah, but to truly succeed in love," replied Curdi, "is such great risk not required?"

"Yeah," said Jackson, "I get it—nothing risked, nothing gained. That's what stand-up is all about. But still, if I flop, I only get booed."

"Perhaps you have never been struck with the love of which the story speaks," said Curdi.

This line of talk sent Billy reeling. *Yes*, he thought to himself, *"faint of heart never won fair lady." That's me. How could I have blown it so bad? I'm just a measly coward.* Sufficiently disgusted with himself, he said to Curdi, "Would you please go on?"

"Are you sure?" Curdi took some pride that his story had acquired the boys' interest.

"Yes, please do," Byron and Jackson agreed.

"Well then," Curdi went on, "Kara, who never liked to displease her adopted father, relented. 'Well spoken, dear father mine,' she said, 'Then one eye only shall be plucked, though we shall choose the eye which we prefer. And we shall keep it in our trophy case.'

"Her father, not enthusiastically, agreed, and soon the news of winning the wondrous shepherdess carried over the countryside and beyond.

"And the suitors came, as love's pang drew them on. But though some felt its strong stirrings, not all would venture for the prize. Was it loss of eye that they feared or some other cowardice? Or was it only love's imitation and shadow that they knew?

"Nevertheless, there were those that ventured. And those that ventured failed. And many an eye trophy was taken. 'A meager purchase,' one lovestruck proclaimed. Said another, 'Mine eye is not lost, for when she looks upon mine eye, her trophy, her, my prize, mine eye will see.'

"And still the challengers came."

THIRTY-THREE

"The fame of the shepherdess traveled and spread," Curdi continued, "and bootless were the assays more. Then, from a country far away, a mysterious stranger came. The trappings of a shepherd had he—a crook, a sling, and a piebald collie dog named Fate. A shepherd, indeed, the stranger was, but with the air of something more. For as a boy he had been to the wars, defending the honor of his king. And blood he'd shed, his own and others' too, and he had lost an eye. To regain health's potency and youth's vigor, he returned to his longed-for flock. And from patient life in pastures high and grassy dales, he did revive and renew. With his faithful Fate, he grew ruddy, strong, and spry again. Wise beyond his years the young stranger grew, as broad experience in nature's book can often give. Some might say wily too, for to cheat the wolf and lion of their drooled-for prey takes more than normal wit. But in the inscrutable ways of love, a wisdom beyond nature lay.

"The old shepherd and his daughter were with the flock when the stranger and Fate approached. When Kara's eyes met his one, something seeming strange occurred. She quickly willed the feeling pass. Who was this tall and one-eyed, scruffy upstart so daring in her presence? The feeling returned, then withdrew again but left a mark. Was it an alarm as if danger neared, as little ever she had known? But were mere alarms meant to bruise and leave a sore? Alarmed she was, she'd run as never she had run before.

"Between her father and the stranger, the rules and terms were confirmed: If said contestant attained first the finish line, the shepherd's daughter would be the contestant's wife and he would gain half the old shepherd's lands and flock. And when the shepherd passed, the lot would be shared forever between the husband and the wife.

"'But when, not if, you lose the race,' Kara voiced her piece, 'your one remaining eye I will have, and my delight it will be to pluck it out.'

"The stranger with calm serenity replied, 'I will you win, sweet shepherdess, and we shall surely be as one. For now I see what I have dreamt from afar and no longer will only dream. On null chance that I the contest lose, you'll have this eye and my other too, which in a box I tote. For no other but you care I to see.'

"Oh, by the way," Curdi interrupted his story, "up there to the right, behind the lodge, is an old-growth live oak forest that natives say is as old as the mountain itself. They say weird creatures have been seen up there. And down there, yonder creek runs from a spring in the mountain that they claim has qualities most strange."

"That's great," said Jackson, "but could you get on with the story? You're doing fine."

"Well, thank you. I am just learning, but I have the best of teachers. You should hear Colin—"

"Could you just please go on," interrupted Byron.

"Well, if you're sure." Curdi was definitely enjoying the success of his tale.

"Yes, you're doing great," Billy said. "Please, go on."

"Okay, where was I? Okay, so Kara chose for the course an old goat trail, some twenty furlongs long, that wound up, down, and through the hills, sunken vales, and grassy pastureland and then wound back up to finish line, where they started from."

"A furlong's how long?" asked Byron.

"It's what they use in horse races," Billy answered. "Two hundred and twenty yards. My grandmother used to take me to Santa Anita—she thought she could communicate with the horses."

"I wouldn't doubt it," Byron said.

"The race was set for the next morning," Curdi continued, this time without being asked, not appreciating being interrupted. "As the sun crested the eastern mountain ridge, the stranger and Fate were on the course, studying the route and planning strategy.

"At the appointed time, the parties met at the starting line. The stranger and his dog stood on the right. The old shepherd and his daughter were on the left, and with her stood her own favorite pup, named Free. She was a collie too, like the stranger's Fate. The stranger gave a hearty laugh when, as her mistress sneered at him, her Free sneered at his Fate.

"The old shepherd again reviewed the terms. Their masters sent the hounds away. The racers removed their cloaks and took to the starting line. Finished stretching, the stranger offered to shake the shepherdess's hand. She, with a frown, haughtily declined. He replied, with a contented smile, 'No matter, dear, I'll have it soon enough.'

"The old shepherd then said, 'Ready now.' After a pause, a shrill whistle he gave from his shepherd's pipe. And before the sound had faded, the shepherdess was gone eight full lengths ahead.

"The stranger marveled at the pace she set and at the ease and grace with which she ran. Her strides were smooth and long; her feet seemed to barely touch the ground. Soon she was thirty strides ahead. *It is a joy*, the stranger thought, *just to watch her run.*

"After a bend in the trail, the course climbed a steep hill. And with the hill, Kara's lead increased to forty, then to fifty, strides. When she began to descend the hill, the stranger lost sight of her. Reaching the hilltop, he stopped for breath and saw in the distance, like an arrow shot from the bow, the shepherdess flying along the trail below. Turning to measure her lead, she saw him on the hilltop. *Who is this audacious upstart to dare think he can best me in the race?*

"The course now ran through a meadow long, bordered on one side by a creek, a forest on the other. A narrow path, one Kara had not seen before, trailed off from the course into the forest. She stopped, seeing on the trail fresh tracks that gave her concern. Had one of her lambs wandered off into the wood, where lurked the long-toothed wolf and clever fox? Thinking her lead sufficient, she detoured off, following the trail into the forest.

"Some minutes later, she emerged from the trees to find the stranger up ahead, having taken the lead. But on the next uphill, she caught him again and came up to the stranger's side.

"'Ah, there you are,' the stranger said. 'Thought perhaps you'd quit the race and were off to ready our wedding feast.'

"'Not likely, sir, I heard in the trees a one-eyed crow moaning his funeral song. I hope my memory soon shall be shun of it as I shall be of you.' And having said her say, she was off again, leaving the stranger in her dust.

"Now near the race's halfway point, the course swung to wind its way back to the starting line. Here, the course ran to the top of a steep ravine. As the shepherdess flew along, another narrow, newly tracked trail she saw. The tracks were fresh and cloven as the ones she'd seen before. Fearing some mishap to her flock below, she flew off the course into the depths below.

"Some minutes later, she trudged back up to the course, muddied and empty-handed, and in the marsh had lost a sandal. The stranger was now a full furlong in front, but she fretted not. Swift as a springbok chased by the wolf, she tore off in pursuit.

"She caught him atop the course's last crest, eight furlongs to the finish line. From there, downhill it ran, then through a grassy meadow to the goal.

"'The mud becomes you well, my love,' the stranger said as she passed him again. 'But your foot looks like it could some comfort take. Should we not rest and further our acquaintance make?'

"'Most gladly would I give you talk, if only you were not such a brute. For what kind of man are you to let a maid run on without her shoe?'

"'If only you would wait a space,' the stranger cried out after her, 'I would not only fetch it but wash it clean as new.'

"But she pressed on hard, and calling back, she cried, 'At the finish gate, like the slave you are, you can wash my feet, and I will clean your eye.'

"'I am your slave,' he offered back, 'but master too, as to each other and forever we shall be.'

"A laugh was all he heard in return as she was long past by.

"Now to the final meadow the racers came, the shepherdess three furlongs in the lead. But suddenly she halted, for again fresh tracks she saw. But two pairs these were, and one of a marked different kind. The first, hooves of the cloven sort, the kind a lamb would leave. The other of paws—not cleft, and of more concern, with claws a wolf would make. Deep into a thicket these led, out of the course's route. As the stranger was far behind and out of sight, to leave the course to investigate was no concern to her. For this could be the thieving wolf that long she had sought—the one that often stole her hens and, once, a favorite lamb from the flock. Into the thicket she tore, following the tracks. And when she came back through the briar and scrub, the stranger had caught up with her.

"Now the runners closed fast on the finish line. The shepherdess had nearly lost the lead, burdened with the weight she now bore: a baby lamb of two months' age.

"'Drop the lamb,' the watching crowd called out. 'It will not much hurt the babe. If you don't, perchance you'll lose the race.' But the crowd she would not heed.

"The stranger now dashed up alongside her with a speed he had not shown before and slowed to her pace. 'May I not relieve your burden, love?' said he. 'Would you not win your prize?'

"'You are my burden, rogue. The race is not over yet.'

"'A burden, love, you shall love to bear, for if I go on, I will win the race.'

"'What of love, of things so high and elevated, would such a one as you know?'

"'Enough to know that when I saw you first, I saw a ray divine.'

"'Not only a fool you are, but silly too.' And tossing him her woolly load, she said, 'Here's your pretty lamb you lent; now you can have her back.' Burdenless now, she quickened much her pace.

"The stranger didn't bother to catch the lamb, but it landed like a cat on its feet and jauntily chased after him, led by his faithful Fate. The collie dog, in his mouth, a new-washed sandal carried.

"Then, with another burst of speed, the stranger again gained the shepherdess's side. The shepherdess, with a frown, looked over. The stranger smiled back. It was neck and neck as the two raced on. But who crossed first the finish line it was not clear, the winner undetermined, as who should take home the prize.

"And this is how the story ends. For a great mystery is true love."

THIRTY-FOUR

The story had ended and the clopping hooves stopped before the boys realized they had drawn up in the horseshoe-shaped driveway in front of the lodge. Even toward the end of summer, the flora ringing the driveway were blooming—green and white hydrangeas, bluestars, deep-green ostrich ferns, and white azaleas. After a moment of silence, Billy said, "Well, that was quite a story. I mean, it was awesome, but the ending—just to leave the reader in doubt?"

"It reminds me of this old Greek myth," said Jackson. "But I think the guy got the girl in the end."

"I liked most of it," said Byron. "But is it good storytelling to just leave the reader hanging?"

"Don't you get it?" said Jackson. "Love always leaves you hanging—or better, anyone who falls in love ought to be hanged."

"Colin hasn't told the end yet," said Curdi. "If there is one. But I think he would say the art of it is to get you thinking and asking questions."

"Well, that's what this seminar you've dragged us here for is supposed to be all about," Jackson said to Billy. "Art as taught by some crackpot professor who thinks he's found the secret. I think I'd listen to this Colin fellow."

"I love the irony," said Byron, "that Billy had to be bound in chains and put behind iron bars before he could find the secret of art."

"I wouldn't have guessed, sir, that you were a criminal," said Curdi.

"I wasn't bound in chains, just handcuffs," Billy said. "I went to jail to get an experience to write about, and it gave me some insight into an area I knew nothing about."

"Sir, I wasn't referring to the seminar," said Curdi. He hopped down from his seat, and his dog sat up. "Sir, I hope you'll find it a new experience up here." Curdi chuckled.

"That would be nice, and thanks for the ride and the story," Billy said as he and Byron and Jackson also got out.

"I hope you liked it," Curdi said. "Please go in and register, and I'll see to your bags."

The boys stood before the building, which did, indeed, look something like a Greek temple—not one of marble or stone, as it had appeared from a distance, but of great white oak logs and timbers. Three twelve-inch-diameter, eighteen-foot pillars on both sides of the entryway supported the slightly peaked roof over the entrance. The outer walls were also of long, white oak logs.

The portico, as in many classical temples, spanned the whole hundred-and-fifty-foot width of the building. On the second, third, and fourth stories, small balconies reached out before glass doors. And under the peak of the roof, above the fourth story, was a single draped window.

"This place does look interesting," Jackson said.

Ominous, Billy thought, wondering just what his grandmother had gotten him into.

They climbed the steps of the portico. As they neared, the front doors automatically opened, and the soft sound of flamenco guitar music floated out.

"Where are we, Hotel California? 'You can check out anytime you like, but you can never leave,'" quipped Jackson, quoting a line from the song the music reminded him of. There were maybe fourteen people, male and female, drinking in the lounge off to their right.

"Hotel Grad School," Byron said.

"At least there's women," Jackson said.

The flamenco music ended in a flourishing arpeggio, and the song "All I Have to Do Is Dream" by the Everly Brothers started playing: "Whenever I want you, all I have to do . . ."

Billy and his friends approached the registration desk on the left. Behind it, sitting on a tall barstool that accommodated his short stature, was a grinning, plump man wearing thick-lensed wire-rimmed glasses. Though he looked old, it was difficult to tell if he really was. His round-ish, cherubic face was pinkish and hairless. His curly hair started a little too far back from the forehead, and its color was something between a very light yellow and a silvery gray. The color reminded Billy of his own hair after he had tried to peroxide it, surfer-style, in the sixth grade.

"Welcome to the Arrow," the little man said, his eyes squinting behind his glasses. "I'm Robin, here to help make your stay one to re-member."

The boys introduced themselves. Robin found their registration booklets. "We've been expecting you. You have been upgraded to suites with balconies overlooking the meadow." Robin handed them each two printed pages that needed their signatures, including a waiver and some at-your-own-risk declarations.

New music started up. It sounded like the overture from Wagner's *Ring*.

Accepting their signed papers, he held their signatures up close to his glasses. Satisfied, he handed them booklets detailing the features of the lodge and spa and another with information about the lectures that would be given later that night and the next evening. "Your suites are on the west hall of the second floor. The third floor is for the women—and no sneaking up there, you know. Your bags should be up shortly. Please let us know if you have any questions or need anything."

"Yes, I do have a question," Billy said. "Do you happen to know my grandmother, a Mrs. Spiers?"

"Can't say I recall the name," Robin said after seeming to strain his memory.

"Well, she did come here a very long time ago."

"Oh, I've been around for quite a long time."

"So, you don't know if she had anything to do with the seminar getting moved up here?"

"And us getting upgraded," added Byron.

"Oh," said Robin with a laugh, his eyes twinkling behind his glasses, "it just might be it's your lucky weekend."

》———◆

Billy's suite was large and elegant in an old-fashioned way. On the wall behind his bed hung a large painting of a shepherd piping to sheep, three of which were leaping in the air, following the other. Scattered around the room were other bucolic artifacts. On the side table next to the bed sat a lamp with a two-foot-high statue of a woman with a plump, fat-faced child at her feet. Double glass doors opened onto a balcony overlooking the front driveway and the meadow beyond.

The suite alone was worth more than what he had paid for the seminar and room at the other venue in Palm Springs. It was clear his grandmother was up to something. This had to be the place she always talked about. How she managed to get the venue changed in such a short time was a mystery.

The place was certainly interesting; that shepherd boy, Curdi, was cool, and he hoped he would get a chance to meet that Colin guy. Robin—the manager or proprietor or whatever he was—well, he was just weird.

Maybe he would get to meet some interesting people among the guests too—maybe even some like-minded writers. He wasn't up there to find another woman, if that's what Nana had in mind. He was there to hear Professor Fulkles and, hopefully, get inspired.

THIRTY-FIVE

Billy was late getting down to dinner. He had started working on a piece about the adventures he had had in jail and at the Phoenix. He had lost track of time in reliving his experiences and trying to make them vividly take shape on the screen of his laptop. Down at the restaurant, he made a quick trip through the Italian-themed buffet and sat down at the table where Byron and Jackson were having coffee after their meal.

"You almost missed the dinner," said Byron. "Not bad. Interesting way to cook lamb."

"Yes, they have a whole flock out in the front pasture," Jackson said. "I pity the poor beast they must have butchered for us before I enjoyed it. I requested they do mine Pittsburgh-style."

"Didn't seem gamy enough for lamb," Byron said.

"Grass-fed, I'm sure," said Jackson. "I took a walk out in the meadow. Very much like what we saw coming in. I tried to talk to the shepherd tending the sheep, but his border collie almost bit me."

"They're trained to recognize wolves," said Byron. "Strange how often dogs want to bite you."

"Aw, Jackson's no wolf," Billy said, "just a goat in wolf's clothing."

"I'm no goat," said Jackson, "Billy's the goat—I'm a ram, misunderstood."

"Yeah, you're hard to understand all right," said Byron. He and Jackson got up. "We'll save you a seat," he told Billy.

>>————▶

When Billy joined Byron and Jackson a few minutes later, the room was about half full—twenty or so people. They had taken seats at the outside end of the second row. The room babbled with anticipation, waiting for the celebrated speaker to make his entrance. After ten more minutes, an attractive blond woman entered through a side door and strode to the podium. Probably not more than a few years out of college, of medium height, she wore snugly fitting designer jeans with holes at one knee and on a lower thigh. Her V-neck quarter-sleeved T-shirt had *Duke* printed on it just below the smirking blue face of a devil.

She tapped the microphone, which gave a sharp popping sound that made her jump back. She returned to it and tapped again, carefully this time, creating a barely audible pop.

"We'd like to welcome you," she began, keeping a safe distance from the microphone and still blushing a little, "to what's going to be a most extraordinary experience, for you are going to have the privilege to hear the most erudite and original Shakespearean scholar"—the last syllable was more like *law* than *lar*—"on the planet. His discovery of the secret of the Bard's brilliance and creativity will not only shake the English departments of the elite universities of the UK, Europe, and US but the artistic world in general. Undoubtedly, there will be controversy, but in all iconoclasms and revolutions, there is reaction, resistance, and opposition. No matter the controversy, the secret Dr. Fulkles has discovered works.

"Now, y'all should have received copies of the agenda and lecture notes."

"Our professor sure has a fox for an assistant," whispered Byron.

"She's trying to talk Southern," whispered back Jackson. "I love the way Southern ladies talk, even if they're faking it."

"Would you guys be quiet?" Billy hushed them.

"I know y'all are excited to be he-ah," she continued (*he-ah* in New England-ese means *here* in many American English dialects), "and tonight, you shall be let in on the secret."

At this point, she reviewed the professor's résumé and publications, which took about six minutes. "Okay now, with that out of the way, it is with great pleasure I introduce professor Dr. Sydney Fulkles."

After a good half minute of loud and energetic applause, a short, older man dressed too young for his years sauntered up to the podium. He gave the woman an affectionate hug before she left the platform and took a seat in the front row.

The first thing Billy noticed about him was how short he was, at least two inches shorter than the woman who had introduced him. He wore black jeans, a black polo shirt with the Brooks Brothers logo of a sheep dangling in midair from a ribbon around its belly. A lightweight maroon cashmere sweater hung over his back and shoulders, the arms loosely tied around his neck. His cordovan loafers looked soft and expensive. He wasn't wearing socks. His glasses hung below his neck on a gold chain lanyard. He looked to be in his late sixties but could have been older—his hair was a little too black, except just above his ears, where the gray contrasted too sharply with what was above. His puffy, pink skin was clean shaven except for a manicured, graying spade goatee.

"Thank you, thank you," he said to the crowd with what seemed to be a trace of a Parisian accent. He turned toward the blonde and made some hand and finger motions in what may have been sign language.

"He sounds like this French waiter I sometimes get at Clyde's," Jackson whispered.

"That guy's not French," Byron whispered back. "My dad says he's an out-of-work actor who fakes the accent to get bigger tips."

Billy whispered, "Be quiet."

The professor spent the first twenty minutes of his lecture discussing trends in Shakespearean criticism. He briefly reviewed seventeen or eighteen of these that had flourished at the better colleges in France, the

UK, and Germany for the past three decades and were still in fashion at the most elite universities in the United States.

At this point, the professor paused, took a sip of water, coughed a few times as if clearing his throat, took another sip, paused again, and finally went on. "The only new idea in Shakespearean criticism that had serious merit during these years came from a gifted young scholar doing his graduate study at the Sorbonne. There, I posited a premise so unique and iconoclastic that the academic and literary establishments, even in Europe and Canada, were not prepared to receive it, though the United States would have if France had. In fact, they actually tried to squelch it. And frankly, with my then lack of experience on the bloody battlefields of academia, I was not quite equipped to marshal the evidence and supporting facts needed to prove my discovery. But now, after years of further arduous study, both in the old literary texts and in scientific treatises and experiments, I have enough supporting evidence to present my premise beyond refutation. That premise was and is . . ." Here the professor dramatically paused for a couple of seconds, then with great dignity, stated, "that, rather than Francis Bacon having written Shakespeare's plays, as was trending at the time, it was Shakespeare who had ghosted Bacon's oeuvre."

THIRTY-SIX

A hush and stillness came over the room. The audience needed a few moments to mentally digest the rather large morsel of intellectual meat (or gristle) they had just been fed. Then a rumble of *whoo*s, *ah*s, and ahas of recognition broke out.

The professor waited for about forty seconds before quieting the room.

"As academics and critics often do," he finally proceeded, "they had gotten the whole thing upside down. But now, as important as this discovery was, it was what it led to that is so thrilling and important. Something so revolutionary that it will not only convulse the ivory towers but revolutionize the whole concept of creativity. And not only this, but it will also make a significant contribution to our knowledge of neurophysiology."

The professor paused to take a sip of a brownish-gold liquid in a crystal tumbler and place it back on a shelf in the podium.

"He's moved on from the water he was drinking—to scotch, I bet," whispered Jackson.

"As you know," he continued, "Lord Bacon was known for being many things, including a high-ranking courtier in the court of King James, a politician, and an attorney general who unfortunately had a weakness for bribes. His raison d'être, however, as all agree, was science. He is generally considered one of the founders of scientism, the detailed abstract analysis of everything. And here is the obvious point that we all know and, as Orwell says, is evident in everything scientists and most academics write (yours truly excluded): They don't write clear, understandable, concise English prose.

"Ergo, the elegant prose of most of Bacon's writing and especially what are known as his *Essays* could not have been written by him. It's simple logic."

The professor paused to let the audience chop the logic for themselves.

"This was one of the clues," he went on, "that led me to discover that it was indeed Shakespeare who wrote under Bacon's name—at the very least Bacon's so-called *Essays*. And understanding this is what eventually led to the discovery that, tonight, I christen and launch like a great ship. Does anyone need a short 'bio break' before we go on?"

"We don't need a break," a female voice in the audience called out. Turning their heads, the boys saw a young East Indian female toward the back of the hall who had stood up.

A large young man with unruly hair at the other end of the second row also stood and said, "No, please continue. You have us on the edge of our seats." The young man's corpulence suggested to Billy that, when sitting, he took up all four edges of two seats. This thought, in turn, caused Billy to remember a tale his grandfather had told him about Chesterton, who excitedly came home one day and boasted to his wife of the chivalric deed he had done: He had given up his seat on an omnibus to three ladies.

"He's baiting us," Byron whispered. "They taught us the very thing in my law school rhetoric class."

Billy shushed him again, trying to keep his attention on the lecture.

"Do get to the point," spoke up a middle-aged African American woman with graying hair that almost looked frosted. She was quite attractive and, in Billy's mind, looked like a cross between Condoleezza Rice and Alison Krauss. She had a slight gap between her two top front teeth, like the Wife of Bath and Ms. Rice, and appeared to be quite intellectually formidable. She must have been very beautiful in her youth. Her faded blue denim shirt had white pearl snaps for buttons, the topmost two open, revealing a gold chain with a cross on it. Though she wasn't smiling, she wasn't frowning either. She seemed something between annoyed and amused. She was close enough that Billy could read her name tag: "Anita Rowls," and under that, "Poet." Kari had that same aura of intelligence, maybe the thing he valued most about her.

"If you insist." The professor smiled confidently and took another drink of the golden-brown liquid. "It is generally agreed that the so-called Bacon was an assiduous student of the medieval and early Italian Renaissance scientists and alchemists. The point is that they had a much greater influence on the Italian poets—and on Shakespeare—than has been understood. You see, the great Italian Renaissance poets such as Ariosto, Boiardo, Tasso, Petrarch, and even Dante to some degree, as well as the medieval troubadours whom they learned from, were all poets of romantic love, or *amore*, as it was called. And here is the critical clue: Almost all the heroes and heroines so vividly conjured by these great and insightful writers were, by and large, frustrated lovers. My great insight was understanding that this frustration was autobiographical, and in a peculiar way. I will get to this peculiarity in a moment. But this was a major step toward my next great discovery. It only took combining this insight with what Shakespeare, under the guise of Bacon, had learned on the scientific side for me to confirm my discovery. These early scientists—of whom Shakespeare, as Bacon, was a devotee—led by Gorganicus Blascicius, had discovered and developed new ideas and theories on the circulation of blood to the brain."

Here, again, the professor stopped and raised his eyes to the audience. Ms. Rowls spoke up again. "Are you ever going to come to the point, or don't you have one?"

"I do appreciate your enthusiasm, madam," the professor said.

"You can call it that if you wish," she returned.

"Please go on, Dr. Fulkles," the large young man with the unruly hair said.

Dr. Fulkles turned to the next page in the notebook from which he had been reading and cleared his throat. "Now," he said, "you shall hear the decisive piece of evidence that has led to the discovery. It is from Bacon's so-called essay on love, which it is clear, as I have shown, that Shakespeare authored. I have included the whole essay in the handout available after the lecture, but I will read with some elucidation the most germane parts:

"Shakespeare as Bacon: 'The stage is more beholding to love than the life of man. For as to the stage, love is ever matter of comedies, and now and then of tragedies; but in life it doth much mischief: sometimes like a siren, sometimes like a fury.'

"In other words," the professor clarified, "love makes you crazy. But going on, the essay says, 'You may observe that amongst all the great and worthy persons (whereof the memory remaineth, either ancient or recent), there is not one that hath been transported to the mad degree of love; which shows that great spirits, and great business, do keep out this weak passion.'

"In other words, people who accomplish great things, including works of art, shun this passion. Going on, the essay suggests that even a mighty, hardened soldier, such as Mark Anthony, who had his heart 'well fortified' against love's madness, had his career destroyed because of his insane passion for Cleopatra, which drove him to destruction.

"And summing up what he basically says in many of his plays, Shakespeare under his own name writes, 'Reason and love keep little company.'"

A pale young man with hollow cheeks and a balding comb-over, sitting three rows behind Billy, let out a mournful groan so loud that most of the room heard it.

The audience let out a nervous laugh.

Turning and looking at the young man, Billy noticed the young lady, similar in age, was sitting as far from this man as possible while still being in the chair next to him. Her arms were crossed, and her head was turned away from him.

"Now, at last, we come to the secret," said the professor. "What Shakespeare learned and has cryptically kept hidden for over four centuries."

He paused again.

"Please, please, please," a number of voices from the crowd, one after another, called out.

"He is totally baiting us," Byron said under his breath.

"His theory might be full of beans, but he's a master of melodrama," Jackson said. "It's like the damsel is strapped to the railroad tracks, and a freight train is roaring in on her."

"I will keep you in suspense no longer," the learned educator said. "I just mentioned that in the great epic poems of the Renaissance poets, almost all the heroes and heroines were frustrated lovers and that my great insight was understanding this frustration was autobiographical of the poets themselves, but in a peculiar way. That particular way was . . . that it was a *self-induced* frustration—while the poet was *innamorato*. For those of you from a public school education, that means 'madly in love.'

"What Shakespeare discovered from his study of the poets and the great scientific treatises was that something unique was happening in the brains of these poets. That chemical and electrical or otherwise unnamed reactions occurred in the brains of these poets when they deliberately frustrated themselves in love. And furthermore, that when their passionate *amore* was willfully constrained by ceasing all verbal communication with the beloved, this cerebral reaction increased exponentially.

"You see, this incredible creative pressure and commotion in the brain would ordinarily be released through the vocal apparatus, through vocal communication with the beloved. But when not released for an extended period of time, the results were marvelous flows of creative energy and intuition and a fluidity of literary expression that hitherto the poet had been incapable of."

There was a gasp, then a rumbling and murmur in the audience as the professor paused and took another drink.

"In short, it is this commotion in the brain caused by the passion of *amore* and the huge amount of creative energy needed to resist its madness that fomented in Shakespeare his torrents of brilliance and verbal fecundity. The tremendous resolve Shakespeare had to exert, for he was a voluble man and quite popular among the ladies, must have been incredibly efficacious. For when words are kept and stored in this way, they seem to fructify into a creative harvest."

With this, the professor closed his notebook and said, "Some say he almost went insane because of it. Indeed, do not think it was hyperbole when he wrote that famous line, 'Lovers and madmen have such seething brains.'"

He paused again, exuding the countenance and poise of a gymnast who had just perfectly landed from a triple gainer with a 360 twist from the high bar. "Rather than succumb to total madness, he chose to retire, back to Stratford."

The audience was silent.

"In tomorrow evening's lecture, we will further elaborate on the discovery, present the data from our experiments illustrating the science behind it, and suggest some practical applications for unleashing your own creativity. This and other data and details will be the subject of a paper to be delivered at a symposium in Prague sometime before the end of the year. To give you time to absorb the lecture, we will hold off on questions and answers until tomorrow evening. For those who wish to attend, as it will be somewhat esoteric, tomorrow morning I will give a brief talk on medieval scientific and alchemistic influences. Thank you for your attention. Have a good night."

THIRTY-SEVEN

Billy and his friends had left the lecture hall and taken seats at a table in the lounge. Four academic-looking young women sat at the only other occupied table. A female bartender, dressed like she was ready for Oktoberfest, was behind the bar at the rear of the lounge, washing glasses.

"Well, what do you think?" Byron said.

"It kind of could make sense in some crazy way," said Billy, "if you have enough imagination to see it. I mean, with the state all our relationships with women are in, what do we have to lose?"

"The problem," Jackson said, "is that to get enough imagination for it to make any sense, one would already have to be deep in withdrawal from female communication. So, it's whatever they call one of those things, like the dragon eating its own tail."

Jackson got up and came back with a tray carrying three bottles of a strange brand of beer and three shots of tequila. Standing, he offered a toast: "To the professor, who is obviously from another planet or another dimension—or just totally off his rocker. He'll probably make millions from this."

They shot their tequilas and chased them with pulls on their beers.

"There is a kind of logic to it," Byron said.

"It is certainly creative," added Billy. "And if you noticed, he didn't actually speak to his assistant. Maybe the more temptation, the better." They took another pull on their beers.

Byron got up and made another run to the bar, coming back with more beer and tequila.

The three friends toasted and shot their tequilas.

"I think it has to do with the physics of the brain," Jackson said, and took a savoring tug on his beer. "Hmm, this is good, I wonder if they brew it here. Where was I? Oh yeah, it causes something like an atomic reaction—you know, like squishing the urge is like squishing atoms to make atomic bombs."

"Yeah, it could cause our brains to explode," said Byron, looking concerned.

"It doesn't matter anyway," said Jackson. "Neither of you could do it even for a week, even given the fact that your girlfriends have dumped you. If they hadn't, there'd be no chance."

"Bianca didn't dump me—we're just taking some time off," said Byron.

Billy just mumbled something inaudible, got up, and came back with more tequila. They toasted, shot the tequila, and chased the shots with their beers.

After a pause, Byron said, "Billy, are you really serious about this?"

»———➤

Behind them, a middle-aged man and woman with two children entered through the front doors and approached the registration counter. The children—a preteen girl and a boy a little younger—were holding the woman's hands. The woman looked like she had been crying. As there was no one behind the counter, the man hit the bell on the front desk four times. After a few moments, Robin came out of a room behind the counter.

"You must be the Abelsons," Robin said to them. "We have you in a two-bedroom family suite for two nights."

Mrs. Abelson moved up to the counter and said, "We've heard so much about the lodge. Our therapists told us that if we mentioned their names, we would get special consideration?"

"Yes, yes, that's already been taken care of," said Robin. "I see you're from New York."

"Westchester County," Mr. Abelson said. "We've flown three thousand miles to spend two nights in this place." He seemed very inconvenienced.

"Well, we do try to have an impact on our guests," said Robin. "We hope you will enjoy your stay. Your suite is on the fourth floor, the east hall—reserved for married couples and families. The elevator is down the hall to the left. Your luggage will be sent up shortly."

>>——▶

By now, the alcohol had made Billy feel even more sorry for himself. Not talking to another girl would be easy because he didn't want to talk to another girl. "I'm willing to go for it," he said.

"If you're serious, how much are you willing to put on it," said Jackson, "that you won't talk to a female for a month?"

"For a month?" Byron said. "Maybe we ought to think this through a little more."

"Okay, then, no talking with any female for two weeks," Jackson said. "I doubt you'll last beyond the weekend."

"Why not a year?" Billy said.

"That's insane," Byron said.

"Okay, three weeks," Billy countered. "We have to give the chemical/electrical reactions time to have their effect."

"All right then," Jackson said. "What happens to the one who breaks the agreement? The penalty should be egregious."

"Not too egregious," said Byron,

"I don't care. Whatever," said Billy.

"He just said *verbal* communication, right?" asked Byron. "Writing is okay?"

"Okay, no verbal communication," said Jackson, "except with one's mother." Jackson talked with his mother almost every day.

"And grandmother," Billy said.

"How about just this weekend?" said Byron.

"No, three weeks," Jackson said.

"Okay, no verbal communication with women for three weeks," said Billy, "except with mothers and grandmothers."

"Agreed," said Jackson. "What are we going to put on it?"

"How about dinner and drinks at Clyde's?" Byron's law firm had an account there, and he figured he could put it on their tab. It was an expensive place and could easily run several hundred dollars a person.

"Still not egregious enough," said Jackson. "How about dinner with dates? By definition, we will be beyond our vows then, so we must get dates." Jackson usually didn't have a hard time getting at least a first date.

"What if I don't want to bring a date?" Billy said.

"Then I'll set you up with my little sister," Jackson said. "You can talk surfing with her." Jackson's sister was eight years younger, a better athlete than he, and a highly rated surfer on the UCLA team.

"Whatever," said Billy. "I'll probably still be on my female fast. You'll have to explain to her so I don't appear rude."

"Let's do it in the Dolphin Room," said Byron, even though he knew it would cost more.

"Sure," said Billy. "Maybe we'll get that waiter who fakes the French accent."

"Okay, it's a deal; we are agreed," said Jackson. "For three weeks. First to break the vow pays for dinner and drinks at Clyde's with dates in the Dolphin Room. I'm in."

"No problem," said Billy.

"I'm in," said Byron. "I can do this."

"This should be amusing," said Jackson. "In your moments of weakness, I'll be there for you." He went and got three more shots of tequila.

When he returned, they stood and lifted their shot glasses. Billy offered the toast: "To our female fast and activating our creative intuitions." They shot their tequilas.

"This really shouldn't be that hard," Billy thought aloud, slurring his thoughts and thus his words. At the moment, slurring thoughts was indeed possible. *I don't have a girlfriend and don't even want one.*

"I totally got this," said Jackson. His pronunciation of *this* came out something like "sisth."

"You think you got this?" Byron said to Jackson, more boldly than was usual for him. "You talk big, but are you going to quit whining about Amanda throwing your records out on the bike path?"

"What about you?" Jackson said. "When are you going to get over that your girlfriend beat you in the Strand 10K Bike Sprint?"

"It was just a sprint," Byron mumbled. "I blew her away on the Peninsula 26-miler, where there's hills."

The alcohol, and maybe the altitude, was not only affecting their speech but had obviously affected their mental apparatuses.

It would be true that Billy took a modicum of solace in hearing his friends bickering over their difficulties with their girlfriends. Misery did love company. He got up and came back with another round of beers.

"This idea"—Jackson took a long slug of his beer—"which is growing on me, seems to strike a blow at the irrational rationalism infecting the current age."

"I can get into that," said Byron, "and thus the existential leap into . . . into wherever." This combination of incongruities suggested some of the trends in modern theater that Byron was trying to capture in his own writing.

They stood and toasted again.

Just as they were settling back down, the front doors of the lodge opened. They turned their heads to watch three very attractive young women enter the lodge. The three young men almost fell out of their chairs as Bianca, Kari, and Amanda walked up to the registration counter.

THIRTY-EIGHT

"Welcome to the Arrow," Robin said from behind the counter. He adjusted his glasses, and reading from something on the desk, he went on: "You must be Ms. Russell, Ms. Porter, and Ms. Hall. We've been expecting you."

Bianca stepped up to the counter. "If this is the place with the spa that does wonders, then I guess we're in the right place."

"Oh, yes, we do try to please. Will you also be attending any of the lectures? Your reservations are all-inclusive, covering more than just spa services. If you're interested, here is the précis and schedule of the lectures being offered." He handed the girls brochures. "You missed the first session, but I'm sure those young men would be happy to give you a summary of the lecture and bring you up to speed."

The girls turned and looked toward the lounge. Only two tables were occupied, one of them by four women. At the other, three men sat cowering with their backs to them. There was no mistaking who they were.

>>———▶

"Can we cancel the vow?" Byron said under his breath.

"No way," said Jackson. "Which one of you is going to cave first?" He was trying to hide between his shoulders.

Byron peeked over his shoulder. "They really look great."

"Don't look," said Billy.

"If both of you fail," said Jackson, "then it's two dinners."

"Shoosh," said Billy, but dared a look too. He groaned.

Seeing the girls' reaction, Robin said, "Are you familiar with those gentlemen?"

"I don't think *familiar* is the right word," Bianca said.

"Neither is *gentlemen*," Amanda said.

Kari backed away from the counter and turned her head away.

"Strained relationships are unfortunate," Robin said.

"We're here to have ourselves a jolly good time," Bianca said, "and to enjoy the spa."

Kari turned back with a determined look.

"We'll do our best to accommodate," Robin said with a wide grin. "Here are your suite keys. You are on the third floor, the west hall, which is reserved strictly for women. The elevator is to your right. I will have your luggage sent up."

"If this is one of Jackson's sick jokes," Amanda said as the girls moved away from the counter, "I'm never talking to him again." In truth, she thought it was wonderful he was there, but she needed to be cool in front of her friends.

"It's Billy's grandmother," Bianca said. "She said this was her gift for me helping get Billy out of jail. I assumed she was only talking about the spa . . . But it is kind of cool they're here. I mean, for you guys."

"Maybe for Kari," said Amanda. "I'm going to avoid Jackson totally—unless . . . Oh, never mind."

Kari had all sorts of things going on in and all over her. She so wanted Billy back, but she also remembered how much he had made her suffer. Maybe she had been too easy. Maybe she should play it cool and see if he would make the first move. But what if he didn't? Everything just coalesced into a big ache in her pounding heart.

Bianca sensed Kari's confusion. "Buck up, sister. Now's the time to be strong!"

Instead of heading off toward the elevator, Bianca went straight to the table where Billy and his friends sat with their backs turned. The other girls followed. "What a coincidence finding you here," Bianca said to Byron. "Well, your scheme is not going to work. And don't worry, I'm never talking to you again."

"And me to you," Amanda said to Jackson.

It took her a few seconds of the two other girls looking at her for Kari to get it out. "And me to you," Kari said to Billy. She didn't even get the grammar right.

The girls turned and stormed away to the elevator.

Once its door closed, Kari's lower lip started to quiver.

Bianca was silent, trying to put on a resolute face.

Amanda said, "I'm sure that was the right thing for us to do." But she wasn't sure at all.

»———▶

"Definitely my grandmother's doing," Billy said, after the girls had entered the elevator.

"The world truly is a stage, and your grandmother the director," said Jackson. "My part in this farce will be that of the unaffected observer." He stood and offered a toast with his beer: "To our vows. And to the one or two who first breaks them, eternal shame and calumny."

Billy and Byron rose, joined the toast, not as enthusiastically as Jackson, then sat down.

After a few moments, Billy said, "She really did look great."

"So did Bianca," said Byron. "Are you having second thoughts?"

"Why should I? You heard her—she's never talking to me again."

"I propose we up the ante," said Jackson. "*Two* dinners at Clyde's."

"Not a problem," said Billy, which couldn't have been more opposite to what he was then thinking.

"No way," said Byron, "I do enough gambling in the stock market."

THIRTY-NINE

The two Abelson children, who had arrived with their parents the night before, were up before sunrise. It wasn't that early for them. They had just flown in from New York, so 4:00 a.m. was to them 7:00 a.m., the time they usually got up for school. After dressing, they quietly left their room in the family's suite and took the elevator down to the main floor.

No one else was in the low-lit lobby.

"This old building's awesome," the young girl, Chelsea, said.

"Yeah, let's go exploring while there's no one else around," Freddie, her brother, said. "Do you think Mom and Dad will get mad when they find us gone?"

"Nah, they both took sleeping pills and won't be up for a while. And if they do, it might give them something to agree about."

"Cool," said Freddie. "This place kind of feels like it could be haunted." Seeing no one at the registration counter, Freddie started to go behind it.

"Freddie, no," Chelsea said. "Someone could show up here any minute."

He came back around, and they meandered back toward the eleva-tor, stopping in front of a closed door with a sign that read "Facilities."

Freddie tried the door. It was unlocked. He opened it and peeked in. Seeing no one in the room, he entered, his sister following him. The room was about twelve feet square. A small wooden table with two chairs sat in the middle. At the far end was a divan and toward the back of the room were closed doors on either side. A wooden cabinet with a glass front—full of bottles, ledgers, and a brass urn—stood against the right wall. On the left wall, shelves were stocked with various lodge activity gear: a couple of volleyballs and softballs, darts, cornhole bean bags, and horseshoes. At the end of the rows of shelves, next to the rear door on the left, was a large bucket holding three softball bats, three unstrung bows, and three quivers full of arrows.

Freddie stopped to inspect a small slingshot that looked to be fash-ioned out of part of a white-and-brown antler. He figured that as he was a guest of the place, he could borrow it for a while. He put it in the side pocket of his cargo pants and quickly passed on to the basket with the bows and arrows. An unstrung wooden bow half the size of the others got his interest. It looked old and had carvings on it. It looked like maybe it was made of antler too.

Chelsea was investigating the vials through the windows of the glass cabinet. When she looked back and saw Freddie unwinding the bow-string from the upper tip of the small bow, she quickly went to him, told him to stop, and put it back the way it was. Then, standing in front of the door on that side of the room, she opened it a crack and looked in.

"It goes into the counter where we checked in last night," she told Freddie. Freddie looked in too.

She went to the door in the other wall and opened it. After about five feet of empty hallway, a darkened stairway led upward.

"Cool," said Freddie, who had joined her at the door.

"Quiet," said Chelsea, who found a light switch on the wall to her right and flipped it. At the top of the steps, a soft light flickered on. Freddie started up. Chelsea closed the door and followed, whispering, "Wait up."

At the landing, they found a bolted door on the right. Freddie unbolted it, and he and Chelsea peeked in. A row of rooms with numbers on the doors spanned to the right and left. Freddie closed the door, and Chelsea relocked it. The next landing had a similar door leading to another hallway of guest rooms.

They climbed to the fourth floor. At this landing, a little broader than the others, the stairway ended, and there were two doors. Freddie unlocked the door to the right and looked in.

"It's our floor," he said. "Our room's just down the hall." He closed the door, and she relocked it.

Freddie then tried the door to their left and saw a spiral staircase a few steps in front of him. They quietly climbed the stairs to a landing and found a dark hall where a line of light shone from under a door thirty feet away.

Freddie looked at Chelsea, hesitating. She put her finger to her mouth, and they crept forward, Chelsea leading. She put her ear to the door and couldn't hear anything beyond it. She backed off a step and shrugged.

She moved back to the door and started to turn the door handle.

Footsteps approached.

She turned and, grabbing Freddie's hand, ran back to and down the stairwell.

They didn't stop until they were back in the room on the first floor where they had started. "What did you hear?" said Freddie.

"Someone was coming."

Chelsea cracked open the door leading to the lobby and, seeing no one, said, "The coast is clear." The two of them came out, and she gently shut the door behind them.

A few moments later, to their left, they heard the door of the elevator start to open. Robin came out. Seeing the children, he said, "Oh, out and about already, my young friends?"

"Oh, hi," Chelsea said, with what could have been interpreted as a guilty smile. "We couldn't sleep."

"Probably a lot on your mind?"

"What do you mean?" Chelsea asked.

"You looked very sad last night."

They were both relieved he didn't say anything about their excursion in the stairwell. "Our parents are getting a divorce," Freddie said.

"That's not for sure yet," said Chelsea. "Our grandmother said coming here might help."

"There's always hope," Robin said. "Could be the air up here or the mountain water—it's artesian, you know."

"She says there's someone up here who can do wonderful things for relationships," Chelsea said.

"Hmmm," Robin said, putting his finger on one of his fat cheeks. "How would you like some hot cocoa? And we'll put a little thought into this situation."

Freddie looked at Chelsea.

"Do you really think you might be able to help?" Chelsea said.

"Meet me at the counter. I'll be back in a flash."

After he left, Freddie said, "Do you think it was him up there and he heard us?"

"Maybe, but he came down awful fast."

Robin returned with a thermos and Styrofoam cups and then led Chelsea and Freddie into the room behind the counter that they'd already been in. Robin had them take seats at the small wooden table that wasn't much bigger than a card table. He pulled in his stool from the registration desk, climbed up on it, and poured them cups of cocoa.

"So, how are your parents doing this morning?" Robin said. Even sitting on his tall stool, he was only about half a head taller than Chelsea sitting in her chair.

"They're still asleep," Chelsea said, "and haven't started fighting yet."

"I would do anything for them to make up—even try to be good for the rest of my life," said Freddie.

"You know, their problems have nothing to do with you."

"That's what our shrinks told us," said Chelsea. "Both our parents are shrinks too, but they make us go to these other ones. I hope it's true, but a lot of other stuff they say doesn't make any sense at all."

"You know, there are experts, and then there are *experts*," said Robin with a grin.

"My grandma says coming up here changed everything for her and my grandpa," Freddie said. "She said it was like magic. He's dead now."

"Are you an expert?" Chelsea asked.

"Relationships can be complicated," Robin said. "Maybe we should try to *un*complicate things a bit."

"Oh, please, if there is anything you can do," said Chelsea.

"Well, there might be a few things we could try."

The children looked at Robin with sad but hopeful eyes.

"Okay, okay," Robin responded. "But you're going to have to do something for me too, okay?"

"We'll do anything," Chelsea said.

"Good. You come back here in twenty minutes, and we'll give it a shot."

After the children left, Robin waddled over to the wooden cabinet and opened the glazed door of the top shelf. Inside was a row of nine glass jars about the size of moonshine jars or Claussen pickle jars, filled with various colored liquids. Peering closer, he tried to read their labels. Pulling back, he counted from the left end of the shelf and took up the fourth jar. He brought it up close to his face, adjusted his glasses, then pushed it out at arm's length. He put it back and took up the jar to its right and repeated the process, putting it back too. He next picked up the jar to the left of the first one he had selected. He inspected it from far away, up close, and in between.

"Got to be it," he said to himself. The jar was about half full of a deep-purple liquid, and on its label were the words "*Amore in ozio*."

He took the jar to the table and waddled back to the cabinet. On the bottom shelf was a brass urn, fourteen inches tall, bulbous in the middle, narrowing to a three-inch diameter at the base and two inches at the neck. He took it up and looked inquiringly at it. He swirled the urn and put it up to his ear as if to gauge how much liquid was in it. It seemed less than a quarter full. He removed the porcelain-covered cork from its mouth and sniffed inside.

"Should be fine," he said.

He looked around the room, first glancing at the quivers of arrows, then at the dartboard, and shook his head. "That won't do." From a different cabinet, he took a shallow wooden bowl and a tin about the size of a deck of cards. The tin's top and sides were spangled with white, green, and red stars. He brought the bowl and tin to the table. The wooden bowl was filled with white tablets about the size of Altoids mints. He dropped five of these into the tin, thought for a moment, and dropped five more in.

He lifted and swirled the urn around again, removed the cork from its mouth, and poured its silvery clear liquid into the tin over the tablets. He shook the urn, then emptied what was left onto the tablets. They fizzled a little but then stopped after they had absorbed all the liquid. They retained their bright white color.

Next, he drizzled the purple liquid over the tablets until all ten were completely covered. After a moment, the substance started roiling and fizzing and then began to be absorbed until all that was left were ten bright purple tablets. The inside of the tin was completely dry.

Robin laughed, pleased with himself. He shut the tin's lid and, with a cloth, carefully made sure the outside was clean.

FORTY

Chelsea and Freddie used the twenty minutes to check on their parents. They were still asleep, lying on the far sides of their king-sized bed, with their backs toward each other. The down comforter barely covered their father, most of it now on their mother.

When the children returned to the room behind the counter, they found Robin sitting at the table in front of a very pretty light-blue tin decorated with colorful stars that seemed to be bursting.

"Ah, you're back," he said. "Come in and shut the door."

After they had taken a seat, he said, "Are your parents still asleep?"

"Yes, but my dad looked like he might be a little cold," said Chelsea. "My mom's got most of the covers."

"That happens, shouldn't matter. Now listen carefully." He opened the tin and showed them the ten bright purple tablets. "These little mints are very special. They should have a positive impact on your parents. Make a pot of coffee for them—you know how to make coffee, don't you? There's a machine in the room."

"Yes, I make it for my dad all the time," said Chelsea.

"Good. Drop a single tablet in each of their coffees—they dissolve quickly, and the color will fade. More than one would probably be too much; the effect can be a little volatile at times."

"What does *volatile* mean?" asked Freddie.

"Doesn't it mean unpredictable?" asked Chelsea.

"Oh, they're predictable, all right," Robin said. "On some people, though, the effect can be a little more intense than on others, and sometimes the effect can fade."

"You mean, like, wear off?" said Chelsea.

"Once in a while, in hard cases, it might take another mint. So I've included a few extras for backup."

"What if our parents are extra-hard cases?" Freddie asked. He was prepared to give them all of the mints if needed.

"These can affect even the hardest hearts. Now, you need to be there when they wake, so run along. Oh, yes—and this is important—please make sure you don't touch the mints directly with your hands." He handed them a couple of small plastic spoons from off the table. "Use these, and then throw them away."

Chelsea and Freddie hurried back to their suite, entering as quietly as they could. Chelsea listened at the door that led to their parents' room. All she could hear was her father's slight drone of a snore. They waited almost a whole half hour and finally couldn't wait anymore. Chelsea put her ear to the door again. Still nothing but her father's light snoring.

She backed away, and looking toward Freddie, she put her forefinger to her mouth. Motioning for him to follow, she walked over to the counter that held the coffee maker and related accoutrements. She brewed two cups of the Italian roast and, after rinsing out the thermos with the hotel's logo on the side, poured the coffee into it.

Freddie opened the tin. She shook her head and whispered, "Not yet." She then went back to their parents' door and opened it quietly— they were still asleep on opposite sides of the bed; their dad had gotten much of the comforter back. She closed the door loud enough for it to be heard a room or two down the hall. The children cracked the door open again and looked and listened for their parents' reaction.

Mr. and Mrs. Abelson stirred. They weren't happy. Barry, with his back to Ruth's, looked over his shoulder to see her back to him. She rolled farther away, tugging the down comforter off him.

"Do you mind?" he said. "You've been hogging it all night."

Ruth glanced over her shoulder at him and mumbled, "After you had done the same to me."

Chelsea watched for a moment or two more, then silently shut the door. After waiting a few moments, she knocked on their door, and she and Freddie entered without waiting to be invited. Their parents were about as far away from each other as they could be without falling off the bed.

"Good morning," said Chelsea. "Hope you slept well. It's a beautiful day."

"We've already been out," said Freddie. "This place is awesome."

"What's so good about it?" Barry grumbled. "The air's so thin up here, I've got a headache."

"You kept on stealing the covers," Ruth said. "I almost froze."

You froze a long time ago, Barry thought, but only grunted.

"I need some coffee," Ruth said, starting to get up.

"We just made some for you a few minutes ago. It's strong, the way you like it," Chelsea said, running into the other room. She poured two cups of coffee from the thermos. Then, as her brother held the tin open, with a plastic spoon she dropped one purple tablet into each of the ceramic cups.

"Mom, you like yours with cream and one sweetener, right?" Chelsea said from the adjoining room. "And Dad, you like yours black?"

"Yes, just black, sweetie," her dad said.

"Stevia, if they have it, and just a little cream," her mom called out.

"Yes, they do. Just one?"

"Just one, dear," her mom said.

Chelsea emptied a packet of stevia and a pod of cream into one of the cups. She stirred both cups to make sure the tablets were dissolved and, putting them on a tray, took them into her parents' room. She gave the cup with cream to Freddie to serve their mom, and she took the other to their father.

"It's still hot and fresh," she said. "We just made it. This place has everything; it's Italian roast and real cream."

"Thank you," Ruth said, sitting up and taking the cup from Freddie. "It's very thoughtful of you both. Too bad that trait isn't more prevalent in this family." She swung her head toward her husband.

"Thanks, sweetie," Barry said, and then to his wife, "I guess you could write a book on thoughtfulness."

The kids quickly retreated to their room and shut the door. With their ears to the door, they waited. After about seventeen seconds, they heard something that neither of them could describe very well. It was like the sound of someone trying to suck the remains of a milkshake with a straw from the bottom of a glass—but amplified about a thousand times. The center of the door the kids' ears were against was sucked away from them a couple of inches concavely. Then came propulsions like swooshes of air expelled from a jet engine, and the door bulged back convexly toward them, slapping against the sides of their heads.

Then there was stillness—for about ten seconds.

Then adult giggles erupted. Ruth giggled, "Honey!" Then came more giggles from both of them and words the kids couldn't believe they were hearing.

After another couple of minutes, they heard their mother's voice. "Chelsea and Freddie, come in here for a second."

They entered to find their parents snuggled very close to each other.

"Why don't you kids go do a little exploring?" their father said.

"We've already been exploring," Freddie said. Chelsea wished he would shut up.

"Go explore some more," their mother said.

"And if we aren't here when you get back," their father said, "I'm taking your mother antique shopping in the village."

"I thought you hated antique shopping," Chelsea said.

"Can we play on the computer in the business center?" Freddie asked.

Chelsea pulled Freddie's arm to go.

"Yes, this once. We're on vacation." Their mother turned to her husband, smiling.

"And if they charge you anything to use it, just charge it to the room," their father said.

"Can we get a soda too?" asked Freddie.

"Okay, but only one," their mother said.

"And a candy bar?" Freddie said.

Chelsea was pulling on his arm to leave.

"Just one. We're on vacation," their father said. "Now scram."

"Awe—" Freddie had started to say *awesome*, but Chelsea yanked him toward the door. She waved at their parents as they exited.

FORTY-ONE

After finishing their drinks the night before, Billy and his friends retired to their rooms, though *staggered* would be more descriptive. Despite all he drank, or perhaps because of it, Billy started to compose a letter to Kari. It wasn't a great idea to write such a letter in the state he was in. But their vow was about not speaking to females; there was nothing in it about not writing to them. Seeing Kari again brought back intensely that longing ache he had for her. He was going to be honest with her—and to himself—and let her know his true feelings.

Trying to find the right wording, he wrestled with his laptop, which was being recalcitrant and wouldn't say what he wanted it to say. For two hours, he struggled not to overdo it or underdo declaring how madly in love he was with her, to say what a fool he had been and that he would surely perish without her. Finally, he just gave up and didn't care what he sounded like.

His alarm sounded at eight the next morning. He fumbled to shut it off, despite knowing he would miss Dr. Fulkles's morning lecture on the medieval scientific and alchemistic influences of his theory. Twisting and turning from one side of his body to the other, he tried and failed to get back to sleep. He felt miserable, but his mind was racing. Fortunately, there was coffee and a coffee maker in his room. He took a shower, drank two cups, and began to feel almost alive.

After dressing, he went back to his laptop, reread his full-page missive to Kari, and resaved it. He then sent it to himself as an email attachment. Hopefully, he could find a printer. He wanted to hand deliver it to her today—reading it electronically wouldn't have the impact of seeing it on paper. After checking that the email had been received with the attachment to his account, he left his room and took the elevator downstairs.

Finding Robin behind the registration counter, Billy asked, "Is there some place where I can get to my email and print out a letter?"

"Our business center has an online computer and a printer and is just down the hall. Usage for guests is, of course, complimentary. If there's anything else you need, please let me know."

"Oh, yeah, do you happen to have an envelope?"

"There are complimentary envelopes in the desk drawer in the business center. Will you be needing a stamp?"

"No, no, thanks, an envelope is all I need," Billy said. "But I think I will try a cup of your coffee." He poured himself a cup from the dispenser at the end of the counter, nodded a friendly glance to Robin, and headed off down the hall.

Seated in front of the computer in the business center were the two children he had seen at the registration counter the night before.

"There, shoot the Uruk-hai," the little girl said to her brother, pointing to a place on the screen. And then, turning to see Billy, she said, "Oh, hi," her braces showing out through her smile. She was sitting to the left of the boy, who was focused on warding off the attacking Wargs, Orcs, and Uruk-hai of the *Lord of the Rings* video game he was playing.

The young girl's blond hair hung down to the middle of her back in a braid. She was outfitted in gray designer sweatpants and a light-blue

T-shirt with a picture of Galadriel from *The Lord of the Rings* on the back. Her black Converse All Star high-tops went nicely with her stylish outfit.

"Hi. I saw you and your parents get in last night," Billy said.

"We're from New York. I'm Chelsea," the girl said, standing up and offering Billy her hand. "This is my nerdy little brother. Freddie, have some manners and say hi to the gentleman."

"I go there sometimes to see plays," Billy said.

"We're from Westchester County," Chelsea said. "We don't go down there much."

After hitting pause on the keyboard, Freddie stood up. "Hi, sir," he said with a quick smile, extending his hand to Billy. "I'm Freddie. Glad to meet you." He also wore a *Lord of the Rings* T-shirt: his dark blue with Gandalf fighting the Balrog on the back. He was a head shorter than his sister and had pudgy cheeks. His light-brown camo cargo shorts hung just past his knees, not too far above his multicolored Curry Flow 9 high-top basketball shoes. Billy accepted his hand, and Freddie gave it a hearty shake. Then Freddie sat right back down, taking hold of the mouse to the right of the computer. Just above the mouse sat a small, light-blue tin ornamented with white, green, and red stars.

"You two must have had a good night's sleep," Billy said. "You didn't look like you were doing so well last night."

"Our parents are getting along better this morning," said Chelsea.

"They kicked us out of our suite," said Freddie, "and they weren't yelling at each other and even told us to come down here to play video games, which they hardly ever do." He said this without taking his attention away from shooting the digital attackers.

"Then they're going antique shopping, which my dad usually hates," said Chelsea.

"I'm not wild about antique shopping either," Billy said.

"I kind of like it," said Chelsea. "Sometimes there's old, interesting books, the kinds they don't print anymore."

"Cool T-shirts," Billy said. "When I was a kid, I was really into *The Lord of the Rings* too."

"It's not just for kids," Freddie said without turning around.

"Okay, you're right," Billy said. "I always wanted to be a Dúnadan."

"You either are or you aren't," Freddie answered.

"Freddie!" Chelsea said.

"Hey, do you think I could use the computer for a minute to print something out?"

"Is it on a thumb drive?" Freddie said. "I'll print it out for you."

"It's in an email attachment."

"Can you email it to me?"

"I'd rather not. It's personal."

"Freddie, let the man use the computer!" Chelsea said.

"Okay, sorry. Give me a minute."

"It won't take long," said Billy.

Freddie shot a few more Orcs, paused the game, and put it in the background, bringing up the computer's home screen. He got up and offered his chair to Billy. Billy sat down, careful to put his cup of coffee up beyond where the mouse rested, next to the light-blue tin ornamented with the white, green, and red stars.

Logging in to his Gmail account, Billy was asked for his password. He quickly typed it in and hit return in case the kids were looking. He found the email he had sent to himself and downloaded the Word document attachment.

"Dearest and only love and heartbeat of my existence. I can no longer endure the thought of life without you," the letter began.

The kids giggled.

"Do you mind?" Billy raised his hand in a futile attempt to hide the screen.

The kids looked away, trying not to smile. *Maybe there is something about this place*, Chelsea thought.

Billy printed out his letter. Then he closed Word without saving the document, deleted it from the Downloads folder on the hard disk, and logged out of his account.

In the desk drawer, he found an envelope and on it, with a pen, wrote: "Dearest and only love and heartbeat of my existence." He folded up the letter, put it into the envelope, and glanced at Chelsea, who was standing behind him at his left. She grinned. He didn't risk looking at Freddie.

Getting up, he reached for his cup of coffee and accidentally knocked the multicolored tin off the table. Hitting the floor, the tin popped open, and some of the bright purple "mints" spilled out.

"Oh, sorry—but five-second rule," said Billy, putting down his coffee and gathering them up quickly. "What are these, candy? They smell good." He dropped them back into the tin.

"Robin, the man at the desk, gave them to us," Chelsea said, not smiling.

"We do the five-second rule too," Freddie said.

"Freddie does the five-*minute* rule," Chelsea said.

"I do not," Freddie said.

"They're kind of special," said Chelsea. "They're supposed to soften parents' hearts."

"Huh! We all could use a little heart-softening," Billy said. "Do you mind if I take a couple?"

Freddie looked at Chelsea, who shrugged.

"I guess it would be all right," she said.

Freddie said, "They're only for grown-ups. The man said sometimes they're volatile."

Billy took three of the tablets from the tin. "I'm a grown-up. They smell like cinnamon."

"That's what I thought," Chelsea agreed.

"Okay, thanks a lot," Billy said. Not wanting to put them in his pocket, he dropped the three mints into his love letter's envelope. "And thanks for forgetting anything that you . . . didn't see in my letter—and for never mentioning it to any living human being."

"We didn't see anything," Freddie said, giggling.

FORTY-TWO

As he left the business center, Billy took a sip of his coffee and grimaced. When the coffee was hot, it was decent, but lukewarm, it was revolting. He tossed the cup in a garbage container he passed by. Realizing he had a bad case of coffee breath, he took one of the mints out of the unsealed envelope and popped it into his mouth. It tasted strangely wonderful, like cinnamon and sassafras and something else he'd seemed to have dreamed about but never experienced before. It dissolved quickly in his mouth.

It took about two seconds, and then it felt like he'd been hit in his upper aorta by the Randy Johnson fastball that had blown into smithereens the poor bird that had strayed into its path. The shock dissipated after ten seconds, morphing into a euphoria of amorous bliss, surging throughout his body, searching for an object—or victim.

He looked up, and it was like Botticelli's portrait of Venus with dark hair had come to life and alighted through the lodge's front doors. How could so much beauty and sweetness and such perfect proportions be compacted into so small a frame? She wore an old pair of black gym shorts, a droopy gray T-shirt with its sleeves cut off, and a runner's pink fanny pack at her waist. She couldn't have been outfitted by a Parisian fashionista better. Much of her hair had escaped from the pink scrunchie holding her ponytail. Her face was flushed, sweaty, and makeup-less except for the residue of moist mascara under her eyes. Everything about her was magnificent. Sweaty and breathing heavily, Bianca was just returning from her morning run.

Inside Billy, explosions started, like a fireworks factory had been set off—rockets and mortars and cannons and cherry bombs and M-80s and Piccolo Petes exploding all at once. Then there was a rumble down somewhere between his kidneys, front and back, and another great explosion, and it was like a dam that had been holding back an ocean of delight had burst. He reeled at the vision before him.

She still hadn't noticed him as he tried to fathom what he was seeing and feeling. Even the way she moved was outrageously wonderful. He lost his breath and had a hard time finding it. His knees quivered. His head dizzied. He could hardly believe his bulging eyes. But he did. He was finally seeing perfection. How had he not recognized such a thunderously gorgeous creature before? Kari was not in the same universe as the goddess who was walking toward him.

He panicked. He un-panicked. He must declare his love to her; he must tell her. But that stupid vow!

If he didn't say something, he would explode. But his friends! His friends would never let him live it down. And what about Byron? His grandmother would probably disown him for stealing Byron's girl. He didn't care. He couldn't help himself. Wasn't all fair in love and war?

Then he thought about the letter he held in his left hand. Everything he had said in it—though it came infinitely short—now applied to the exquisite five-foot-two beauty that was only forty feet away and coming closer. Remembering how the kids giggled at the first line, he realized he hadn't actually used Kari's name even once in the letter—just a plethora of too-weak descriptions of his passion.

Bianca finally looked up and saw him gawking at her.

It didn't register to him that her look suggested that she wasn't at all pleased to see him.

She stopped about seven feet in front of him. "You have been such a creep to Kari—" She cut herself off, startled and grossed out. He was smiling broadly, his head slightly tilted to his left, his puppy-dog eyes seeming to be sending pleas for amorous pity. *That ludicrous look couldn't be for me*, she thought, she hoped.

She didn't smell very good, but he didn't seem to notice and wouldn't have cared if he did. How had he been such a blind fool, such a dunce, not to have seen before the harmonious grace, the poetic beauty, the sublime compact elegance in the knock-kneed epitome of womanhood now standing before him. His heart pounded. It was difficult to breathe. His mouth was so dry that it would have been difficult to talk. But he didn't need to. He had the letter.

Smiling a toothy smile that reached from below the far corner of his right eye to the top of his left ear that showed off his gold cuspid, he winked his left eye at her—and handed her the envelope.

"You're unbelievable," Bianca said. Taking the envelope, she glanced down and saw it was addressed to "Dearest and only love and heartbeat of my existence." She turned and ran off in the other direction.

He started after her, but his throbbing legs were like mushy spaghetti. He stumbled and fell.

At the other end of the hall, Amanda, who had just come from the spa, had a hard time believing what she had just seen.

***

Billy got up slowly. Bianca was gone. He floated back to the elevator, up to his floor, and into his room. She was all he could think about. All along, it had been Bianca who was the answer to his longings. This was what true love was all about. What Professor Fulkles was saying made perfect sense. He already felt his creative juices flowing.

He was in the bliss of love, and everything in the universe was in order. He was blissfully happy that he was able to communicate his love, even if it was only in a letter. Watch out, Tolstoy; get out of the way, Edgar Allen Poe—there was nothing now that could hold back his talent. Refraining from communicating with the woman you loved really did enhance your creativity. If he could only confine his communication with her to writing a little while longer, he felt he could be a genius like Shakespeare.

But at the moment, Bianca overshadowed everything—that gorgeous, wonderful, coquettish little shrimp, Bianca. In not having spoken to her, it was like viewing the most beautiful painting in the world and just contemplating it—but at the same time devouring it. He would compose lyrics and sonnets to her—mere spoken words wouldn't do; they would just float away.

He hadn't eaten breakfast, but he had *another* hunger. Oh, that glance she had left him with! He could feed on that forever. The thought of any other food was disgusting.

He had slept less than five hours the night before, but he dreaded sleep because he might lose the glorious, vivid image of Bianca's beauty he held in his mind. But he did lie down on his bed just to daydream of the two of them together, walking hand in hand on the wet sand, the small waves breaking gently on the shore, chasing them up from the water to the dry land.

Though he didn't want to sleep, he soon did, drifting off into a very surreal place.

FORTY-THREE

Bianca needed to be by herself. What had just happened couldn't have happened. It was absurd. Rather, it was insane. Was she imagining it? She'd fled back out the front entrance and walked around to the grounds at the rear of the building. The staff was already preparing for the barbecue lunch that would begin a few hours later.

She was trying to be charitable. It's not wise to jump to a conclusion because of another's body language. But the way he was acting was way beyond body language. When he gave the envelope to her, wouldn't he have said something about passing it along to Kari? She flapped the envelope. It wasn't sealed, and there was something other than a letter inside. She looked again at how it was addressed: "Dearest and only love and heartbeat of my existence." No, it couldn't be for her. It had to be for Kari. She would deliver it to her. But she did wonder what Billy said in the letter.

She turned and headed back to the front entrance to deliver the letter to Kari.

As she waited for the elevator to come down, she flapped the envelope again. The elevator arrived, she entered and pushed the button for her floor, and the door closed behind her. Unable to resist any longer, she pulled the letter out, and two small tablets popped out with it and fell to the floor. She quickly picked them up. They smelled delicious. She put both back in the envelope.

She scanned the letter. A love letter, all right. She kept reading. Wow! Some love letter. No way could it be for her—even with all those silly looks he'd given her. As the elevator settled on the third-floor landing, she folded up the letter and put it back in the envelope. Getting out, she walked over to Kari's room and knocked on the door. After knocking again, she waited a few more seconds.

The delicious smell from the tablets lingered, and she could not resist. She took one and dropped it into her fanny pack. Then she closed the envelope, slipped it under the door, and walked off toward her room.

At her room door, she looked in her fanny pack and realized she had left her key in her room. She looked up and down the hall for a house phone to have a key sent up. There was none. She headed back to the lobby.

"I need a key to my room," she said to Robin at the registration counter. "I locked myself out."

"No problem," he said, smiling at her unkempt appearance. "Looks like you had a healthy run."

"Yes, thank you. I'm in room 307."

"Do you have some ID?" Robin asked, typing a few keystrokes into the registration computer.

"I was on a run. I didn't take my ID with me."

"We do have our policies."

"Can you just ask me a few questions or something from my registration info, please? I really want to shower and change."

"No need," Robin said, laughing. "I was just having some fun; I remember you from last night, Ms. Russell." He hit another keystroke and took a plastic card and held it against a small, flat electronic device for about three seconds. Then he handed the key card to her. She headed off to the elevator, holding the key.

From the hall around the corner, Jackson came into view. Returning from the fitness center, he wore spandex gym shorts that were too tight. So was the sweaty white tank top with a picture of a muscular mouse hefting a barbell. The white-and-black checkered Vans he wore were okay, but the mid-calf black socks made his lower body seem even more ill-proportioned to his muscular chest and arms. *Oh, the vanity—to go out in public like that*, she thought.

Generally, she thought he was a sardonic ass, and he had been especially so lately to Amanda. In the mood she was in, she decided to confront him; she would let him know just what she thought of him. But she remembered she might not be smelling so great, and as she was thinking this, a wonderful, sweet aroma drifted up to her from her fanny pack. She dropped her key into her pack and took out the tablet. The scent was strong and wonderful, like cinnamon and something even more delightful. *This might help.* She rubbed it on her hands, hoping the fragrance would linger, then popped it into her mouth. She did start smelling better.

Her heart took off like Byron's Tesla S Plaid, pedal to the metal, and her head whiplashed back. She almost blacked out. She gasped a couple of deep breaths. Her eyes bulged wide open. Her mind felt like a Midwestern tornado had just passed through it.

The statue of David wearing spandex and black socks was walking toward her. It strode like a Roman general leading a triumph, and she was the conquered. Her head cleared, and she saw Jackson as she had never seen him before. All her previous disdain was merely an effort to resist his incredible animal attraction. He was a paragon of confident manliness.

How could I have never noticed how handsome he is? she thought. *But not just handsome—beautiful . . . And his physique!* Her pulse increased to a hundred and ninety beats a minute. *He is the most gorgeous man I have ever seen. That isn't a sneer, it's just him protecting a precious and delicate heart behind a shield of whiskers, lips, and—oh, those teeth! If only they would take a bite out of me. How have I not seen him before! How could I have ever wanted Byron?* The thought of that spoiled brat appalled her.

She quickened her pace toward Jackson.

He saw her. *Yuck!* Because of the vow, he wasn't going to say any-thing, but he would have to bite his tongue not to make some snide remark. Instead, he let out a sneering laugh at her disarray.

She didn't stop. With a huge, totally uninhibited grin, she lunged to enfold him in her arms.

He ducked out of the way. She looked out of her mind.

Her arms wide open, she lunged at him again. "At last, my darling, my love, at last," she said. "I must possess you forever."

He just stepped away, out of her reach again, amazed. He didn't say anything. Even without the vow, it wasn't difficult. He couldn't believe what he was seeing and hearing. Ordinarily, he would have laughed, but this was beyond funny. A ravenous, disarrayed mini vampire was trying to pounce on him.

When she tried to grab him again, he ducked out of the way, pivoted, and sprinted off toward the elevator, the door of which was just opening.

Freddie and Chelsea stepped out, with Byron right behind them. Jackson dodged around them and started frantically pushing buttons.

"No, no, my heart, my soul, my life," Bianca cried out, but she bumped into the children and Byron, getting entangled with them. In the melee, Chelsea dropped the tin she held, and the mints spilled out, bounding about the floor.

"Oh, if you only knew how much I love you," Bianca cried out as the elevator door closed. Bianca untangled herself from the children and took a few steps back.

Byron smiled contentedly at her. He always knew, despite what she had been saying lately, that she was crazy about him. She didn't look great this morning, but when all dolled up like she was last night, she was the cutest thing in the world. He decided to play it cool and coy, and he wasn't going to break the vow—yet. But he did turn on his best love smile.

She sneered back at him. "Not you, you spoiled, conceited, obliv-ious dork." She turned and ran off down the hall, toward the stairway.

Byron bent down to pick up the mints scattered in front of him.

Chelsea and Freddie just stared at him.

Looking up at the children and seeing Chelsea's expression of pity and Freddie's amusement, he said, "She's actually crazy about me. She just has a hard time expressing it."

"I don't think my mom ever called my dad a dork," Freddie said.

Chelsea elbowed Freddie.

"When you're in love," Byron said, "it makes you do crazy things. What she said at first were her true feelings, then she caught herself. She's just trying to play it cool. I mean, I might be a little spoiled, but conceited?"

He put three of the mints back into the tin, but before putting in the fourth he brought it close to his nose. It smelled delicious.

"Mmm, these smell wonderful." He added the mint to the tin, closed it, and handed it back to Chelsea. The delightful fragrance of the bright purple coloring lingered on his fingers.

"She didn't seem like she was kidding to me," said Freddie. "I can tell."

"What do *you* know?" said Byron. "You're only a kid." He headed off to find the fitness center.

All the while, Robin was cleaning up in the lounge, observing and amused.

FORTY-FOUR

The children saw that Robin had witnessed the collision in front of the elevator and the spilling of the tablets and walked over to him.

"Meet you in my office in two minutes," Robin said.

A few minutes later, Freddie and Chelsea sat at the table in the back room, waiting for him to enter. Freddie was playing with a four-inch-high white marble statuette of an old-fashioned man with a hooked nose and a cap that was more like a shawl banded around his head. Chelsea stood examining the contents of the cabinet.

Robin waddled in and, seeing Freddie handling the statuette, said, "What do you have there?"

Freddie showed it to Robin. "Who is it?" Freddie asked. "I can't tell if he's happy or sad."

"Huh! Where did you find this?"

"It was in the barrel with the bows and arrows. It looks old."

"Could have been left here by former management. He probably looks sad because he wrote about sad things and happy things."

"You mean like relationships?" Chelsea asked, turning toward them.

"Most everything's about relationships. His was both sad and happy,"

Robin said. "Now, my young friends, how is it going with your parents?"

"We put one mint in each of their coffees," said Chelsea. "We think it might be working."

"All of a sudden they're acting all weird and lovey-dovey," said Freddie. "They made us leave our room."

"Excellent," said Robin. "That's always a good sign."

Chelsea opened the tin and showed the four remaining tablets. She set the open tin on the table.

"Do you think we're going to need some more?" asked Freddie, picking up the tin.

"We only used two like you said for our parents," Chelsea said. "But this man in the computer room took three of them, so then we had five. One must have gotten lost just now when that dorky guy bumped into me at the elevator."

"He only put four of them back. We didn't want to touch them ourselves."

"He picked them up with his bare hands, and you think he kept one?" Robin said.

"It looked like he put all the ones he picked up back in the tin," said Chelsea. "But some of the color came off on his hands."

"Hmm, that could be interesting," said Robin.

"What do you mean, 'interesting'?" said Chelsea.

"In these types of things, there can be some collateral damage."

"What does that mean?" asked Freddie, idly tapping the tin against the table.

"Oh, no big deal. It might be a good idea for me to take those though," Robin said, taking the tin from Freddie.

"Maybe we should keep a few, just in case?" said Chelsea.

"Not a bad idea for you to have some backup. Give me an hour or so and meet me back here. Let me see about getting a fresh batch."

>>———▶

After Chelsea and Freddie left his office, Robin went to his cabinets to make up another batch of his heart-softening potion. He found the jar with the purple liquid about a quarter full. "That should do," he said out loud.

He put the jar back and retrieved the brass urn from the lower shelf. He shook it. It was empty. "Not going to work without this." Often his most interesting conversations were with himself. He stuffed the urn into a backpack, but the backpack wasn't deep enough. He zipped it up anyway, securing the urn well enough with only four inches of it sticking out the top.

He called one of his assistants on his walkie-talkie to watch the front desk.

"Curdi told me I needed to take his place getting the barbecue ready," the assistant said. "There's another visitor coming in that he has to go pick up."

"Oh, I guess I forgot we had another guest checking in today," Robin said.

"We didn't. This one didn't have a reservation. She just called from the gate, but we have plenty of room. Boss, your mind has been skipping quite a bit lately."

"Do you think so?" said Robin. "It seems to me it dances rather than skips. Whatever. I'll cover the desk. I guess those children are going to have to wait."

>——▶

Byron had called down that morning to confirm the fitness center had spinning machines. They even had a couple of Pelotons in good condition connected to the internet. He'd worn his tight black cycling shorts padded in the crotch, and a bright-yellow short-sleeved Bedin Prosecco cycling shirt. His cycling shoes had cleats on the soles toward the toes, which caused him to stride heel first. Walking awkwardly down the hall, that enticing aroma from the mints he had picked up came strongly on him.

As he reached the fitness center, he saw in the glass door his reflection.

He had a good-sized smear of purple on the right side of his nose and cheek. He looked at his hands and saw that the fingers of both were similarly stained with something that looked like purple dye. He sniffed, realizing it was the source of that delicious smell.

He licked his fingers to clean them, then tried to rub the stains off onto his riding shorts. Seeing there was plenty left, he went through the process again, enjoying the taste very much. He hardly noticed the rumble that began building somewhere down below his diaphragm. He went through the process a third time, then licked his fingers several more times and tried to wipe the smears off his face. His face was now clean, but a good portion of the purple was still on his fingers. He licked that off.

His stomach began to growl, but this was no ordinary digestive growl. It shook his whole body and escaped through his mouth in a loud burp that shook the glass in the door in front of him. A roaring gale surged up from his abdomen, rising through his chest and esophagus, and then hit his sinuses like a gigantic wind-blown dose of ultra strong wasabi. Reaching the top of his skull, it swept back down through his whole body to the tips of his toes.

A sudden elation filled him as he looked past his reflection in the door and saw a face that would have launched a lot more than a thousand ships. No, this Helen would have launched ten thousand ships. Empires, not merely city-states, would have gone to war for this Helen. No, Helen couldn't compare to the gorgeous vision in baggy gray sweatpants, pink tank top, and Boston Red Sox baseball cap that had just walked from the spa's workout room into its lobby. He lunged forward, smashing his face into the glass. It didn't hurt that much. He stepped back, without taking his eyes off the vision.

She walked up to the fitness center counter and started signing something. Her every movement was like the flow of beautiful music and poetry. She turned. Her stature was stately, not short like Bianca's, nor was she too tall. She was the perfect height, perfectly proportioned, shoulders slightly back. Her feet barely touched the floor as she now glided toward him. He envisioned Mercury's wings on the sides of her red Converse All Stars. The old Boston Red Sox cap hid part of her glorious dishwater-blond hair. She was still breathing a little deeply from her workout.

She floated closer. Her glowing, radiant skin, a little flushed, was makeup-free. It needed none.

The door's window was steaming up in front of him from his breath. He wiped the glass clear.

Her perfectly fitting pink "Lowell YMCA" tank top revealed perfectly shaped feminine shoulders, trim and slightly bony, with just the right amount of muscley definition protruding from her biceps.

He lunged forward, smacking his nose against the glass again.

Kari looked up and froze. Her light-blue sapphire eyes with hints of aquamarine burned through the fog on the glass to see Byron gawking at her with a very unflattering grin on his face.

His finger slowly drew a large heart on the steamy glass. With lips puckering, he leaned forward to plant a kiss in the center.

Kari pushed open the door, smacking Byron's nose and lips. He bounced off the door and slammed the back of his head against the corridor wall behind him. He slid down the wall, a blissful smile on his face.

Kari sprinted past him, thinking that whatever Byron was up to, it wasn't funny. Well, a little funny, but absurd. She was glad she had smacked him with the door.

On the floor, Byron's expression turned determined. He staggered to his feet and tried to run after her. But the awkward cleats on his cycling shoes slipped on the tile floor. He crashed to the ground again, his right arm reaching out for the fleeing angel. He started to call out his love for her but remembered his vow.

FORTY-FIVE

Jackson lay shirtless on the bed in his room, eyes closed, trying to settle himself.

After he had escaped from the insane advances of Bianca, he'd found a small purple tablet on the elevator floor. When he'd picked it up, a sweet and tangy smell rose up to him. Entering his room, he placed the tablet on one of the overturned glass tumblers the hotel provided, and then proceeded to the suite's spacious bathroom to shave and take a long, hot shower. After the shower, he donned white boxer briefs and skinny jeans and lay down on his bed for a power nap. He was tired when he closed his eyes, but he couldn't stop thinking about that little tablet sitting on the upside-down glass. Even after his shower, its fragrance still lingered on his fingers.

Finally, he could no longer resist its tantalizing attraction. He rose and strode to the table. Tiny droplets of purple bubbles sparkled from the tablet's surface. He picked it up. It smelled wonderful. He brought it closer to his nose. Something like the strongest and most pleasant nasal spray surged through his sinuses and cascaded through to his eardrums, making the inner channels to his ears, then the whole inside of his skull, tingle delightfully. Switching the tablet to his left hand, he noticed that some of its purple color had come off on his fingers. He tasted them, then licked them. Licking wasn't enough—he had to have more of that taste. He chomped on the tablet. It dissolved, and the moisture mixed with his saliva and trickled on and over his tongue.

For a moment he savored it like a sip of fine wine from Byron's dad's cellar: "Ambrosia of the gods!" he marveled. The delicious nectar seeped down his throat and esophagus into his stomach. Barely having time to enjoy the delightful taste, he felt something like the shakings that anticipated the coming of an 8.5 magnitude earthquake. The waves of quaking grew stronger and stronger, until there was a moment of calm. Vesuvius erupted.

The lithospheric tectonic plates of the two sides of his brain split violently apart. The right side of his brain, the intuitive part, rose exuberantly while the left, the analytical part, sank. Then they both rose and dropped again in opposite directions. They kept on moving. He thought he was about to be launched into the atmosphere. He felt marvelous.

He staggered to his right, reaching for the table to steady himself. He struggled to breathe deeply, felt even more marvelous. He stepped up to the glass door leading to the balcony. His attention was drawn down below to the area in front of the fountain at the entrance to the lodge.

He staggered again and fell over. He strained to get up on his knees and peek through the glass to see the apparition again. Or was it a mirage—a mirage more desired than an oasis in the most bleak and barren desert? The tumult raging through his body and head blurred his eyesight. He blinked and rubbed his eyes. She was no mirage. It was like his blind eyes had suddenly been opened. He was in love.

Billy's ex-girlfriend was the most gorgeous, attractive, appealing being, living or otherwise, on the face of the earth. Even if she and Billy were still together, he had to have her. He now understood crimes of passion. But none would be needed. Of course she would love him, though it might take some wooing; such beauties often played hard to get. But she wouldn't be able to resist him—he barely could resist himself as he saw afresh his own beauty and elegance reflected in the door's glass. He stood and opened his mouth, crying out, "My love, my dearest, can you possibly know how much I . . ." He caught himself. That vow—that stupid, moronic vow he had boasted so foolishly that he would be the last to break. But the door was closed. She hadn't heard him.

Below, Kari was stretching, bending over, grabbing her toes with straight legs, and pulling isometrically against them. She still hadn't seen or heard him. He had to get her attention without saying anything. He opened the door and stepped onto the balcony. As his stomach was still echoing with the explosions that had torn through him, he let out a great roaring growl, and throwing his arms wide open and bending his head slightly to the right—the opposite side of his now out-of-whack brain tectonics—he smiled his most uninhibited Casanova smile.

Kari straightened up, scanning for where the gross sound had come from. Jackson stood on his balcony without a shirt, in too-tight skinny jeans, with his arms wide open, flexing his latissimus dorsi muscles.

Kari almost laughed, the pose was so absurd. What was he doing, and that imbecilic look on his face?

He moved to the edge of the balcony and reached out his arms as if he were offering himself to her. Yes, his upper body was built, if you liked that look, and some might consider him handsome. But to her, he was totally gross. She felt like vomiting.

What was going on? First Byron, and now Jackson? She detested the thought of them, but why couldn't Billy be so open with his emotions? She picked up a rock and threw it at Jackson. It nicked him on the side of his chin. *Not a bad shot*, she thought, taking pride in her athleticism.

Jackson barely felt the pain and smiled broader. That rock was clearly a gesture of love.

Seeing his ridiculous response, she took off in a run toward the back of the lodge.

FORTY-SIX

"You've already spent over an hour on that stupid game. Your brain is turning to mush," Chelsea told Freddie as they crossed the lobby. In truth, she had her preferred games, but they were on her Xbox at home, and she was bored watching Freddie blast waves of Saruman's army.

"What else are we going to do? Let's go for a walk down to the parking lot to see if our car is still there. If it's gone, that means they really did go antique shopping."

Out on the cobblestone lane, the sun was shining, and the sky was clear except for clouds out to the west. To their right, they had a pleasant view of the meadow in front of the lodge. Out in the distance, a couple of flocks grazed, their shepherds and dogs lolling nearby. A little farther along, two lambs of another flock had strayed up to the holly hedge bordering the lane and were sniffing but not eating its bright red berries.

Freddie walked up and started talking to the sheep.

"They can't understand anything you're saying," Chelsea said. "They're just as dumb as you are."

"I'm talking Sindarin to them," Freddie said, referring to one of the Elvish languages in *The Lord of the Rings*. "These could be Elvish sheep."

"No, they look too dumb."

Hearing Chelsea, the herd's shepherd left the rest of the flock in the care of his dog and walked up. "Now, now, miss, my lambs aren't dumb," he said. "Ignorant, but not dumb—just lambs. They're smart enough not to eat these berries that only the birds can eat. They're even learning to come when I call; they'd rather me not send Walter to fetch 'em." He gave a low whistle, and Walter, his collie, turned from watching the rest of the flock and jogged up to the shepherd's side.

"My brother was speaking Elvish to them," Chelsea said. "He thinks he can communicate with animals."

"*Some* animals," Freddie said.

"Wouldn't be that unusual. But that language would be new to me. The boss might know something about it though. As far as communicating with my sheep, Walt's the one who knows the language."

"Your dog knows sheep language?" asked Freddie.

"Course Walt knows sheep language." The shepherd patted his dog on the head. "He's awful smart, wasn't worried with Sal and Ellie coming to see you. Saw right away you was no wolves in little people's clothes. But Walt can be stern sometimes too."

"I think it's the Wood Elves that can talk to animals, at least to smart ones," said Freddie.

"As I said, I don't know 'bout that, but Colin might. He's been around a long time and paid his dues."

"Who's Colin?" Freddie asked. "Is he like the head of this place? Or is Robin?"

"That's an interesting question. Colin's my boss anyway."

"If he knows Elvish, I'd like to talk with him," said Freddie.

"He don't talk to just anyone, but talking to animals might be a subject he's interested in talking about. Well, me and Walt best be getting back to the flock. Have a nice day."

"You too," said Chelsea.

The shepherd turned and started walking back, whistling a three-note call. Walt responded by nosing at the two lambs to get them moving, then chasing them back to the flock.

"I hope we can talk again," Freddie called.

The shepherd just waved back.

"You sure ask a lot of dumb questions," Chelsea said as they continued their walk.

"I bet that dog and those sheep know at least a little Sindarin or Quenya."

"Maybe the dog," Chelsea said, "but not the lambs. They're too young and dumb—like you."

As they drew near to the parking lot, an Audi sedan was leaving. At the gate, the horse-drawn coach was turning around to head back to the lodge. The same young man they had met when they arrived was driving, and in the back of the coach was a young woman of about thirty with freckles on her cheeks and reddish-auburn hair. Her jeans had a few holes in the legs, and she was wearing a Seattle Seahawks jersey.

"Good morning," Curdi said, stopping the coach next to them. "Beautiful morning for a walk." His dog, who had been resting at his side with his head on his lap, sat up and seemed to greet them too.

"Hi," said Chelsea.

"This is Ms. Vivian, our new guest who's just arrived," Curdi said, motioning to the passenger in the seat behind him.

"Hi," Vivian said, with not quite a full smile. "Vivian is good enough."

Chelsea and Freddie returned her greeting.

"We wanted to check if our parents' car is still here," Chelsea said to Curdi. "They said they might be going off shopping."

"The only two folks that I've taken to the lot this morning are the lad and lass who just took off in that fancy car. They've become betrothed."

"Does that mean they got married?" asked Freddie.

"I believe it's that they have made an agreement to that purpose. But such relationships can sometimes get complicated and don't always work out."

"Complicated—I'll say," Vivian offered. "That's not the half of it. Me and my old man have been engaged five times and never tied the knot. That train might have left the station."

"Oh, you never know," Curdi said.

"We should be getting back. Do you think we could have a ride?" Chelsea said. "We need to see Robin again. He's been trying to do some stuff for our parents."

Curdi hopped down from the driver's seat and helped Chelsea into the coach. She took her seat next to Vivian. He offered to help Freddie in, but Freddie declined the offer and pulled himself in, struggling as he was barely tall enough to reach the stepping rail. Curdi laughed to himself, seeing the little boy's effort. He hopped back up and took his seat next to his dog, and the carriage started off back to the lodge.

"Cool shoes," Vivian said to Chelsea once they got going. She, like Chelsea, was wearing black high-top Converse All Stars.

"Are you up here to try to fix your relationship with your husband too?" Freddie asked.

"Freddie!" Chelsea said.

"That would take some fixing," Vivian said.

"Our mom and dad always used to fight but weren't fighting this morning," said Freddie.

"I'm not up here for that. I'm here to hear this professor dude who thinks he knows the secret to good writing. I'll believe it when I hear it, but my old old man thinks there's something to it."

Curdi started humming a pleasant tune as they rode on, which he kept up till they came to the flock and the shepherd that the children had talked with earlier. The shepherd raised his staff in greeting, which Curdi, with a nod, acknowledged. Curdi's dog sat up and gave an approving bark.

"Do you think dogs can talk to sheep?" Chelsea asked Curdi. "My brother does."

"How else do they get them to do all the stuff they do?" Freddie said.

"What do you think, Gus?" Curdi said, looking down at his dog. Gus looked up and wagged his tail.

"Do you think they understand Elvish too?" Freddie asked. "I think they do."

Chelsea rolled her eyes.

"Oh, do you?" said Curdi.

"Do you think that Colin would know? Sounds like he's really smart."

"He might."

"I hope we get a chance to meet him," said Freddie.

"He generally keeps apart from the guests, but you never know," Curdi said.

"Where does he stay?" Freddie had the feeling that maybe it could have been Colin behind that door at the top of the spiral stairs.

Chelsea elbowed Freddie. "It's rude to ask so many questions."

Freddie turned away from her and frowned. In his imagination, this mysterious Colin was becoming something like Gandalf or maybe Elrond, king of the Elves. It was something that needed investigating.

FORTY-SEVEN

When the carriage got back to the lodge, Curdi helped Vivian with her bags and led her to the front desk to get checked in.

For Chelsea and Freddie, it was still a few minutes before they were supposed to meet Robin, so they went to check on their parents. Not hearing any stirring when they entered the suite, they pressed their ears to the door of their parents' room. Still no noise. Chelsea opened it slightly, and they peeked in.

Their parents were fast asleep, their father's arm over their mother's shoulder and their mother's face nestled on their father's chest.

The children backed away and quietly closed the door.

"What should we do?" whispered Freddie.

"I don't know. Nothing, I guess," said Chelsea. "This is amazing." She went back to the door to peek in again, Freddie following.

Hearing a noise from the door, or just feeling the presence of the kids, Mr. Abelson's eyes opened. A couple of seconds later, Mrs. Abelson's did as well. For a second or two, they seemed to be pleased they were snuggling.

Then Mrs. Abelson shrieked, lifting her head off his chest and moving away. "What are you doing?"

"What do you mean, what am I doing?" Mr. Abelson still had his arm around her. "What are *you* doing?" He pulled his arm away.

"I'm mad at you," she said, moving farther away.

"And I'm mad at you too." He moved away and turned his back to her.

She tugged on the covers and pulled them fully off him.

"I don't feel like going antique shopping anymore," he said. "Go by yourself."

"I wouldn't go with you if you asked me." She moved so far from him that she had to reach her leg out to keep from falling off the bed.

"Well, you don't have to worry about that."

The children closed the door. They looked at each other, their countenances having crashed.

"We better go back and find Robin," Chelsea said.

»———▶

Billy had been asleep for over an hour. Not a REM sleep, where one's dreams, often anxious, usually occur. This sleep was something closer to deep sleep, where one's mind is very much at peace. But this sleep did have its own kind of dreams. Images of Bianca would come before him. Her beauty unearthly, her movements graceful, her demeanor ethereal. She sang a song soothing and enchanting that made him giddy and sent him in conquest of her love. She beckoned him with her hands outstretched. He kept running toward her. But just out of his grasp, she would vanish like an idea, only to take shape again.

Outside, in the hallway, Jackson walked determinedly up to Billy's room. Byron was standing in front of Billy's door, talking to himself, rehearsing what he was going to say.

"What are you doing here?" Jackson said to him. He wasn't happy to see Byron. "I have to talk to Billy. Could you give us some time?" His tone wasn't friendly.

"I need to talk with him too. I was here first." Byron's tone wasn't friendly either.

Inside his room, Billy's visions had ceased, vanished beyond memory.

A blissful rest enveloped him in that place between deep sleep and wakefulness. He had no memory of what he had been dreaming or what had occurred to him after tasting that aromatic mint. A new and fresh vision of Kari had appeared.

A faint pounding on his door interrupted his heart-aching vision of her. He fought to deny the intrusion and retain her radiant image. His deep longing for her tugged at his heart, a pain that he would not exchange for anything. She was all he had ever wanted, and he must—

The pounding on the door broke out again, louder.

He stirred, groggy and angry at being distracted from the ache of his vision.

"Go away," he hollered. "I don't need room service. Just leave an extra towel and some more coffee."

"It's not room service," Jackson spoke loudly through the door. "It's me, I have to talk to you."

"No, it's *me*," said Byron, even more loudly. "And I got here first."

Billy got up and opened the door. Jackson, elbowing Byron out of the doorway, barged in. He was still shirtless and shoeless, in only his skinny jeans. Byron came slipping in after him, trying to hold back Jackson by the shoulder. He still wore his cycling outfit and shoes.

"Would you guys mellow out?" Billy said. "What's going on? Have you already broken your vows?"

"I have to talk with you," said Jackson. "Man to man." He was more serious than Billy could ever remember him—the snide, ironic look he perpetually wore was gone. "This is more important than any stupid vow."

"Don't listen to him," said Byron. "What I've got to say is more important—our friendship might depend on it."

"Never mind him," said Jackson. "I'm in love with Kari, and I always have been. Now that I've come to realize it, I have to be honest. It shouldn't matter. It's clear why she dumped you—it was for me."

It took a few moments for what Billy was hearing to register—had his friend been wooing his true love behind his back?

"What are you talking about?" said Byron. "*I'm* in love with her, and she is with *me*."

"You're out of your mind," Jackson said. "She's in love with me."

Billy was getting madder and madder; jealousy was rising like a bear and, with it, a disdain he had never felt for either of his friends. "What makes you think that she could possibly have such bad taste to like either of you?"

"Bad taste? You bourgeois philistine!" Jackson said. "I'll tell you, just like Romeo and Juliet, she threw a rock up to my balcony to get my attention. When it accidentally hit me, it was like Cupid had struck me with a dart. I'm sorry, Billy, but we are meant for each other. It's obvious that she dumped you for me."

"You think hitting you with a rock means she loves you?" said Billy. "It was Juliet who was on the balcony and Romeo below, and he just tossed pebbles—or *a* pebble. I can't remember. Anyway, you're no Romeo. I doubt you could hit the side of a cow with a rock if you were standing inside it." This was probably true.

"Jackson's out of his mind," said Byron. "When a woman loves you, she shows it by *not* showing it, like Kari is doing with me."

There might be some truth in that, but in no way does it apply to Byron, Billy thought. His jealousy was starting to boil.

"She slammed the fitness room door into my face when I drew a heart on it and was about to kiss it," said Byron. "That's how I declared my love, without breaking the vow. It was like she was kissing me back with the door." There was a remote chance that this could be true as, in the old tales of courtly love, the beloved would often enjoy inflicting pain, at least emotionally, on their pursuers. But Billy quickly shunned the idea as, in this case, it was absurd.

"You're out of your mind," Jackson said to Byron.

"I'm so much in love that even if we don't modify the vow, for my love's sake, I will make the sacrifice." Byron sighed.

"It's true that sometimes women show their affection in different ways," Jackson said. "But she's a woman of taste, culture, and sensibility. I am the only one for her, and she for me. I tell you, you morons, she's crazy about *me.*"

"Did you break the vow?" Billy's fury neared eruption.

"No, but she knows," said Jackson. "She knows without the trifle of words. She knows by the smile I gave her, which I only use for special occasions. I'll cherish the rock she gave me as a memento of our love."

"You don't even know how to smile, you conceited, pedantic beast," said Byron. "It's like you have a permanent case of indigestion."

"I'll hit you with something more than a rock," Jackson said, lunging forward, then hauling back to take a roundhouse swing at Byron.

Byron, at the same time, was preparing to charge Jackson, but unfortunately, he still wore those cycling shoes. Lunging forward, he slipped and crashed into Jackson's midsection with his head and shoulders.

To keep from falling over, Jackson wrapped his arms around Byron's torso and bent forward, forcing Byron's head down by pushing his chin into the top middle of Byron's back. This didn't feel very good to Byron, whose head and own chin were now down around Jackson's knees. He grabbed Jackson's legs, pulling Jackson toward himself as he tried to do something like a football tackle.

Jackson, with his arms cinched around Byron's belly, tried to flip him up and over his shoulders, legs first, in what is called, though he didn't know it as such, an "inverted suplex." That didn't work, Byron being too heavy or Jackson too weak, despite his physique. He tried rolling him to his left, and they both tumbled to the floor, causing a crash heard and felt down to the main floor. Byron somehow ended up on top, but it didn't take long for Jackson to inadvertently pull off something like an Olympic-style wrestling reversal—which now put him on top of Byron.

Fuming with jealousy, Billy yelled, "You rotten backstabbers! Leave my woman alone!" And he leaped, flattening Jackson on top of Byron to make something like a three-stack of pancakes or a ham sandwich. The three of them wrestled for predominance. Loud insults, grunts, and curses spewed from each.

Soon, a firm knock rattled the room door. It was unheeded. The knocking started again.

Billy, who was trying to grind both their faces into the carpet, considered answering the door but didn't want to give up his advantage.

Finally, the electronic lock on the door clicked. Robin waddled in.

"Now, now, boys," Robin said.

Billy looked up, releasing some of the pressure from the backs of his now rivals' heads. Jackson let go of the stranglehold he had on Byron's neck. And Byron took his thumbs most of the way out of Jackson's eyes.

"After lunch," Robin went on pleasantly, "there will be time for fun activities and plenty of competition too. I think you ought to take a break for a while. Let's all meet outside at the barbecue in a couple of hours, eh? A shower, a cold one, and a nap should do you all some good."

Billy took his hands off their heads and stood up. "These traitors woke me up from my nap and told me—"

"I just took a shower," interrupted Jackson, rolling off Byron.

"I suggest you take a *nap* too," Robin said. "It will help you think more clearly."

"He's the one who needs a shower." Jackson pointed to Byron as he got up. "You smell terrible."

"He needs a nap too," Robin said. "This thin mountain air sometimes takes getting used to." He went to the door and opened it.

"Just get out of here," Billy said to his ex-friends as he pushed them out into the hall. Robin followed them. "And leave me alone." He slammed the door, then banged his head hard up against it.

His thoughts swirled and seethed. What was going on in this place? His two best friends were challenging him for the only woman he could ever love. Was he going insane? No, loving Kari was the sanest thing he had ever done. But he had lost her. Did the blissful expectations he had had in his relationship with her have to end in such pain?

FORTY-EIGHT

After the unpleasant incident she had with Jackson, Kari had returned to her room to find a letter that had been slid under her door. As she reread it for the third time, her heart throbbed, and she was swooning with joy over the pure passion it expressed. Could it be true? She dropped all her defenses. She deeply loved him too. If the letter were addressed to Billy, it would just *begin* to capture her feelings for him.

She brought the letter up to her face and kissed it. He'd even scented it with something like cinnamon. She sniffed the envelope and found the scent there even stronger. She looked inside—he had put a wonderful-smelling mint inside. What a lovely romantic touch! She got up dreamily and swooned around the room until she caught her reflection in the mirror. She could use a little attention. She would dream about getting back together with Billy while taking a luxurious hot shower.

After her shower, she donned jeans and a Jack's Surf Shop T-shirt Billy had given her and her New England Patriots jersey. She giggled to herself, "If only I had a Seahawks jersey." Sitting down, she could smell the delightful fragrance emanating from the envelope and letter on the table next to her.

She was rereading the letter, delighting in every phrase and word, when rapid knocks at her door disturbed her. Still holding the letter, she got up and answered the door. Bianca, flush-faced and animated, stood in the doorway. She was still in her sweaty running clothes.

"You look adorable in that outfit," Kari said. The letter had put her into a benevolent mood. She had always thought Bianca adorable and her stature preferable to her own, even though Bianca thought the same of her. "Have you been eating blueberries? You've got purple all over your lips."

"This is important," Bianca said, entering the room and letting the door swing shut behind her. "It has to do with that letter."

"What do you know about my letter? Are you okay? You look frazzled."

"It's what's *in* that letter."

"You've read my letter?"

"Billy gave it to me."

"Oh. I wondered how it got here. I could just see the doll sneaking up here to deliver it."

"I'm the one who delivered it, and I shouldn't have."

"Why not?" said Kari. "It's addressed to me."

"It's addressed to the true love of his life."

Kari, still holding the letter, looked at it and then at the envelope. She hadn't noticed it, but neither mentioned her by name. *Who else could it be for then?* she thought.

Another knock sounded. The glow in Kari's mood was fading fast. She opened the door—Amanda was standing there. The tall beauty had already dressed for the barbecue, makeup and all. Amanda's expression, which was concerned to begin with, changed when she saw Bianca in the room. Her large blue eyes seemed to want to pop out of her head. One of her blue-tinted contacts did, in fact, slide slightly, revealing a touch of brown. She raised a forefinger to her eye to adjust it.

"So, *she's* here," Amanda said, shooting Bianca a look that could have cut diamonds. She stormed into the room, taking a stand on the other side of Kari, away from Bianca. Even though she was a head taller than Bianca, Amanda knew she could be fierce.

Just then, there were loud voices and a crash and a shaking from the floor below them.

"What was that?" Kari said.

"Never mind that," Amanda said. "I need to talk with you, and I'm glad that little vixen is here."

"I was here first," said Bianca. "And what have I ever done to you that I'm a 'vixen' now? Fine friend you are."

"I thought you were," said Amanda, "and were Kari's friend too—until what I saw today."

"I thought you were both my friends," Kari said. "What are you talking about?"

"I was here first, so I'll tell you," Bianca said.

"Yeah, I want to hear this," said Amanda.

"I was coming back from my morning run, and I'm walking through the lobby, and I see Billy coming toward me, almost at a run, and his eyes are bulging out, and there's this ridiculous smile on his face, as if we are long-lost lovers, and he lunges toward me, trying to embrace me."

"And you were just getting back from your run," Kari said, "dressed as you are now?"

"Yes, he even tried to kiss me right on the lips, I think. I got out of his way and just stared at him. And he stood there, like a dog in heat, grinning at me and, like, pleading his love for me. He was so lovestruck he couldn't even talk. He just handed me that letter as if to explain everything. I took it and ran off, trying not to believe what I had just been through. I so wanted the letter to be meant for you, but the way he acted . . . well, that's why I'm here. I wanted to let you know about that two-timing boyfriend you have, or had, or whatever he is. And I want you to know that I want nothing to do with him. 'Cause I'm your true friend."

"You deceitful little shrimp!" Amanda hissed at Bianca.

"Who are you calling a shrimp?" Bianca said to Amanda, striding toward her, fists clenched and sneering. "You, you beanpole."

"I saw the whole thing," Amanda said to Kari. "That's why I'm here. She was teasing him, playing him, like a kitten plays with a spool of thread; like a spider plays with a fly, the poor puppy."

"Kari, you need to believe me. I did nothing to lead him on, but he's out of his mind in love with me. You should have seen the way he attacked me. I tried to believe it wasn't true. Then I read his letter."

"You opened my letter?"

"I saw what I saw," said Amanda. "The way you were coyly playing with him."

"Your contacts must have been unadjusted again," said Bianca. "I couldn't care less for Billy, though he does have nice hair and pretty eyes. How could I be in love with him when—and I'm glad Amanda's here to hear it." Bianca paused. "I know now that I'm in love with Jackson."

"So, you like Billy's eyes and hair, do you?" Kari said to Bianca. "I knew I couldn't trust you."

"Jackson's aloofness," Bianca gushed, "his sarcasm, his dry and sophisticated sense of humor—I can't get enough of him. He's my dream come true; I can't stop thinking about him. I couldn't care less about hair and eyes. I'm in love with Jackson, despite his bald spot."

"What? I don't believe it," Amanda said to Bianca. "And what's the matter with a little bald spot? I think it's cute. By the way, you've got purple drool coming down your chin."

"I'm going after him with all I've got," said Bianca, wiping the drool away.

"Well, that doesn't scare me," Amanda said, wiping her own mouth just to make sure she wasn't drooling too. "You're going to need more than what you've got. You aren't even a scampi."

"You think so?" Bianca moved even closer to Amanda. "You cornstalk."

"Well, I've got news for you both," Kari said. "Jackson couldn't care less for either of you. You should have seen the way he just acted toward me. It was, and he is, totally disgusting."

"With you?" said Bianca.

"Impossible," said Amanda. "He loves *me*. I know he does."

"But I'm not interested in either of those creeps." Kari cringed.

"How dare you call Jackson a creep!" said Amanda.

"Byron and Billy are both super disgusting compared to Jackson,"

Bianca insisted. "And you can keep that letter from your two-timing boyfriend, even though I know it was meant for me."

"There's no way this letter is meant for you," Kari said.

"I know the truth hurts," Bianca said.

"You're out of your mind. Just keep your grimy little hands off Billy. Now get out of here and leave me alone."

"My hands are petite, not little," Bianca said, and stormed out of the room.

"You get out of here too," Kari said to Amanda, starting to tear up. "How could you be so blind to think Billy was hitting on her!"

"I saw what I saw," said Amanda. "And you better stay away from Jackson."

"Get out of here," Kari said, chasing her out the door.

To the sensitive soul deep in love—amid turmoil, angst, and the painful fear of true love being lost from a relationship that once abounded in hope and seeming certainty—common sense can be a casualty. It was absurd to think that Billy could be in love with Bianca, as Kari had just proclaimed, and even shouted. But Kari feared it anyway. Maybe the letter *was* for Bianca, and Billy *did* hate her. But it didn't matter. She might perish, but she would go on loving him.

PART 3

Men have died from time to time, and worms have eaten them, but not for love.

William Shakespeare, *As You Like It*

FORTY-NINE

Gwendolyn Spiers woke up Saturday morning from her night's sleep more anxious than usual. She had had another of her dreams, and she needed to talk about it with her husband. But he had already left for an early-morning breakfast meeting at the yacht club.

By the time he came home at ten forty-five, she was ready to burst.

"Darling, finally," she said. He had barely had time to put his captain's cap on the hat rack. "I had another dream last night."

"Yes, my love. Those often happen in one's sleep."

"But this one—it was about our grandson."

"Many of your dreams lately have been about our grandson. Are you feeling guilty for trying to manage his life?"

"Of course not. I'm just trying to give it a nudge."

"Perhaps, like Scrooge, your bad dream was from 'a crumb of cheese' or 'a fragment of underdone potato'?"

"This is serious. It concerns me greatly, and I woke up perspiring."

"Oh dear, I'm glad you weren't sweating."

"Would you please be civil and let me tell it to you?"

"You know I don't put much stock in your dreams."

"But this one was about Billy at the lodge."

"So, you are feeling guilty?"

"No, not at all . . . just a little."

"Well, go ahead. I'm all ears."

"I dreamed he had fallen for a girl with holes in her pants—and with freckles."

"What's the matter with freckles? I adore freckles. You used to have freckles and still have a few when you don't cover them up."

"But Kari doesn't have freckles."

"Are you sure?"

"No, but what if Kari isn't the girl for him?"

Elrond was waiting for his transport from LA County Jail's Venice annex to Folsom Penitentiary when he was escorted from the holding cell to the front office. He was met there by his lawyer and informed that all the latest charges had been dropped.

Though of concern, the charges alone—assault with a deadly weapon—would not have sent him directly to Folsom. It was that his arrest for this charge broke one of the conditions of his parole that would have sent him there without the preliminaries of a trial.

The lawyer explained that the prosecution would have had to prove that Elrond's teeth were a deadly weapon. They would undoubtedly have tried to equate his teeth with a knife. For teeth, like knives, may be used for tearing apart not only animal flesh but also human flesh.

But Elrond's lawyer had made the case that whereas knives have many functions, including stabbing human flesh, the main function of human teeth is eating. And the few cases where they could be shown to have been used for mortal purposes were either the stuff of fantasy—zombies or vampires—or were attacks of a nature and severity well beyond what the defendant was alleged to have committed.

Now that Elrond's "assault with a deadly weapon" had been dropped, he was no longer guilty of breaking parole, and thus he was a free man.

Elrond's lawyer happily agreed (he was billing by the quarter hour) to drive him down to the Phoenix. Elrond had realized, especially as it looked like he would be spending considerable time away from Vivian, how much he really did want her back. And this time, he wanted her back for good. He longed and ached for her wit, her humor, the ease with which she carried on, and the reserve behind which always loomed her passion. He needed to see her and square things up. And he needed to know if she had gotten the note he sent her by Billy. In it, he'd told her about this conference where she could learn from an important writing teacher and get a chance to meet some agents and big-shot people.

It was a little after 10:00 a.m. when he arrived at the Phoenix. Only five or six customers were inside, two of them at the end of the counter eating breakfast burritos. Louisa, Vivian's roommate, was behind the bar.

"Hey, Lou," he said, "where's Cel?" Cel was what the homies called Vivian—it being short for Celebrían, Elrond's consort and queen of the Elves.

"El, what you doing here?" Louisa responded. "Word was you was going north."

"Just a rumor. Where's Cel?"

"She took off early this morning in your car. Said she was going to some place up in the mountains."

"Good, she got my note. I tried to call, but it's like her phone is off. Did she tell you where?"

"Maybe the coverage is bad up there. We looked the place up on the internet. It's called the Bow and Arrow, or maybe vice versa—yeah, the Arrow and Bow."

Just then, a tall dark figure approached from the back of the room. As he came into more light, it was clear he had a large bandage on his left ear.

Elrond reared back, cocking his right arm and fist to poleaxe Julio Bocardo. Fortunately, a combination of Louisa leaning over the bar and grabbing El and Julio taking two steps back and raising both hands in surrender held him back.

"Whoa, El. Easy, bro," Julio said, his hands still held high. "Aren't you going to thank me for dropping the charges?"

"Yeah, thanks, why did ya do that?"

"Man, I'm through with Cel—for good, El. She ain't my type. I got a new old lady. Plus . . ."

"Plus what?"

"She ain't interested in me."

"How do you know that?"

"'Cause one of my boys saw what he saw."

"What'd he see?"

"Some preppy dude she was with."

"Some preppy dude was moving in on my old lady?" Elrond had uncocked his arm and fist, but he was still seething.

"Yeah, he said they were all ogling each other, and she put her hand on his, and they hugged a couple times. And she followed him out the door and they hugged some more. Thought you'd want to know, El, 'cause I'm your homie. I'm lookin' out for ya."

Elrond looked over to Louisa for confirmation.

Louisa just shrugged—like she knew nothing.

Elrond didn't need confirmation. *So, she's gone up to this lodge to meet him*, Elrond thought. *That Hollywood rat who got dumped by his old lady is now moving in on mine.*

"Lu, get me the address of that lodge." To Julio, Elrond said, "Put some aloe on your ear, it might help it to grow back, and the scar won't be so bad."

Elrond hastened to the apartment where he kept his things, took a quick shower, dressed, and threw some other things in a duffel bag.

As Vivian had used his car to get to that lodge place, Elrond called on one of his homies, a cousin who owned a restaurant supply company, to give him a lift. As he was used to saying, "It's not *what* you know but *who* you know." Homies always have each other's backs.

FIFTY

After seeing their parents fighting again, Chelsea and Freddie hurriedly left their suite. Not finding Robin behind the counter, they found him in his office, sitting upright, asleep on his high stool, his head tilted to one side. The tin with four remaining mints was sitting on the table in front of him.

Hearing the children enter, he awoke and almost fell off his chair. "Oh, hello, so nice to see you again." He straightened up, pushing his glasses back up his nose, smiling, and said, "What can I do for you?"

"You said to come back in an hour," said Chelsea.

"That's right, now I recall."

"We have a problem," said Chelsea.

"Our parents are fighting again," said Freddie.

"Hmmm, your parents?"

"They were doing so good," Chelsea said. "When we got back to the room, they were asleep, but when they woke up, they started fighting again."

"So they had gone back to sleep, took a nap?"

"We accidentally woke them up," said Freddie.

"It's like what we put in their coffee wore off," Chelsea said.

"Well, I did mention sometimes it can be a little volatile." Robin wore a look like he was saying "oops!" without really speaking it. "Other factors can be involved too."

"Should we give them more of these, then?" Freddie pointed to the open tin with four old mints.

"That's right, I was going to prepare a new batch."

"What's the matter with these? Do they, like, lose their power?" said Freddie, pointing to the tin.

"Not usually. Actually, they seem to become more powerful. It's hard to predict. Best we make a new batch, but we're running a little short of the main ingredient."

Chelsea's expression dropped, and she started to cry. Freddie looked again at the open tin on the table. The mints were no longer soggy, but tiny bubbles of purple moisture oozed from them.

"Please don't cry," said Robin. "As soon as my assistant gets back, I'm going to take care of everything. I can fetch what we need. Don't you worry—I still have this under control."

"When is he getting back?" said Freddie.

"He shouldn't be too long. Then I'll go check on the barbecue and run my little errand."

"Where do you need to go?" said Freddie. "We could go for you."

"No, no. Just be patient. Check back with me after lunch." He hopped off his stool, the twelve-inch drop to the floor causing his glasses to pop off. He bent over and, with his hands, searched the floor for them.

While Chelsea scooted off her chair to get his glasses for him, Freddie closed the lid on the tin and slipped it into a pocket of his cargo pants.

"I should get back to watching the counter now," said Robin, getting up and adjusting his glasses. "Now, don't you worry—I've got this under control."

Chelsea and Freddie left to check on their parents again, not so sure things were under control.

>>———➤

Robin had almost let the barbecue slip his mind. An assistant soon arrived to manage the registration counter, and Robin went out back to check on the lunch preparations. The morning had started out clear and sunny, but as the day wore on, clouds began to move in from the south. Toward the rear of the freshly mowed lawn, the luncheon buffet had been set up with two large grills made from metal barrels cut in half and set on metal stands. A nearby smoker resembled a miniature steam engine with smoke oozing from its stack. Adjacent to the grills were two tables covered with light-blue cotton tablecloths bearing prepared dishes on trays with hinged covers that swung up like the visors on knights' helmets. Past the prepared dishes were stacks of pewter plates, bowls, and cups and a large basin of fruit punch. It looked like the lodge crew had things very much in order, but Robin had wanted to make sure. Like many supervisors, he could at times be an annoying micromanager and at others a lax one.

Chelsea and Freddie returned to their suite to find their mother just back from the spa and their father, dressed in a red polo shirt and blue jeans, at the room's desk, typing on his laptop.

"The damn place doesn't have cellphone coverage," was all he said when they entered.

"The internet's working in the business center," Chelsea said.

"Yeah, thanks, sweetie. It's working up here too," Mr. Abelson said.

"The spa is wonderful, Chelsea," Mrs. Abelson said. "If you want, you can get your nails done."

"Thanks, Mom. Maybe later," Chelsea said.

"Your father ought to go down and get a massage—maybe it would help him be not so uptight."

Mr. Abelson didn't respond, just gave her a glance, thinking, *You're the one who needs to mellow out*, and went back to his work.

The lodge's intercom came on and announced that the barbecue lunch was being served in the park at the rear of the lodge.

"Want me to go down?" Freddie said. "I could bring you up something." He brushed his fingers over the cool surface of the tin in his pocket.

"I need to take a break," said Mr. Abelson. "I'll be down in a minute."

"That's thoughtful of you," said Mrs. Abelson to Freddie. "I'll come down too; it would be nice if we all ate together."

"Oh, good," said Chelsea. "We'll save a table."

Freddie was working on plan B.

FIFTY-ONE

On the way to the barbecue, Bianca and Amanda met at the elevator on the third floor. Bianca had showered and taken a nap in which she entered a sleep like she had never had before—it was like gravity had been turned up, pressing her to the bed. She hadn't dreamed—at least she couldn't remember dreaming. The last thing she could remember was coming back from her run. She felt incredibly refreshed and perky.

Bianca's perkiness sometimes got to Amanda, and now it really frosted her. Amanda almost said, "How can you live with yourself?" She had been in her suite doing yoga, trying to get her mind off how irate she was with her friends. Not only was Bianca toying with Kari's beau, but she was pursuing her Jackson, which made her want him even more now.

She was furious with Kari, too, for thinking Jackson was interested in her. *She was probably toying with him to make Billy jealous, just like Bianca was toying with Billy. Oh, the audacity to think Jackson cares for her! But then, what if he does love Kari, and I've lost him? Oh, what kind of friends are these!*

So, instead of responding to Bianca, she just sneered a pitying look—the kind of pity that wasn't really pity—turned, and walked off to take the stairs.

Wow, what's the matter with her? Bianca thought.

>>———▶

Bianca found a place at a table by herself toward the far end of the buffet, close to where the desserts had been spread out. A couple asked if they could join her, which she allowed. Amanda took a seat at a table a good distance from Bianca.

Chelsea and Freddie had taken seats at a vacant table in front of the buffet and were waiting for their parents to appear before they got their food. Finally, the kids saw their dad in his red polo shirt come through the rear door of the lodge. The kids waved him over.

"We were waiting for you and Mom," said Chelsea. "We didn't want to lose the table."

"She's finishing putting on her face," Mr. Abelson said.

The phrase came across as mean to Freddie. "Is she still coming down?"

"That means she's putting on her makeup," Chelsea interpreted.

"I'm hungry. Let's get in line," Mr. Abelson said.

"Someone could take our table," Chelsea said.

"Shouldn't we wait for Mom?" Freddie said. "I could get you a drink or something."

"Don't worry." Mr. Abelson tilted his chair forward against the table and instructed Chelsea and Freddie to do the same. "That means the seats are taken." He took off his sunglasses and put them in front of his place. "No one's going to take our seats—if they do, I'll sic you on them," he told Freddie.

They got in line—Freddie first, Chelsea, then Mr. Abelson. As they were waiting, a pretty young woman with blondish-brown hair, wearing a New England Patriots football jersey, joined the line behind them. She got Mr. Abelson's attention—and not only for the jersey she was wearing.

He turned, smiled, and said, "What's a Pats fan doing way out here?"

Kari had been looking around, trying to see if Billy had come down, but shifted her attention to the man that had just spoken to her. He was maybe midforties, medium sized, and trying to look younger than he was. His two kids were in front of him.

"I'm originally from the Boston area." She gave him about a quarter of a smile, not wanting to seem rude but not wanting to seem flirtatious either.

"No kidding," Mr. Abelson said. "I went to college in Providence, and even though I'm from New York, I love the Pats."

"That's because New York hasn't had a decent football team in years," Kari said, though she didn't feel much like chatting. She continued scanning the crowd.

"You have a point." He laughed.

Chelsea and Freddie looked at each other, uncomfortable with what they considered their father's overfriendliness.

In the distance, thunder rolled and then cracked.

Just before they were to be served in the buffet line, Mrs. Abelson came outside. The kids motioned to her, and she joined them in line. The young lady behind them made it clear that she didn't mind her getting in line ahead of her.

Back at their table with their food, Chelsea and Freddie tried to interest their parents in conversation. Chelsea told them about the shepherd they had met, and his really smart dog, and that Freddie had tried to talk to the sheep.

"I think they could understand me a little," Freddie said.

"That's wonderful," Mrs. Abelson said. "Of what I've seen so far of the place, most of it is charming." Whether he got it or not, this was pointed at her husband.

"Yeah, even though they don't have cellphone coverage," Mr. Abelson said, looking around the lawn. "I'm going to do some exploring before it starts raining. Those clouds look ominous."

"Yeah, me too," Freddie said. "It was an awesome morning earlier when we were out."

"I think I'll get a little more brisket first." Mr. Abelson got up.

The children glanced at their mom. She took a deep breath and tried to smile. "I'm going to get a few more blueberries," she said. Mr. and Mrs. Abelson walked off to different ends of the buffet as the clouds continued to gather and darken.

>>———▶

By the time Billy came down, there was no wait in the buffet line. He hadn't eaten all morning and thought he was hungry. He filled up his plate with a serving of Caesar salad, chicken breast, and an end-cut slice of brisket; he had never cared for lamb. He passed on the scalloped potatoes but took a serving of quinoa infused with bits of diced onion and celery.

As all the tables were full, he walked over to the left and stood not too far from where the kids he had met earlier were sitting and started to peck at his food. He saw Kari standing with a plate of food across the way, talking to a middle-aged man in a red polo shirt. He didn't feel like eating anymore. Billy thought maybe she looked up at him a couple of times.

She had seen Billy, and now she didn't feel like eating either. She thought maybe he had looked up at her a few times too.

Mr. Abelson was trying to engage her in conversation. Mrs. Abelson was at the fruit-and-dessert portion of the buffet, talking to a short man in a black V-neck T-shirt with a maroon cashmere sweater hanging over his shoulders and a pretty black woman wearing a light-blue denim shirt who looked like she might have been a movie star when she was younger. Freddie was watching both his parents.

To the southeast, there was a flash of light. Five seconds later, a moderately loud rumble of thunder followed. Most everyone out on the lawn looked up. The thunder passed, and the clouds seemed to clear a little.

"Do you think Robin knows what he's doing?" Freddie said to his sister. "This isn't working."

"I don't know, but he's weird," said Chelsea.

"He seems totally random," Freddie said.

"That's what you always call someone when you don't know what else to call them. That word went out of style three years ago."

"But he is random."

"Well, I'm out of ideas."

"I'm not."

There was another rumble of thunder, a little closer, and more clouds rolled in. A hint of moisture scented with pine freshened the air.

Freddie got up and walked over to the table where one of the servers was replacing the almost empty punch bowl with a new full one. It had fresh pieces of orange, banana, and strawberry bobbing around on its surface. He waited there while the exchange was made, and after the server left, he hung around a little longer before returning to where Chelsea still sat. He put two full cups on the table.

"I got Mom and Dad some fresh punch," he said.

Chelsea looked at Freddie inquiringly.

He reached into a pocket of his cargo pants and pulled out the light-blue spangled tin.

"You took it!"

"When you and he were picking up his glasses." He opened the tin. Inside, two purple mints seemed to radiate.

"What happened to the other two?"

Freddie motioned toward the punch bowl and then to the two cups.

"You put them in the punch bowl?"

"I used a spoon."

"What if they don't just work on Mom and Dad?"

"It was time for action. 'One does not simply walk into Mordor.'"

"That line isn't even in the book. They made it up for the movie."

Freddie shrugged. "It's still a great line." He handed one of the cups to Chelsea. "Get Mom to try it; I'm going to get Dad to."

>>———▶

The first person to the punch bowl after Freddie had left was the short man in the black V-neck T-shirt with the maroon sweater, Professor Sydney Fulkles. When he went to refresh his drink, Mrs. Abelson started back to her seat.

Freddie reached his father. "Here, Dad," he said. "You gotta taste this new batch of punch."

"Thanks, son." Mr. Abelson took the cup.

This gave Kari an excuse to break away from the mostly one-way conversation the man was trying to have with her. She walked off.

Freddie turned and headed back toward their table.

As Mrs. Abelson sat down, Chelsea offered her the cup of fresh punch.

"Thank you, dear." Mrs. Abelson took the cup.

Long streaks of lightning flashed above the park. Less than a second later, there was a crash of thunder that rolled and seemed to make the ground tremble, then a blast that crescendoed the roll and *did* make the ground tremble, and then, like a denouement, it echoed off the mountain.

A few moments of stillness and silence followed.

Professor Fulkles, holding his cup, wandered over to the edge of the forest to inspect some flowers that he thought were calypso orchids, also known as "fairy slippers," which were usually only found in the Northwest. His interest in botany was closely linked to his interest in alchemy. He took a few steps to his right to inspect a different variety and took a sip of his punch. There was a stirring at the edge of the forest. He looked up. A loud cry of "*Oh la passion de mon cœur enfin!*" was heard echoing off the mountain and back over the lawn. Professor Fulkles sprang away into the forest.

A few moments later, Mrs. Abelson raised the cup of punch to her mouth. "Smells delicious."

As she was about to take a sip, Chelsea reached out and slapped the cup from her hand.

Her mother looked at her, amazed.

"I saw a bug land in it," Chelsea said, realizing she just may have averted disaster.

Freddie's reaction was slower. He was distracted by the man streaking through the woods, his maroon sweater flapping like a cape behind him. When he looked again at his father, he found him barely holding on to the cup that dangled from his right hand, past his hip. He was staring bug-eyed at a blond woman about twelve feet away in a Duke Blue Devils T-shirt. She wore a lanyard and was holding a plate of food. Mr. Abelson let out a growl so loud that Chelsea and her mom heard it.

The woman in the Duke shirt turned at the noise to find a man in a red shirt with a zombie-like expression growling at her. After making another noise, this one almost like a bark, he lunged toward her. She dropped her plate in terror and took off like a zombie really was after her.

Freddie would have tried to tackle his father, but he wasn't close to fast enough. He looked back to their table. At least his mother was still there with Chelsea.

»———▶

Billy hadn't moved from where he was standing. With very sad eyes, he was looking across the way at Kari. She looked up, and their eyes met for a moment.

There was another peal of thunder, the clouds burst, and it started to rain torrentially. Most everyone on the lawn scampered inside, except the staff, who started collecting the bowls and plates of the buffet.

Billy just stood there getting drenched, watching Kari run away in the rain. He loved the way she moved.

FIFTY-TWO

After getting sufficiently drenched to punish himself, Billy went back to his room. He was in a very blue mood. He had taken the stairs up, not feeling like being in the presence of anybody. On his climb up, his right knee hurt from banging it in the brawl with his former friends.

In his room, he got as far as taking off his wet shirt before he started pacing the floor, despite his knee. He limped to one end of the room, then back again. After a few laps, he sat down and let out something between a moan and a sigh, then got up and paced some more.

Though he was wet on the outside, the rain had not dampened the coals of his love for Kari; they had flamed up again into a conflagration the moment he saw her. She was so beautiful. When it started to rain, it was like it gave her a silver aura. Could there have been something in the glance—no, glances—she gave him? The pain in his knee was nothing compared to the ache he felt for her.

And there was another pain that made this ache even worse. He felt the truth of the old saying "There is no greater pain than jealousy." If the Spaniard who said this didn't also say that jealousy can also cloud one's judgment, he should have. Billy was insanely jealous of both his traitorous friends.

An idea had come to him that he rejected at first but was tempted to think again. Was it possible that she had cooled to him because she thought he had cooled to her? Had his cowardly fear of rejection cost him the girl of his dreams?

If that was the case, he knew the one thing he had to do. He must make known to Kari his true feelings, come what may, and let her choose whom she would have. He would not hold back his love for her any longer.

He thought about the letter that he had spent so much time on, that he thought had made his feelings so clear. But every trace of his morning, from the time he left the computer room to sometime in the middle of his nap, had vanished from his mind. He remembered those two kids playing computer games and that he had printed out the letter, but he couldn't recall what he had done with it.

He opened his laptop and found the letter in the Recent Documents list. As he reread it, he thought it did come close to expressing his feelings. But he would revise it just a little, be even more direct. He got to his feet and paced some more. This might just be the most important thing he'd ever write. It had to be perfect.

»———▸

After having coffee, Kari's usual routine in the morning was to get in at least five hundred words on the story she was writing before doing anything else. This morning, she had put it off. But despite the crazy morning and the miserable rained-out barbecue, she would attempt to do some work.

Trying to write, she couldn't stop thinking about the look she thought Billy had given her. *What was in that look? Was he trying to say something?* The letter was still sitting there on the table by the balcony door. She picked it up and reread it. It couldn't have been for Bianca. She was cute and spunky and smart, and so self-confident. She was a good dancer. When Kari first told her about Billy, Bianca mentioned what a catch he was and told her not to let him get away. But then she also told her it was best to slow down, that it wasn't good to let him know too early how much she liked him.

So that was it! Bianca had told her to play it cool with Billy so she could move in. That was clear now. *Bianca had her eyes on Billy from the start. She was just waiting for the right opportunity.*

Well, Kari wasn't going to play it cool anymore. She would tell Billy the truth. Maybe, just maybe, his old feelings would come back, if they were ever there. She had to know either way. She would get her five hundred words in, and then she was going to deal with it.

>>———◆

Back in their suite, Chelsea and Freddie changed into dry clothes and went to their parents' room. Their mother had changed and was sitting in a chair with her hands on her lap as if deciding what to do. She looked up at them. "Thank you for changing," she said. "You're good children." Then she started to cry.

The children had discussed if they should try to explain to her what was behind their father's latest behavior. Thinking it best not to go into all the detail, Chelsea tried to simplify it: "There's something about this place that has an effect on people. Kinda like Grandma said."

"It makes people do weird things," added Freddie.

Their mother didn't respond, just tried to hold back her tears. Chelsea went to the side of her chair, and Freddie came up as well, trying to comfort her.

"I know what I need to do now," Ms. Abelson said. She had stopped crying.

"No," said Chelsea. "Please don't."

Her mother got up to leave the room.

"Oh, Mama, don't," said Chelsea.

"I'm just going to get a massage."

"You already had one," Chelsea said.

"Yes, I know. This time, I'm getting a deep-tissue massage. They hurt more."

FIFTY-THREE

After their mother was gone, Chelsea said, "We better go find Robin."

Not wanting to run into her, they took the secret stairs down.

They found Robin in his office, packing his backpack.

"There you are," he said. "I was just getting ready to go run my errand."

"You haven't gone yet?" said Chelsea. "Things with our parents are getting worse."

"Now, now, there's always hope. What did old what's-his-name say? 'Hope springs eternal.'"

"My dad says everyone gets that saying wrong," said Chelsea. "The rest of the saying goes, 'but never is but always to be blest.' That the guy was really a pessimist."

"Oh, that does sound a bit pessimistic. But what about that chap who everyone is talking about around here? He said something about true love not always running smooth."

"That's Shakespeare," Chelsea said. "I played Ophelia in our school play, and it got pretty unsmooth for her. I had to fall out of a tree and drown."

"Now, now, not to worry. We should be able to fix things right up. I hope to be back in an hour or so. Meet me back here then." He scooted out the door leading directly to the lobby. Sticking out of the top of his backpack was the neck of the brass urn.

Chelsea and Freddie looked at each other.

"What should we do?" Freddie said.

"I guess we should do what he says."

The kids went back to the business center to wait. Freddie sat down in front of the computer. He pushed the left mouse button several times and then Return several times. Nothing happened. He turned the CPU and monitor off and on and waited for the system to boot up. While he waited, he took the speckled little box from his pants pocket, opened it, and checked on the remaining mints. He took a quick sniff and quickly shut the lid and put the tin down next to the computer.

Still nothing was happening on the computer screen. He took hold of the mouse again and pushed both buttons on it repeatedly. Nothing happened. Apparently, the thunderstorm had blown the breaker or something.

"Now what?" Freddie said.

Chelsea seemed to be thinking or almost listening to something. "I have an idea," she said. "Stay here."

"No," said Freddie. He got up and ran after her.

Chelsea got to the side door that led to Robin's office, with Freddie right behind her. They peeked in. No one was there. They went in, and she checked through the door that led to the registration counter. One of the assistants was standing there. She quietly closed the door and went to the one that led to the secret stairway.

"Let's find out who or what is at the top of these stairs," she said.

"Roger that," Freddie said, using some GI Joe language. "Maybe it's that Colin man."

"Yes. If it is, what should we say?"

"Let's tell him we heard he told good stories and we'd come to hear one."

"Well, you say it then." She opened the door, and they ascended the stairs. At the final landing, they stopped. Chelsea put her forefinger to her mouth. Twenty feet down the dark hall they had come to before, the line of light still shone from under the door.

The children looked at each other, then crept forward. Chelsea put her ear to the door.

After a few moments, a voice came from the other side. "You may come in. I've been expecting you."

The children stepped back, frightened.

"Don't be afraid," the voice said.

Freddie moved forward, turned the knob on the door, and opened it just wide enough for both children's heads, Chelsea's above Freddie's, to look through. The room was large and lit partly by sunlight shining through a window high on its left side. Two lamps on the back wall illuminated two large framed pictures below them. Both pictures were of large windows swung open on their hinges. The one on the left had deep-green drapes that were drawn open and an ornate silver casement. It looked out on a frothy, turbulent sea. In the distance lay an island, then more rough sea, beyond which, barely visible, was another island, and another beyond that, until nothing but white-capped sea remained.

The picture on the right showed deep-red drapes drawn open over a gold casement. Through this window were rolling dunes of desert painted in hot, arid colors: yellows, oranges, and reds fading into a dull brownish auburn. In the distance, the sands stretched to a hazy oasis, then more sand and a smaller and hazier oasis, then still more sand to yet another, until the sand reached the traces of what looked like a continent.

Both pictures looked so real that it seemed one could walk through the frames into their worlds. On the base of each picture's frame was a brass inscription too far away for the children to read.

Cast into shadow by the backlighting of the pictures' lamps sat a person at a table. He had a pen in hand, and his head was down, studying something. The children came closer, and he raised his head—it was Curdi.

"Took you a while to get here," he said. "Why didn't you come in this morning?"

"We were afraid," Chelsea said.

"I wasn't that afraid," Freddie said.

"Is it okay we're looking around? We thought we might find Colin up here," Chelsea said.

"You would have this morning. What did you want to see him for?"

"Our parents are fighting again. Things don't look very good for our family," Freddie said.

"Do you think he could help?" asked Curdi.

"Maybe he could try," Chelsea said.

Curdi just looked at them, resting his head on his chin with a look that suggested, *Not bad.*

When he didn't respond, Chelsea said, "What are you doing up here? Is this your room?"

"I'm working on an assignment for Colin—a story."

"What's it about?" asked Freddie. "Is there a happy ending?"

"He hasn't finished it yet."

"Curdi, we're just trying to figure out what to do," Chelsea said. "That man, Robin, has tried to help, but now it seems like it's getting worse."

"Do you think he knows what he's doing?" Freddie asked.

"What do you think?"

"He seemed to help for a while," said Chelsea, "then . . . I don't know. I don't understand."

"Sometimes he can be helpful, if you realize his limitations. He's like stories: Some end happy and some not so. And some stories are hard to understand."

"Yeah, like the book I read where the girl's horse died," Chelsea said.

"Stories can be like riddles, like pictures can be like riddles," said Curdi.

"Like riddles?" said Freddie. "I like riddles."

"You mean like those pictures behind you?" said Chelsea.

"I don't know if I'd call them riddles."

"Can we look at what's written on the bottom of them?" Chelsea asked.

"If you like."

Freddie and Chelsea walked over to them. The inscription on the picture to the left read, "Magic casements, opening on the foam of perilous seas, in faery lands forlorn. John Keats."

The inscription on the other one read, "From perfect love light does proceed which as apprehended aright more apprehends while drawn to proceed. Dante Alighieri."

"I don't understand," said Freddie. "Is it like a sea of sand?"

"What do they mean?" asked Chelsea. "Are they like mirages? And I don't get the stormy-sea one at all either. Is it like it's impossible to get through the sea to the islands?"

"Probably a good ques—"

"I know, 'probably a good question for Colin,'" Chelsea said.

"If we ever get to meet him," said Freddie.

"Maybe you give up too easily."

The children stood there trying to understand what this meant.

After a pause of about ten seconds, Curdi said, "I think you have spent enough time up here asking questions. Now listen carefully: You need to follow where Robin has gone. Sometimes he can point you in the right direction."

"Where has he gone?" asked Freddie.

"Up in the forest. After the rain, you'll be able to follow his tracks. It's the northernmost trail."

"Won't it be all muddy?" said Chelsea.

"It only rained a short time, and there'll be many pine needles on the trail, which will show his tracks." Curdi handed Freddie a leather pouch with a nozzle at one end. "And take this."

"What is it?" asked Freddie.

"It's a skin for carrying wine or other liquids. You might need it."

FIFTY-FOUR

Kari had been sitting at the desk in her suite, trying to get her five hundred words in, but if there was a coherent idea in her brain that related to her story, it wasn't getting through to her fingers and to the keyboard. Her mind was in what seemed like a million other places, though most every thought came back around and landed on Billy. Some of the thoughts were almost pleasant. She remembered the discussion they had after watching Laurence Olivier's version of *Hamlet*. They were sure they had discovered what Shakespeare was cryptically saying in Hamlet's famous "To be or not to be" speech. He was speaking of his own indecisiveness in deciding what one of his characters was going to do or say. Shakespeare, too, got writer's block. It was crippling. They laughed and decided that, in the future, they wouldn't hesitate to run Claudius through or make him drink poison.

She wondered if her priorities were out of order—perhaps she couldn't write because her subconscious was trying to tell her something important. She may have lost Billy by not taking action when she should have. If she was getting another chance, she couldn't delay or mess it up. Some old writer had said, "The one who hesitates is lost."

Not only did she need to be honest and declare her love for him, she needed to do it now—today.

Still shirtless and in his damp pants, Billy was sitting at the desk in his room in front of his laptop. At least he had taken off his wet socks and shoes, which, being leather, weren't that bad. He had reread his newly edited letter in full twice and wasn't entirely satisfied. A real writer is hardly ever satisfied with his work. It lacked nuance and something more.

He remembered the times he and Kari had laughed at each other's writer's block and how they determined that was what Shakespeare's cryptic "To be or not to be" speech was really about. The trouble with writer's block is that you think you know what you want to say but just can't get it out right.

The letter was too much about him. He didn't like people who were self-absorbed narcissists. Was that the way he was coming across? It was supposed to be about how madly in love he was with her, but the emphasis should be on her. It should be about how it was she who made him who he now was, how he was incomplete without her.

Why had he never fallen so hard for another girl? Was it because he didn't want to settle for being less than totally in love? For some short-lived infatuation? The type of love he was after was the kind that, though they might not always be flaming, the embers would always be smoldering, ever ready to be stirred a little to burst into flames again.

But that still wasn't it. It wasn't about him just having some abstract feeling. It wasn't about him getting transported to some ethereal place. No. It was about them getting transported together. To some degree, the person had to have similar feelings, if that was the right word—not necessarily in quantity but in quality, in their sensibilities toward literature and cinema and music and imagination, and spiritual things, and in their general attitude toward the adventure of life. That's what he and Kari had. Not that they always had to agree, but in a strange way, it was there even when they didn't.

Was this kind of love even possible? Was it an unattainable ideal that no one could ever find? That out-of-their-minds medieval troubadours and Renaissance poets only dreamed of? Was he out of *his* mind? That kind of love was the love he longed for, and it had always been just out of reach. The kind of love that would take him out of himself. That was what she did for him. Could she, even a little bit, feel the same?

He agonized some more, made some edits, and finally he started to feel good about it. He read it through again. Yes, this letter was better than his first one. Now all he had to do was print it out, find Kari, and give it to her. If she gave him even a hint of encouragement, he would break the vow, be a man, and tell her in simple terms that he loved her and would most probably shrivel up and die without her.

FIFTY-FIVE

Chelsea and Freddie hurried down the stairs to Robin's office to make sure he was not there or at the reservation counter.

"We're going to do this?" Chelsea asked her brother.

"You shall not pass!" Freddie said, trying to imitate a deep, authoritative voice. "Fly, you fools."

"What are you talking about? That doesn't make sense," Chelsea said. "Gandalf said that to block the Balrog."

"I know, but it just came to my mind. Like, we have to be determined—don't you think?—and not give up."

"Well, okay, then let's go."

They went through the lobby and out the back door to the lawn where the barbecue had been. The weather had indeed cleared up. Beyond the lawn were three different trails leading up into the forest.

"He said to take the northernmost one, right?" Chelsea said. "Which way do you think north is?"

Freddie looked up in the sky. The sun was at about a sixty-degree angle toward the left end of the mountain. "That must be west," Freddie said. He had done Boy Scouts for a while before he dropped out to concentrate on tae kwon do. "So that way must be north." He pointed toward the trail at the far end of the lawn.

"You sure?"

"Pretty sure." They ran off to the trailhead.

A few yards in, Freddie stopped. The floor of the trail was moist, but on it were scatterings of pine needles and fern leaves that kept it from being soggy. In places, diminutive footprints led up the trail.

"Wait a sec, there could be wild beasts up there," Freddie said. He looked to the side of the trail and picked up three roundish stones.

"What are you doing?"

He pulled from his pocket the antler slingshot he had borrowed from the lodge supplies in Robin's office. "I'll be ready," he said, and took the lead.

The trail twisted and turned up the mountain, in some parts fairly steep and in some parts rather flat; in some stretches it was narrow, in others wide enough for two or three people to walk side by side. There were times, especially in the flat parts, where they could see the trail rising up ahead through the trees two hundred or more yards. Robin was not in sight, though his tracks still led forward and upward.

They trudged on. After a quarter mile, they came alongside a brook. As they hiked higher, it widened into a stream. A little farther up, the trail crossed over the stream on a narrow rope-and-wood bridge wide enough for only one to cross at a time. The stream flowing five feet beneath the bridge was twenty feet wide at this point and shallow and clear enough to see the stones at its bottom.

Not far beyond the bridge, the ground leveled off and they could hear the sound of cascading water and something else, which they could not quite make out. Soon they came upon the source of one of the sounds, a waterfall twelve feet in height, narrower by half as much as the stream that fed it. The falls splashed into a pool of swirling aqua water. Sitting on a large rock next to the falls, playing a shepherd's pipe, was the source of the high-pitched sound they had heard.

"Curdi!" Chelsea exclaimed. "How did you get here before us?"

The children walked closer, and the strain from the pipe didn't stop until a suitable place in the tune was reached.

"Greetings. You are mistaken: I'm Ralph. I do resemble my brother—or he me. I think."

"You do look like him," said Chelsea. The young man was dressed very similarly to the way Curdi was and he did look remarkably like him.

"Are you as nice as him?" said Freddie.

"He seems to have made an impression on you."

"What are you doing here?" Chelsea said.

"Colin has me making sure Mrs. Pulchritude isn't getting into any more trouble."

"Who is Mrs. Pulchritude?" asked Freddie.

"She's our bear, who thinks she owns the forest. Most of the time she behaves herself, though earlier today she got into some mischief. She spends most of her time higher up by the spring. Colin also said that since Curdi is busy, I should keep an eye on you."

"He knows about us?" said Chelsea. "We'd very much like to meet him."

"I think he likes you."

"Curdi told us to follow Robin," Freddie said. "We've been tracking him."

"He was here. You just missed him."

"We didn't see him coming down. Could Mrs. Pulchritude have got him?"

"I don't think Robin would be to Pulchritude's taste. There's more than one way to get up and down from here."

"Are we safe?" asked Chelsea.

"As safe as anyone."

"Robin had a jug in his backpack," Chelsea said. "Is there supposed to be something special about this water?"

"And Curdi gave us this," Freddie said, showing Ralph the goatskin.

"It's called a bota bag," Ralph said.

"I guess we're supposed to get some of this water?" said Chelsea.

"Is that what Curdi told you?"

"He just said we might need the bag," Chelsea said.

"Has Robin been helpful?"

"He often seems confused, but he seems to be trying," Chelsea said. "He gave us these purple mints, which I think he makes with this water. They did seem to work a little, but not for very long."

"If he gave us this thing," Freddie said, lifting the bota bag, "I guess we're supposed to get some of this water." He walked to the edge of the pool, where the water was running down over some rocks, and knelt to start filling the skin.

"Wait a minute," Chelsea said. "What's that noise?"

Freddie stopped, listening too.

"What's up beyond the waterfall?" Chelsea asked. "It's like there's more music coming from up there."

"I hear something too," Freddie said. "Like birds singing."

"Are you sure it's not just the waterfall or its echo?" Ralph said.

"Yes," said Chelsea. "It's beyond the waterfall."

"Is that where the water comes from—like the source?" asked Freddie.

"Maybe you should go up and find out, if you think you could make it."

"Is it a difficult climb?" said Chelsea. "Did you say that bear could be up there?"

"That's where the water comes from," said Ralph. "The source is usually best. But it's not easy."

"My sister and I do tae kwon do; we can make it."

"Did Robin go up there?" asked Chelsea.

"That's beyond his limits."

"Do you want to come with us?" asked Chelsea.

"Nah, I need to stick around here."

"Good enough," said Chelsea, determined. "Freddie, let's do it."

Freddie got up from the bank.

Ralph started playing his pipe again as the children started up.

FIFTY-SIX

As the trail bent up and around the falls, Chelsea and Freddie first had to negotiate a set of large boulders, then a steep and narrow patch before the trail swung back alongside the stream. Flowers of red, pink, yellow, blue, and white bloomed along its bank. The stream was a little wider than it had been below the falls but still quite shallow, and the water was so clear they could see schools of tiny fish darting about.

In depressions on the trail, those sounds coming from up above seemed to almost wane out of hearing. But the farther up they went, the clearer and more distinct they became. It was hard to tell what kind of instrument the melodic tones were coming from. At another steep part, the trail swung away from the stream and deep into the trees. The trees muffled the sounds of the water running over the stones of the shallow stream. But they could still dimly hear the music, which seemed to be drawing them on.

The thickness of the trees blocked much of the sunlight, and it grew eerily dark.

"Do you think these kinds of trees are alive like Ents?" asked Chelsea, referring to some of the trees in *The Lord of the Rings*. "If they are, they seem awful grumpy."

Freddie whispered, "Most Ents are grumpy 'cause they don't like being woke up. We should probably be quiet till we get out of here."

Neither of the children said anything more, though they did quicken their pace and Freddie handled his slingshot.

After ten more long minutes of darkened forest, the trail bent again toward the stream, and ahead they could see the trees opening up. They came to a small plain with a garden in the midst. Within the garden were various fruit-bearing trees and vines and flowers of many colors and in different stages of budding and blooming. Amid the lush flora was a gurgling fountain sprouting five feet high, sometimes higher, out of something like a pile of large dark rocks. It was like the water had just more or less exploded out of the ground and expelled the small quarry in the process. The water from the fountain flowed through the rocks, forming a small pool of shining clear water that fed the stream that flowed down from it.

On a slab of stone beyond and to the side of the fountain sat an old man dressed in shepherd's attire, like Curdi and Ralph—or rather, they like him.

As the children came out of the trees, the man lowered the stringed instrument he was playing, but the tune lingered before slowly fading into the air. He took off his straw hat, tipped it to them, then placed it back on.

"Of course the trees are alive—and they're very old, and their roots run deep," the man said, as if he had heard their earlier discussion. "Living things are by definition alive." He had silver-gray hair and a beard that was closer to white. He had a friendly countenance without diminishing his august stature and seemed to be teeming with controlled vitality. The children were very much taken aback.

"I knew they were," said Freddie. "I mean the trees were."

The man smiled, as if to put them at ease.

"Are you Mr. Colin?" asked Chelsea.

"No need to be so formal," the man said.

"We've heard a lot about you and wanted to meet you. I'm Chelsea and this is my brother, Freddie."

"I know."

"This place is awesome," Freddie said. "It looks like it got blasted by lightning."

"Could have been," Colin said. Something about the man made Freddie feel almost comfortable, but not quite. For one thing, he seemed to know that there was more to trees than just their being trees.

There were a few moments of silence.

"What you were playing was beautiful," said Chelsea. "I take piano lessons, and it was something like these old folk songs my teacher is trying to make me learn." Sometimes one just needs to say something, and his music did remind her of old songs that could make you happy and sad at the same time.

"Music comes from interesting places," Colin said.

"Freddie quit piano. He wants to be a football player."

"But I like music too."

"You probably know why we're here," Chelsea said.

"Yes. Hope springs eternal," the man said.

"The person who said that," Chelsea said, "goes on to say that it always lets you down."

"You shouldn't let pessimists influence you. Hope can be a wonderful thing, if it's in the right things and mixed with patience. Otherwise, it can let you down."

"You mean like Robin?" Freddie said.

"The best he can do is sometimes hint at the right direction. But often, a lot worse."

"Curdi told us to follow him, and he gave us this." Freddie showed Colin the bota bag.

"What do you think you should do?"

"I feel like jumping in the pool and letting the fountain splash all over me," Freddie said.

"If you're going in, so am I," said Chelsea.

"You are welcome to come back most anytime. Why don't you just fill up your bag and get going. I have a feeling you might be needed down below, but be brave"—he paused and laughed—"one does not simply walk into Mordor!"

"Awesome," said Freddie. This person was totally awesome. He moved over to where the water from the pool spilled into the stream. He pulled the stopper out of the mouth of the goatskin bag and let the water flow into it.

"When we come back, we hope you'll tell us one of your stories," said Chelsea as Freddie was filling up the bag.

"What makes you think that you will like my stories? Some stories can be scary, and some even sad."

"I bet your stories would be good even if they're sad," said Chelsea. "Like Frodo not being able to come back to the Shire and sailing into the West."

"I might surprise you."

"Stories with good surprises are the best kinds," said Freddie.

"But not too scary ones," Chelsea added.

"Make sure you fill it all the way up," Colin said.

Freddie did wait until it was full, put the stopper back in, and stood up.

"I hope to see you again soon," said Chelsea, "and thank you."

"Me too," said Freddie. "Maybe I could even come back and work here someday."

"You better get going," said Colin.

The kids took off back into the forest and down the trail.

FIFTY-SEVEN

Billy took a long shower, a cold one. Cold baths—or in this case, showers—were supposed to be good for you. It did make him feel alert. He donned fresh clothes, including a shirt he had fortunately brought, one that he knew Kari liked, and sprayed on a touch of cologne. Before he left his suite, he read his letter over again and made a few more modifications. He saved and emailed it to his Gmail account.

Leaving his room, he couldn't remember if the elevator was to the right or to the left. He turned to the left and walked down the hall past a couple of rooms that had twos for the first of their three-digit suite numbers. The elevator wasn't down this way, but toward the end of the hall, there was a door slightly ajar that, rather than having a room number on it, had a sign that read "Staff." He opened it a little more and peeked inside. Ahead was a small landing, to the left, a stairway going down, and to the right, one going up. His heart started pumping fast. He remembered that Robin had said the third floor was for women and no men were allowed. He climbed the stairs going up and came to another landing and another door.

He opened the door enough to peek in. His heart pumped even

faster. It was the women's floor. If he only knew which room was Kari's. Was he crazy? It would look awfully bad if he got caught up there. Still, he didn't move away. The love of his life, the fulfillment of his desires, could be behind one of those doors.

A door two doors down started to open. He closed the door he was peeking through as quietly as he could, leaving just enough of a crack to see who was coming. It was a maid carrying a basket. She was walking toward him. He shut the door all the way. He started to go down the stairs. But the stairwell brightened as if a door had been opened. He heard footsteps coming up. He took off, as gently as he could, up the stairs to the next floor.

This landing was a little wider than the others, and here the stairway ended. To either side there was a door. Billy tried the door to his right. It opened to the fourth-floor suites. He tried the door to his left. A narrow spiral stairway rose up to the next level. It wasn't so much that he didn't know what else to do, which he didn't, but that he almost felt drawn to take the stairs up.

At the top of the spiral stairs was a dark hall, and down the hall, a line of light shone from under a door. Not knowing where his boldness came from, he went to the door and gently knocked on it. There was no answer. He knocked again. Still no answer. He knocked a third time and, getting no response, opened the door and went in.

The room was large. Sunlight shone through a window high on the left side of the room, lighting much of the room's middle, including a large desk. The chair behind the desk was empty. Two large pictures, lit by lights just above them, made it look like there were windows on the back wall.

Billy's attention was drawn to the pictures, actually paintings of windows swung open on their hinges. One looked out upon a series of diminishing islands in a turbulent, frothy sea. The other depicted rolling dunes of desert, painted in hot and arid yellows, oranges, and reds, fading into a dull brownish auburn. The sand was interrupted by smaller and smaller oases, until it reached the traces of a continent. Both pictures looked so real it seemed that he could walk through the frames into their worlds.

He moved closer to read the brass inscriptions tacked on to the base of the pictures' frames. On the left: "Magic casements, opening on the foam of perilous seas, in faery lands forlorn. John Keats." On the right: "From perfect love light does proceed which as apprehended aright more apprehends while drawn to proceed. Dante Alighieri."

"It's about time," a voice sounded behind Billy. He froze and raised his hands as if he were being arrested.

FIFTY-EIGHT

When Billy's heart started beating again, he slowly turned around. The voice belonged to a man with silver hair and a mostly white beard.

"I'm glad you finally came. I enjoy conversing with young poets."

Billy was almost as stunned by what the man had called him as he was by initially hearing his voice. After regaining a little of his composure, he said, "I'm not really a poet. I write mostly in prose."

"The word for *poet* in Greek, where much of the concept comes from, means 'maker.' It matters little whether the thing made is in verse or prose. It can apply to a picture or even a loaf of bread, if it is skillfully made. The best stories are *poemas*, well-captured visions that delight while saying something beyond what they are saying. Curdi told me he tried to tell you my 'Perils of Love.' I hope he didn't mangle it too much."

"No, it was delightful, though I'm not sure I got what it was saying beyond what it was saying."

"Funny how that is; the best stories often keep you wondering. It's not quite finished, but I did discover that Free and Fate do get together and have a pup named Fortune. As for the young shepherdess and the stranger, that's still up in the air."

Billy groaned. After a few moments he said, "I hope someday to become skillful at telling stories."

"In order to make and tell good stories the poet must also be a kind of 'seer.' That's what they used to call the most vocal of poets, though not necessarily the most truthful. In some sense, most everyone is a bit of a seer, though they might not realize it. Most everyone gets glimpses of beatitude, but their visions are blurred, stifled, distorted, and often almost cease, though glimpses still can break through. Their prejudices, aggressions, and defenses blur, twist, pervert, and maul what they see into vanities. The more subjective a would-be poet is, the less of a true poet, though the language might flow and delight as if from Parnassus. This is why I have hope for you; you are struggling to clarify and understand your vision, even if it costs you. For there is always a cost. And, as in my story, as in love, one must learn to take risks and make sacrifices."

"I'm not sure I understand you," Billy said. He didn't want to say something stupid. He just hoped it wasn't Kari that it was going to cost him.

The old man strode toward the pictures hanging on the wall and said, "Skillful paintings, like good stories, are also distilled visions."

Though Colin spoke with effortless authority, he also had an almost brotherly or familial quality that gave Billy hope—or was it courage—in his own potential. Colin even likened the process to the distiller's art, as he had conceived it. Billy's grandmother had called it "the moonshiner's magic."

"What do these pictures suggest to you," Colin asked, "or remind you of?" Billy felt that though Colin had asked the question two different ways, they meant the same thing.

"Well, I love the lines from Keats," Billy answered. "I don't know what the other picture means. I don't know if I understand what Keats is getting at either. But whatever it is, the language enchants me."

"It is wonderful when that happens. But go on."

"In both pictures, one must enter through a window, which suggests

a different realm. I guess that is something like the realm of the imagina-
tive. And for both, but especially for the one on the left, not the nursery
room fairyland of sugar plums and frosted cakes, but a scary place of
wearing hopelessness. The vanishing island apparitions suggest maybe
unfulfillment. Though the picture draws you in, the vision, without
the beauty and music of the language, at least to me, is despairing. The
poet's unhappy journey is a trail that must be followed. His beautiful
brooding is his only solace."

"And what of the other?" said Colin.

"Maybe they're both in search of something or following something,
or perhaps, something draws them on. Yes, I like that more: something
drawing one on. In the one, it appears to be islands—barren islands—
that vanish into nothingness. In the other, they're more like alluring oases
that kind of vanish but reappear again, like mirages, but they seem to
lead or draw one on to something more substantial." Billy took a few
steps closer to the picture on the right.

"I'm not sure what this means," Billy went on, contemplating the
picture and the inscription. After a few moments, he turned and said,
"I think I have an idea of what I need to do now. She is my radiance. I
have enjoyed our talk, but I need to get going."

"Do come and visit again," Colin said.

Billy took the secret stairs down to the second floor and then the elevator to the business center. He went straight to the computer, logged
on, and printed out his letter. Taking it from the printer, he scanned it
to make sure it came out formatted correctly. He took out an envelope
from the computer desk drawer and addressed it as he had done before.
He folded the letter and put it into the envelope. As he got up, he noticed, by the side of the computer, that little tin with spangling, dancing
stars on it. He picked it up. A sweet aroma came from it, bringing some
distant and vague memory, or feeling. The fragrance had been lingering in the room, but he hadn't consciously noticed it as his thoughts

were on his letter and what he had just experienced upstairs. But the tin allured him. He opened it to find two sparkling purple mints inside, beckoning at him.

»———▶

Outside, at the lodge's delivery dock, a white Ford panel van pulled up. Stenciled on its sides in large print was "Gomez Organic Vegetables and Seafood," and under that in smaller print, "Visalia, Bakersfield, San Bernardino, OC, LA." A short white man with a blond crew cut and white gardening shoes hopped out of the driver's side. On the other side, Elrond stepped out. He was dressed totally Hollywood: black jeans, black cowboy boots that didn't have those silver toe shields, and a black button-down long-sleeve shirt, the color slightly lighter than the color of his pants. His hair was slicked back in a ponytail and his goatee was neatly trimmed.

He walked over to the crew cut and said, "Make sure you give GoGo my best, and tell him I owe him big-time. A ride all the way from Pedro would have cost me *mucho*." He slung the strap to his leather courier bag over his head across to his left shoulder with the rest of the strap crossing his chest and the bag resting on his right hip.

"Glad to help, bro," said Crew Cut, "and nice getting to know you. Your stories are awesome. And thanks for the Dodgers tickets." They shook hands, thumbs-up style.

Elrond walked into the lodge through the delivery entrance. Now that he was out and a free man, he wanted to hear this famous professor who maybe *did* know some secret about writing. Even more important, he had some business to take care of with Billy.

»———▶

Kari came out of her suite's bathroom having changed into a blue blouse that was near the color of Billy's eyes. She paused to pick up Billy's letter and skimmed over it again. She refused to believe that it could be for

Bianca. But soon she would know for sure. She put it and the mint back into the envelope and put the envelope in the webbing inside her roller bag. If the letter was for her, she would keep it for the rest of her life; if it wasn't, she would burn it.

Before she left the room, she gave herself one last check in the mirror. She fluffed up her hair just a little and left the room.

Waiting at the elevator was a red-haired young lady with a few cute freckles on her cheeks. Her tight-fitting faded blue jeans had a single hole in them at the left knee. Her shoes were black high-top Converse All Stars. She wore a number 25 Seattle Seahawks jersey tied in a knot at the bottom front hem, showing a little of her tummy and her pierced navel. She carried a small nylon valise.

"Hi," Kari said.

"Hi," said the redhead.

"You here for the spa? I was there this morning. It's wonderful." There was a hint of wishful thinking in what Kari asked, though she maybe didn't realize it.

"No, I'm here for the lecture, and to meet my boyfriend." This statement and the Seahawks jersey gave Kari a stir.

"Love your jersey. You wouldn't be interested in selling it, would you?"

"No."

"I'll give you a hundred dollars for it."

"No."

The elevator opened, and they got in. Kari pushed the button for the lobby. The door closed, and the elevator descended.

FIFTY-NINE

Still in the business center, Billy was struggling. The tin didn't belong to him. Yet he wanted those mints. The ideas spawned by those pictures he had seen upstairs battled with his desire for the mints. Their fragrance gave such an exotic air, one that might appeal to Kari. He wouldn't take the tin. That would be stealing. Instead, he took only one of the mints and dropped it into his envelope. He hesitated. No, he wanted both. He took the other mint and dropped it in too. One for himself and one for Kari. He put the tin back where he found it.

Now he would find Kari, wait for her to come down if he had to, and give her the sweet-smelling letter and watch her response. If there was any hope, he would tell her, in words that could not be mistaken, how he felt, how he had always felt. He didn't care about that stupid vow. Compared to Kari, *sixty* dinners at Clyde's was nothing. The ridicule of his friends he would happily endure.

As he entered the lodge's lobby, rehearsing what he would say when he saw her, the mints' aroma rose afresh to his nostrils, delighting his whole cranial cavity. He could resist no longer. He took one of the mints and popped it into his mouth.

For three steps, as he walked forward, nothing happened. Then he felt like he had been smashed by a twenty-five-foot Hawaiian wave. (Hawaiian waves are way more powerful than Californian waves.) It felt like he was being thrust way down by a great rolling wall of water and was tumbling over and over. He didn't know which way was up. Surfers call this "getting caught in the washing machine."

Across the lobby, the elevator door opened. Kari and Vivian offered each other the choice to exit first. Vivian accepted the offer. Kari followed a few feet behind her. They saw Billy going through weird gyrations that vaguely looked like a very bad rendition of the dance move called the Swim.

From the lobby's rear entrance, Elrond saw Vivian standing a few steps in front of another attractive woman. Twenty feet before them was his former cellmate and would-have-been writing partner—now archenemy—making weird convulsions. *She's conquered Hollywood and made him go crazy*, Elrond thought. *But the dude has made a big mistake and's in for some major pain.*

As Billy was desperately trying to get out of the washing machine, clawing and reaching for air, his letter flew out of his hand. It flittered and fluttered and seemed to almost float before it alighted a few feet behind him.

About twelve feet behind Billy, Elrond reared back, getting ready to pounce, but was distracted by the dance of the falling envelope. Waiting for Billy to stop flailing enough that he could wrap his hands around his neck and strangle him, Elrond's nose was stunned by a strong and delicious fragrance. It was wonderful, refreshing, delightful. He picked up the envelope. It was addressed, "Dearest and only love and heartbeat of my existence."

Elrond's rage boiled, but the scent from whatever was inside the envelope was stronger. Inside it, he found an exquisite purple tablet oozing with an offer of delight. He greedily threw it into his mouth.

It became a luscious liquid trickling over his tongue, over the inside of his lower teeth and gums, past his tonsils, down his throat. His system, his whole being, came to a screeching halt. His mind went blank. His heart stopped pumping, and his circulation stopped.

It could have been an hour, or it could have been a nanosecond, but it revved up again. He looked up and saw the women now approaching side by side. His insides took off again like a jet-powered race car laying rubber and going from 0 to 220 in 0.8 seconds. Crying *"Mi único amor, mi amor,"* he lunged forward, hands outstretched, still holding the letter.

At the same time, Billy came up out of the washing machine and saw the two women approaching. He launched like a projectile shot out of a bazooka.

Though Billy was faster, Elrond had a head start. Running full speed, they were shoulder to shoulder, each trying to push the other out of the way. They crashed into each other, falling, and then groveling at the women's feet.

Vivian's first thought was, *What's Elrond doing out of jail?*; her second, rage at him throwing himself at this other woman. As Elrond was getting up to his knees, she swung her valise, weighted with her 4.3-pound MacBook Pro, at full speed and caught him under the chin. Elrond's head shot upward, then twirled. He limply crashed to the floor.

Kari's impression was that Billy was going for Vivian. Following Vivian's lead, she swung her bag (with a slight amount of reserve) at Billy as he was trying to get up too. Her bag contained her Surface laptop, weighing only 2.84 pounds, but she caught him well on the side of his head, about at his left ear. He went straight down.

Vivian stared at the flattened body of Elrond. "You snake," she hissed. "You centipede, you scorpion, you, you . . . boll weevil!" Somehow the bug from her third-grade science class came to mind. "I forgave you, and now you, you—" She was so mad she couldn't think of another bug. She almost slammed him again. There could be a little truth to the idea that some redheads have volatile tempers.

Kari stood in a daze, thinking maybe she had made a mistake. It wasn't absolutely clear who was throwing himself in front of whom. "I think he"—she pointed to the dark-haired one—"was trying to get to you."

"Oh my," Vivian said. "You really think so? True, it isn't usually his style. But why did you smack Hollywood? No way he was running for me."

>>———▶

Byron and Jackson had not taken Robin's advice. Ever since their fight, they'd been down in the lounge drinking and arguing over which one of them loved Kari more. Their passions had toned down slightly, and their discussion hadn't broken out in violence, only threats of knocking the other's teeth out.

When their attention was drawn to a ruckus in the lobby, they saw Kari standing over two sprawled bodies. They both sprang up and started toward her. Byron, who had put a sweat suit on over his cycler's outfit, was slightly the better athlete and got a head start on Jackson. But Jackson was faster, and the flip-flops Byron was now wearing slowed him up. Kari and Vivian were still discussing their unconscious boyfriends, old men, exes, old old men, or whatever they were, when Jackson ran up to Kari and tried to embrace her. Upset that she might have wronged an innocent, she teed off on Jackson with her bag, catching him right under the nose. He went down fast.

Byron, seeing the blow, tried to veer off, but strayed toward Vivian. She didn't hesitate either and whacked him up alongside the head between his temple and his cheekbone. Byron, in a twirl, went up a little before he went down and quite out.

Kari and Vivian surveyed the massacre before them. Billy, Elrond, Byron, and Jackson all sprawled out motionless on the floor. They looked quizzically at each other. Were all men out of their minds? It was a stupid question.

But then, Kari thought, *Bianca and Amanda weren't exactly acting normal either. Something strange is happening in this place.* She kind of knew that already.

She looked at Vivian and said helplessly, "I love him."

Vivian started to lift her valise.

"No, not him," Kari said, pointing to Elrond again. "Him." She pointed to Billy.

"Oh, you must be Hollywood's homebiscuit."

"I'm not sure what that means," Kari said, sniffing back her tears.

"It means, like, you're his hot sauce. He's crazy about you."

"How do you know?"

"He wasn't running toward me, and I seen it in his eyes."

"You're sure?"

"No doubt about it."

"Who's he?" Kari asked, pointing to unconscious Elrond. "I've never seen him before."

"That's my old man," Vivian said. "He's crazy about me. But sometimes he gets confused and just doesn't know how to show it. He bit off the ear of the last guy that tried to mess with me."

"Oh my, I wouldn't want that," Kari said. "I've told Billy he needs to be a better listener."

"I could use a drink." Vivian motioned over to the lounge area a hundred feet away. None of the tables were occupied. "Let's go get one and talk."

"What should we do about them?" Kari said.

"They look comfortable. We should let them rest."

"Well, I guess that's okay."

"Do you really think he likes me?" Kari said as they took seats in the lounge.

"Sure he does," Vivian said. "Sure thing."

"I wish I could be so sure."

"He got to know Elrond, my old man, when he was in the joint. When he got out, he did El a favor and brought me news about the lecture up here and all, and I got to know him, too, a little. I could tell he was nuts about you."

Kari wasn't thrilled that Vivian had gotten to know Billy at all, even with this assurance. Billy had once told her that he had a girlfriend in high school who had red hair, and ever since, she had been suspicious of redheads.

"Hey, listen, I'll tell you what," Vivian said. "I'm going to give you my Seahawks jersey. He told me he was a Seahawks fan."

"No, I couldn't. Really? You don't want it? I'll give you two hundred dollars for it."

"No, homestone, we sisters ain't mercenaries."

"We could trade. I have a New England Patriots jersey."

"No way! Next to the Raiders, the Pats are El's favorite team."

"Come on, really?"

"El and I were in the Navy—journalists in the Public Affairs Office. That's where we met and decided to be writers. You see, the old coach of the Pats, Belichick, grew up in Annapolis, and he, or his father or something, used to coach Navy—we're Navy loyal."

"You're writers? Way cool. So are Billy and I."

"That's why I'm here—to hear this professor dude talk about what he thinks he knows about what it takes. El said that he and Billy are going to be pards and work on stuff together. I got a lot of good stuff, too, that you might want to look at."

"Yeah, wow!" Kari said.

"Hey, let's go up right now and make the trade before they wake up."

"My Pats jersey is kind of wet, I got caught out in the rain."

"That's cool, I don't have to wear it now."

On the way, they passed the melee still passed out on the floor. The expressions on their faces suggested that they were having pleasant dreams.

"They look awfully comfortable," said Kari.

"Yeah, weird."

They headed to the elevator.

SIXTY

Just after Kari and Vivian left the lounge, Robin entered the lodge through its rear door. He was wearing his backpack with the top of the brass urn sticking out. He came upon the scene of four unconscious young men sprawled out on the lobby floor.

"Interesting," he said, and looked up at Curdi, who had been sitting at the registration counter the whole time, watching the events unfold. Curdi gave him a stern look.

Robin raised his open hands guiltily, as if to say, *I was only trying to help.* He went off to his office.

»———➤

A few minutes later, Chelsea and Freddie came back into the lodge. When they spotted the four men sprawled on the floor, one was stirring slightly.

They crept closer to within a few feet and stopped. Two of the bodies were face down and two face up with strange expressions. Chelsea looked at Freddie, and Freddie looked back. Freddie grinned at Chelsea, and Chelsea grinned back.

Freddie shook the bota bag, confirming it was quite full. "Colin did say, 'Be brave.' I think we can spare a little." It appealed to the surge of adolescent mischief he was having. He stepped closer and popped the stopper out of the bag's mouth. He gave the bodies good squirts on their heads, necks, and faces.

"Fly, you fools," he said to Chelsea, pealing with laughter. They didn't wait to see the result and ran off into Robin's office.

From the registration desk, Curdi smiled as if appreciating a nice goal kick in a soccer game. He was getting an idea for a story.

»———▶

A new designation of sleep category, or dream category, would have been needed to adequately describe what was going on between the ears of the four men who lay on the floor.

For Byron, it was something like the opposite of that Eurythmics song, "Sweet Dreams." Somehow his vision of Kari had morphed into a dream of him sailing the seven turbulent seas with mermaids turning into tantalizing Sirens of Titan, with huge fangs and forked, licking tongues. He had been on the verge of getting shipwrecked on perilously jagged rocks, but escaped the rocks and was cast up on the beach of a barren island. His sleep on the beach was blissful compared to the seafaring nightmare that had landed him there. He didn't want to be awakened.

Jackson's dream had something to do with the song too. But somehow, the blind ancient Greek poet Homer and James Joyce had gotten into it along with Eric Clapton, who was wailing on a guitar. And Ulysses—though it should have been Achilles—was driving a chariot in front of the gates of Troy, dragging a dead body—but the body was . . . he didn't want to look. He climbed into the Trojan Horse, where James Joyce was sleeping, and also went to sleep. He didn't want to be disturbed anymore either.

»———▶

The children entered Robin's office to find him nodding in his high-chair, his head slumped over, his chin on his chest, his glasses balancing on the tip of his nose. His backpack and urn sat on the table.

"Should we wake him?" Freddie whispered to Chelsea as he was raising the skin to squirt him.

"No, don't," Chelsea said. "Save the rest of the good stuff for Mom and Dad. Probably best if we let him sleep."

They left, taking the secret stairway up to their suite.

>>———▶

Billy was the first to revive. It didn't happen all at once. He rose slowly, hardly noticing the others on the ground. He craved coffee and something to eat. He staggered over to the large coffee dispenser at the end of the registration counter and drizzled some into a Styrofoam cup. It was tepid and stale. He looked up at Curdi, who was attending the counter. "Any way you could get some fresh coffee?"

"My pleasure," Curdi said. He took the dispenser and went off to fetch a fresh batch. Billy waited, leaning on the counter. A few minutes later, Curdi returned with a new dispenser and drew a cup for Billy. "You look like you could use this," he said.

Billy took too big a sip and scalded his tongue slightly. Without waiting for it to cool, he took a couple of smaller sips. His head cleared a little more.

Curdi said, "Have you been enjoying your stay?"

"This place is having a weird effect on me. Hey, aren't you the guy who drove us up from the parking lot and told us that story?"

"I believe so."

"I liked it a lot—nothing dared, nothing gained."

"It was about lots of things."

Elrond staggered up to the counter. He had taken a little longer to revive, possibly because Vivian's laptop weighed a pound and a half more than Kari's, or perhaps it was because she had nailed him under the chin instead of upside the head.

"Wow, Elrond, what are you doing here?" Billy was still too groggy to be totally amazed. "You don't look so good."

"Hey, homestone." Elrond drew himself a cup of coffee and took a gulp. It scalded him too. He was more careful with his next few sips. "My lawyer did, like, a Johnnie Cochran for me—made the dude whose ear I bit off drop the charges. I got out early this morning. Haven't got a lot of sleep lately, feels like I just woke up. You don't look so good either. You get caught in the rain?"

"I got caught in a cloudburst," Billy said.

"It usually doesn't rain indoors," said Curdi.

"But what are you doing up here?" Billy asked Elrond.

"Remember, you told me about it—and how you and me could work on some stuff. It made sense when I got out I should come and attend the seminar with you to hear that dude who's got all the goods."

"Oh, I see," said Billy, finishing off his cup of coffee and drawing himself another. "I think I need to sit down. Let's go over to the lounge." Billy was wondering what he had gotten himself into.

»———▶

Chelsea and Freddie were in their parents' part of the suite, reading books. Their mother hadn't returned from her deep-tissue massage, and their father had been missing since the barbecue. When either of them came back, they wanted to be demonstrating good behavior.

The electronic lock on the suite's main door started making a whirling noise. The door handle clacked a few times as if someone was unsuccessfully trying to enter the room. The children put down their books. The door finally opened. Their father staggered in, muddy and so drenched that his red shirt looked dark brown.

His countenance was different too. The children were taken aback. They rushed to him, careful, but not too careful, not to get wet and muddied.

"I don't know what happened," he said. "I must have slipped in the mud." His feet were bare, and he was holding his mud-splattered Italian loafers with his wet socks stuffed in. Chelsea looked on compassionately and patted him on the back, not knowing what to say. Freddie didn't know what to say either. He took the wet shoes and socks and rushed them into the bathroom.

A few moments later, the electronic lock on the door whirled again, and the handle turned. Freddie, Chelsea, and Mr. Abelson looked toward the sounds. The door opened, and Mrs. Abelson took two steps into the suite and stopped abruptly. The heavy door slammed on its own behind her. She was wearing a light-blue terrycloth bathrobe from the spa with little pink and yellow stars all over it, and her hair was wrapped turban-like in a white towel.

"Darling, oh, darling," Mr. Abelson said, distraught and shaking his head.

"Yes?" Mrs. Abelson wasn't sure he was talking to her.

"I've been such a fool—such a huge, dumb, selfish, idiotic fool. I thought I had lost you." His head stopped shaking and just tilted to one side.

"Tell him he hasn't lost you," blurted Freddie.

"Mama, tell him, please," Chelsea said.

"Tell me I haven't totally blown it." He raised his muddy, otherwise empty hands palms up to about waist level.

"Are you yourself?" Mrs. Abelson said to her husband. "You look like, like you've been through . . . like you've been rolling around in the mud."

"I don't know what happened." He looked like a wounded, drenched puppy. "I must have slipped and hit my head. I don't know how long I was like that, but then it rained and kept on raining all over me, and it was soothing and fragrant and refreshing. Then there was something like a rocket going off in my head, exploding like fireworks into a multitude of stars, constellations that in turn exploded into smaller constellations and finally turned into snowflakes and jewels and diamonds and then a huge, beautiful rose. And I realized what a fool I had been. It was like you were the rose, and the kids the petals. I woke up at the edge of the woods, next to a stream, in a puddle of mud. You should have seen me before I cleaned up."

"You're cleaner than Freddie is after he gets a bath," said Chelsea.

"Chelsea," her mother said.

"Darling," Mr. Abelson said, "I've been such a fool."

"You know I haven't been all that perfect either," Mrs. Abelson said.

"Yes, I know, but I've been worse."

"I don't know about that."

"No, not even close."

"Yes, not close. I've been way worse," said Mrs. Abelson. "I know I can be a . . ." She paused, not wanting to say the "B-word" in front of the kids.

"No way," said Mr. Abelson.

Freddie interjected, "Are you going to have an argument over who's more worse?"

"Less bad," Chelsea said. She had a habit of correcting her little brother, picked up from their mother.

"Well, at very least, I have been not-all-that-perfect more than you have been not-all-that-perfect," said Mrs. Abelson.

"So, does it come down to quantity versus quality of bad behavior?" asked Chelsea. She had learned the important distinction between quantity and quality in economics class.

"Darling, it comes down to this: I love you and the kids more than anything in this world," Mr. Abelson said. "Especially more than myself, whom I am not fond of at all. I want you to forgive me and want us to start over, even if we might need to start over every other day."

"Are you asking me to forgive you?" asked Mrs. Abelson.

He paused. "Yes."

"If you will forgive me?"

"Wait a minute. Relationships that have contingencies are in trouble," said Chelsea. She had heard that from their shrinks.

"Okay, I forgive you," Mrs. Abelson said. "But I hope you will forgive me, even though you don't have to for me to forgive you."

"That's close enough. I do," he said. They embraced.

Chelsea and Freddie sighed. Freddie said, "Is it okay if I go back down to the computer room and shoot Orcs?"

Mrs. Abelson took her husband's muddy hand in hers, nestled up even closer to him, and gave him a kiss. Breaking from the kiss, she said to the kids, "Yes. You too, Chelsea. Run along."

SIXTY-ONE

Vivian returned to the lobby. She had changed into a black corduroy vest that went well with her short-sleeved gray Phoenix Bar and Grill T-shirt and her blue denim jeans, a look she knew Elrond liked. The men were no longer sprawled on the floor. Instead, Elrond and Billy sat at a table in the lounge drinking beer, and Byron and Jackson sat at another.

Seeing Vivian approaching, Elrond had a feeling he was in trouble.

Billy's first thought was that he was worried for Elrond.

She stopped a few feet in front of them and said to Billy, "Homestone, tell your old lady to keep away from my old man." She knew Kari wasn't doing anything of the sort. She slid a quick look at Elrond.

Elrond's eyes lit up, and he breathed a sigh of relief.

She knew calling Elrond her old man, given the circumstances, would surprise and please him. Her words might also make Billy jealous and fire up his desire for Kari—though that wasn't needed.

Elrond rose. "Hi, babe, I see you got my message." He went to hug her, but she stepped just a little back.

"Yeah, Whitesauce there delivered your note."

"Listen, sweets, we need to talk," Elrond said.

"I'd like that," she said. "Something we ought to do every once in a while—like a lot more."

"You got the tab?" Elrond said to Billy. "We'll square it later."

"Sure," said Billy.

Elrond took Vivian's hand, and they walked off to the lodge's front door.

Billy didn't feel like finishing his beer. He asked the bartender to charge it to his room. He was used to getting stuck with the tab. He wandered off to the rear of the lodge.

The sky was clear again and bright blue and the earlier dark clouds were gone. The sun had another hour and a half before it dipped down beyond the mountain to the northwest. A hint of evening crispness was already in the air. The park was empty except for a few people playing croquet at the other end of it.

Unlike the sky, Billy's mind was not clear. A horrible thought was disturbing him. Was what he was chasing merely the experience of being in love, the exhilaration the poets wrote about? Was it Kari that he really longed for and joyed in, or merely the feeling of being in love? Was love just a myth, a pathetic psychological disease, a vanity that the whole human race was plagued with? One that never got— could never get—satisfied? And it did seem that human beings—real ones anyway—were plagued with trying to find it, or at least something like it. It was a crude example, but it was like an itch everyone was trying to scratch in some way, even if they weren't always conscious of it. Was that rapture he so ached for ever attainable, or was it a phantom, a mirage that vanished as you grasped at it, only to appear again just out of reach?

But what he experienced with Kari was different from every other relationship he had ever had. As much as possible in this world, she did satisfy his longings. Merely thinking of her was wonderful, even with the forlorn expectation that he had lost her forever.

>>———▶

In the lodge, Byron, then Jackson, had gone through much the same process of waking, getting coffee, and staggering over to the lounge.

"I think those tequilas snuck up on me," Byron said after swallowing a sip of a beer he had ordered but didn't feel like drinking.

"Must be the altitude," Jackson said. "My head feels a little strange too. Hey, what happened to your face? You've got a bump on your forehead the size of a golf ball."

"I don't know," Byron said. "Maybe I fell out of bed."

After the barbecue, Amanda did an hour and a half of yoga to calm herself. But she was still having a hard time dealing with the fickleness of her friends. She wished she didn't have to ride home in the same car with them. She was determined to be aloof but somewhat cordial.

She and Bianca met again at the elevator on the way down to the lobby. Bianca, seeing Amanda, said hi. She was cleaned up and dressed in blue jeans and a dark V-neck sweater that went well with her dark hair.

Amanda didn't verbally respond. Bianca could be so irritatingly perky.

"Did you get enough to eat at lunch?" Bianca said. "There was so much good food, but I just wasn't hungry. Crazy, it must be this mountain air. But now I'm starving."

"Oh, I'm sure it's the mountain air," Amanda said.

When they reached the lobby, they saw Byron and Jackson in the lounge. Bianca chose a table at the far end, away from them. Amanda didn't want to sit alone and followed.

"I took a great nap," Bianca said after taking a seat, "but I had the strangest dreams; I guess 'cause I ran out of protein bars. I hope they have a lot of leftovers."

"How could you even sleep?" Amanda said, not resisting taking a dig. She sat down and took up a menu.

Bianca frowned at her. "Maybe a nap would do you good."

Dropping the menu from in front of her face, Amanda replied, "I did my hatha exercises and am quite refreshed."

—————————

On the other side of the lounge, Jackson said, "Don't look now, but guess who just sat down?"

Of course, Byron looked.

SIXTY-TWO

Kari was checking herself out in the mirror in her room to see how she looked in the Seahawks jersey Vivian had traded her. The dark blue with the gray number twenty-five outlined in light green went well with the blue of her eyes and her light-blue jeans. She tucked the front of the jersey in and let the back hang out. She hoped Billy would interpret her wearing the jersey the way she wanted him to.

She started to leave to go downstairs but hesitated. She went back into the bathroom and looked at herself again. She changed her earrings to a pair of gold-and-turquoise ones that Billy had given her. The turquoise kind of went with the light green outlining the numbers on the jersey.

She left the room and waited for the elevator. Her stomach felt like it used to feel before an important lacrosse game—her coach called it "the butterflies." But this case was worse. She took a couple of deep breaths. Was what Vivian told her really true? Why else would she have traded her Seahawks jersey? But what if it wasn't? She laughed to herself, remembering the line she and Billy joked about the first night they met: "Get thee to a nunnery." *Seriously*, she thought, *I might as well. I'll never care for anyone else the way I do for him.*

In the elevator on the way down, she rehearsed what she would say when she saw him: *"I'm sorry things haven't been working out between us, but I would very much like to see if we could try again." No, no—stiff, bland. How about, "I'm crazy about you and can't live and will dry up like a prune without you." No—though true, and I like the energy.* After four or five other ideas, she gave up. *Hopefully, he'll say something first, and depending on what he says, I can respond. If he doesn't say anything, I don't know what I'll say. But even if I make a fool of myself, I'm going to say something. I'm going to tell him the truth.*

>———▶

Kari walked into the lounge, looking for Billy.

"Hey, sister," Bianca called out from where she and Amanda were sitting.

Kari saw her and looked away—not vindictively, she was just pre-occupied.

Amanda was especially interested in Byron's and Jackson's responses as Kari walked by their table. They paid her next to no attention. Seeing this, Amanda relaxed.

When Kari didn't see Billy, she walked to the rear exit without saying a word.

"This place makes people act weird," Bianca said. She glanced at Byron, who was staring at her.

>———▶

Billy was still wandering around in the park at the rear of the lodge. He finally concluded he was overthinking his feelings. All he really knew was that he cared for Kari very much and missed her terribly.

He walked a little more and sat down on a bench in front of a bird feeder. Two hummingbirds were flitting around it, darting in and out to take nips of its nectar. He remembered sitting out on one of his grandparents' balconies and watching one of those tiny aeronauts with a bright red throat nipping at one of his grandmother's feeders. A blue jay came bullying in, trying to poach some of the drink. The humming-bird flew off for a moment. Then shot back, dive-bombing the much larger bird, pecking at the back of its neck until the jay abandoned its looting and flew off.

That was courage, Billy thought. That's what he needed. If she rejected him, he'd never get over her. But as much as he wanted her, he didn't want her if she didn't want him too, even though he never would quit wanting her. This might seem contradictory to some who haven't been in love the way Billy was, but it made perfect sense to him.

He sensed her nearness even before he saw her. He turned to see the lodge's rear door open and then—Kari, wearing a Seahawks jersey. His heart started pounding, his stomach mashed up into his esophagus. She was walking toward him. He looked behind him to see if there was someone else she might be walking toward. No. She slowed a little but kept on coming.

What should he say? He remembered the letter he had written to her. But he didn't have a clue where it was. He got up and started walking toward her.

She slowed a little more.

He didn't slow up until they got within about twenty feet of each other. He risked a small smile.

She gave him what was, hope against hope, a demure little smile.

They took a few more steps toward each other.

She was the most wonderful thing he had ever seen.

Things often get uncomfortable when two people don't know what to say to each other. The silence between them now was not like this.

"Cool Seahawks jersey," Billy finally said.

"Yeah, I'm warming to them."

"It's interesting, the Pats are growing on me too."

"Yes?"

"A whole lot." This wasn't an outright fabrication. It fitted with Billy's literary understanding of symbolism.

"That's the way I'm feeling about the Seahawks," Kari said. This type of symbolic expression is a good way for two people to get a little momentum going before they get more to the point.

"It looks great on you," Billy said, taking a few steps closer.

"You really think so? I hoped you would like it. I like your shirt."

"It's my favorite; you bought it for me."

"I'm glad you like it."

They made a few more minor compliments to each other, such as Billy liking her hair, and Kari liking his tan. (She was fully aware he had gone surfing in Mexico with Jackson.)

Billy stepped closer until he was just three feet from her. "I need to say something to you."

"I need to say something to you too," Kari said, almost tearing up. "I'll go first."

"No, I'll go first," said Billy.

"Should we write it on napkins?" Kari smiled.

"That didn't work out so well last time. Maybe we should just speak at the same time."

"We might not be able to hear each other."

Billy didn't wait any longer. "I've played the total absolute moron and imbecile."

"I too," Kari said. Being a writer, she knew her pronoun cases. "Thanks for going first."

"The only reason I became a criminal was because I thought I was losing you."

"You mean you became a burglar for me? That's *kind* of romantic." She smiled and sighed; she also had an artistic imagination.

"I would do anything for you." It would have been out of place to mention that going to jail was also to give him something to write about.

"I didn't know you hated cats. It was my insensitivity to your sensitivity. But I'm willing to give her away."

"I don't hate cats." He took another step closer.

"But your grandmother said you're allergic to them."

"Mac's an Abyssinian—I looked it up, and short-haired cats aren't so bad for me. If I get used to her, she might hardly affect me at all."

There was a crack of thunder not that far in the distance. A few clouds had appeared.

"Still, I'll give Mac to Mrs. Martin. She lives right in front of me, and I can see Mac anytime I want."

"I even got a prescription for allergy medicine."

"I think she will like it at Mrs. Martin's. She would be uncomfortable being the third wheel."

"Kari," Billy said, taking a step closer. Now they were at arm's distance.

"Yes, darling?" Kari said.

"I've missed you so much."

"Me too." She didn't care about the grammar.

"I've been a total wreck without you. It hurts when we're apart." He took her left hand with his right, and they inched closer. She put her right hand somewhere between his left shoulder and his neck, but closer to his neck. He let go of her hand and put both hands around her waist. They inched up even closer. In their minds and bodies, a glorious peace had finally come—amid a raging storm of delight.

There was another crack of thunder, and it started to sprinkle. They probably needed to be cooled off.

»———➤

Bianca and Amanda were still at their table on the other side of the lounge from Byron and Jackson. The parties would occasionally glance at the others' table, and sometimes more than just glance. Occasionally, some eyes would meet.

"Stop staring at her," Jackson said.

"I can't help it. She's so hot," Byron said.

"Having doubts about the vow?" Jackson was having his own doubts and was doing his share of staring.

Byron just groaned. "You having doubts too?"

"I might be open to renegotiating the agreement."

"Wait a minute," Byron said. "Look at what's coming into the lobby."

Jackson turned. Billy and Kari, hand in hand, were walking in.

"Do you think they talked?" Jackson said.

"Of course they've talked—look at them." Byron got up.

"Awesome!" Jackson got up too. But then slowed down. "Hold on, we gotta be cool."

They casually strolled over to Bianca and Amanda's table.

"Can we buy you ladies a drink?" Jackson said. To some, the way he said it might have come across a bit conceited, but the girls didn't seem to mind.

"That would be nice," the girls agreed. Byron and Jackson took a seat. Their hostilities seemed to melt away—mostly. True friends always try to be forbearing.

SIXTY-THREE

In the early evening, the sky was clear again. The moon hadn't risen yet, but the stars were out. Many of the guests had departed on hearing of the disappearance of Professor Fulkles and the cancellation of his second lecture. There had been reports of him wildly dashing off into the forest, the lodge's pet bear chasing after him, and conflicting accounts in which it was the professor chasing the bear. The management wasn't alarmed and assured those concerned that the professor would show up eventually. It wasn't unusual for guests to become enamored with Mrs. Pulchritude.

The remaining guests had gathered outside on the back lawn of the lodge for a fireworks display. Chelsea and Freddie sat with Curdi between them. Their parents had gone antique shopping and weren't back yet. Next to Freddie sat Vivian and Elrond. The couple had run into Freddie at the business center's computer, shooting Orcs, and found they had similar interests in Tolkien's world. Elrond turned out to be even better than Freddie at shooting Orcs and Uruk-hai, and Vivian was pretty good too. Freddie decided that Elrond was not Elrond but Celeborn, and Vivian was Galadriel. He thought she was pretty and liked her freckles.

Elrond was open to accepting the new designation as some would say Celeborn was a promotion. Curdi, who was a fan of Tolkien too, said he wasn't sure but was inclined to think they were more like Elrond and his wife Celebrían, but it was open to debate.

Anita Rowls, the woman from the lecture who looked like a younger Condoleezza Rice, was seated between Elrond and Professor Fulkles's assistant. On hearing the talk of Tolkien, she chimed in about his influences—especially the King Arthur legends, whose influence on him was not as well known as that of Norse mythology. She thought him a master storyteller and that being able to create a whole universe—including its history, geography, and even its languages—was truly amazing.

Curdi said, "My boss tells good stories too." A burst of light exploded overhead. "He also makes fireworks."

Rockets began shooting off and blasting high into the air every twenty seconds, exploding into multitudes of constellations of diamonds, rubies, emeralds, and sapphires, which in turn would boom and explode into smaller constellations of different colors, which boomed and exploded into yet others and finally crackled into tiny snowflakes that fell from the sky.

"Like Gandalf," Chelsea said, excited and delighted.

Anita and the professor's assistant got to talking. "You didn't seem too excited with the professor's discovery," the assistant said.

"Just like so many trends: here today, gone tomorrow. Probably will get some traction, though, for a while."

The last of the fireworks exploded in a grand finale. A series of booms flowering and spangling into light blues and pinks and purple starlike things popping into further brilliant colors and into further booms, flowerings, and spanglings and then fading and popping like popcorn. And then, rather than fading completely away, there was a great explosion, and something like a dragon blasted out of the dark and grew and grew and grew and then, as it passed the lodge, exploded into a huge multicolored butterfly.

The party on the porch thrilled and ducked as it shot over them.

Curdi said, "I told you my boss was good at fireworks."

>>———▶

Billy and Kari watched the display from a porch atop the lodge. They had met an old man who had shown them the way up by a private stair. Billy didn't let on that he had met him before. On the porch were two chairs and a table holding a bottle of wine and glasses. They enjoyed the view but not as much as they enjoyed each other. "Awfully kind of that old guy to let us come up here," Billy said.

"He really did seem nice," Kari said. "He kind of reminded me of your grandfather."

»———▶

Billy's grandparents were at a dance at their yacht club. They had just returned to their table after Arthur's feeble attempt to lead Gwen in the rumba. Gwen said, "You would think, after all these years, you would have learned to keep off my toes."

"I use them as coordinates, to keep track of where I am," Arthur said, suggesting a sailing metaphor.

"Oh, darling, must you?" Gwen was self-conscious about the size of her feet. Changing the subject, she said, "I wonder how Billy and Kari are doing up at the lodge?"

"You know what I think? You ought to listen to your own advice: that would-be lovers, not to mention their grandmothers, not take themselves too seriously. They need to see and enjoy the wonderful silliness of the whole thing."

"Yes, yes, I know, but love is such an important thing. It's so important that it's easy to forget."

»———▶

Early the next week, Billy's grandmother got a text message: "You owe me for eight dinners at Clyde's restaurant. Love, Billy"

EPILOGUE

Well I can discern how already within thine intellect
The Eternal Light is shining,
The mere sight of which ever enkindles Love.
And if aught else seduces your love,
It is no other than some vestige of this,
Ill understood, which shines through there.

Dante Alighieri, The Divine Comedy

ACKNOWLEDGMENTS

I'd like to express my appreciation to those who, from the inception of the idea that eventually became this book, gave encouraging support and advice, particularly to the young lady who liked the first chapter when there wasn't anything else—I might not have gone on without that encouragement. Allison Prizlow was most helpful in the sailing lingo. VJK at times was helpful with her critical eye, and down the stretch, DJJ gave some provocative input. To Christina Boys, my editor, whose encouragement, patience, and expertise were extremely helpful; to Michael Krohn at Blackstone for his excellent contribution on the "print editing" side of things; and to all the other folks at Blackstone for their contributions, especially to Josie Woodbridge for shepherding this project along, and to Candice Roditi, who I could always go to when I needed most anything.

ABOUT THE AUTHOR

John J. Jacobson is the author of three novels, including *All the Cowboys Ain't Gone* and *California Fever*. Born in Nevada, he grew up in the West, surfed big waves in Hawaii, circled the world thrice, and survived the sixties and seventies, corporate America, and grad school. Among other degrees he has an MA in Renaissance literature from Claremont Graduate University. He lives in Nashville, Tennessee.